Snowbone

'I want to know about our people. How we live, how we grow, how we die.'

'I can tell you that,' said Figgis.

'And I want to know about the slave trade.'

'Do you now? And why might that be?'

Snowbone's eyes hardened. She held up a stubby finger and thumb, and squeezed them close, like a crab's claw. 'Because I came *this close* to being one myself,' she said. 'And if it takes me the rest of my life, I will find the people who did that to me. And they will be sorry.'

Cat Weatherill is a performance storyteller, performing internationally at storytelling and literature festivals, on national radio and television and at schools throughout the country. She lives in Wales.

catweatherill.co.uk

Books by Cat Weatherill

BARKBELLY
SNOWBONE

CAT WEATHERILL

Snowbone

TO Reese
Best Wishes!
Cat Weatherill
x.

PUFFIN

PUFFIN BOOKS

Published by the Penguin Group
Penguin Books Ltd, 80 Strand, London WC2R ORL, England
Penguin Group (USA) Inc., 375 Hudson Street, New York, New York 10014, USA
Penguin Group (Canada), 90 Eglinton Avenue East, Suite 700, Toronto, Ontario, Canada M4P 2Y3
(a division of Pearson Penguin Canada Inc.)
Penguin Ireland, 25 St Stephen's Green, Dublin 2, Ireland (a division of Penguin Books Ltd)
Penguin Group (Australia), 250 Camberwell Road, Camberwell, Victoria 3124, Australia
(a division of Pearson Australia Group Pty Ltd)
Penguin Books India Pvt Ltd, 11 Community Centre, Panchsheel Park, New Delhi – 110 017, India
Penguin Group (NZ), 67 Apollo Drive, Mairangi Bay, Auckland 1310, New Zealand
(a division of Pearson New Zealand Ltd)
Penguin Books (South Africa) (Pty) Ltd, 24 Sturdee Avenue, Rosebank, Johannesburg 2196, South Africa

Penguin Books Ltd, Registered Offices: 80 Strand, London WC2R ORL, England

penguin.com

First published 2006
Published in this edition 2007
004

Text copyright © Cat Weatherill, 2006
Illustrations copyright © Sarah Dearlove, 2006
All rights reserved

The moral right of the author and illustrator has been asserted

Set in Monotype Baskerville
Typeset by Palimpsest Book Production Limited, Grangemouth, Stirlingshire
Made and printed in England by Clays Ltd, St Ives plc

British Library Cataloguing in Publication Data
A CIP catalogue record for this book is available from the British Library

ISBN: 978-0-141-31873-8

www.greenpenguin.co.uk

Penguin Books is committed to a sustainable
future for our business, our readers and our planet.
This book is made from Forest Stewardship
Council™ certified paper.

To Gary, my very own Manu

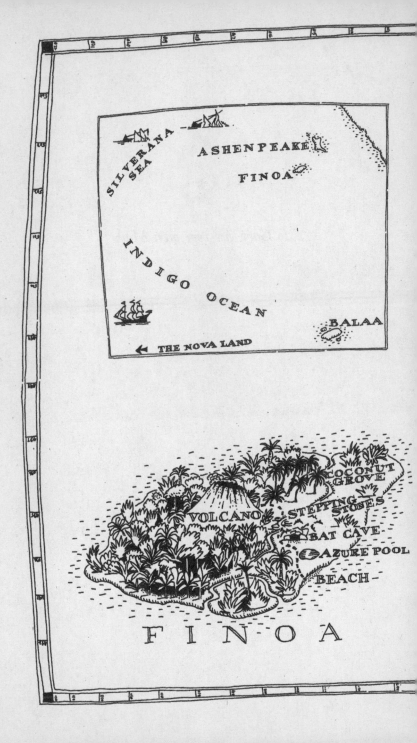

SILVERANA SEA

ASHENPEAKE

FINOA

INDIGO OCEAN

THE NOVA LAND

BALAA

COCONUT GROVE

VOLCANO

STEPPING STONES

BAT CAVE

AZURE POOL

BEACH

FINOA

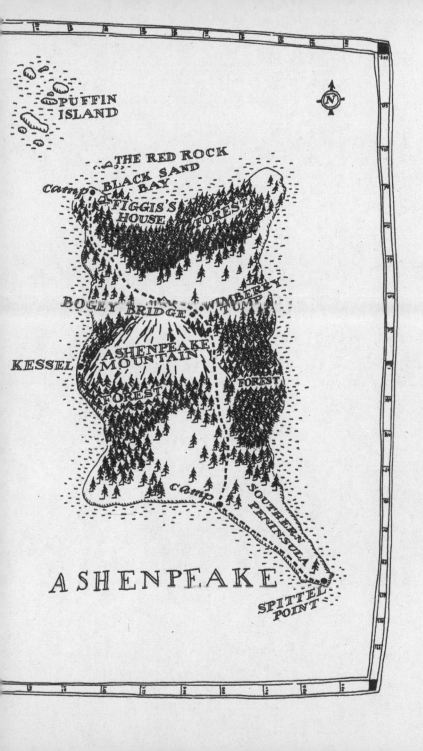

At that moment Barkbelly would sooner have kissed a wild dog than this strange, pale, wooden girl.

Barkbelly, *Chapter 45*

PART ONE

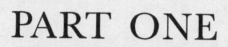

1

The galleon sailed through the afternoon, alone on the butterfly-blue ocean. Only she wasn't alone. Not any more. Because the strange ship that had been following her for days, lying low on the horizon like a great, grey wolf, was coming closer.

'PIRATES!' The lookout shouted so loudly, his teeth rattled. 'PIRATES! PORTSIDE! GAINING FAST!'

The First Mate stormed to the quarterdeck, knocking sailors down like bowling pins. 'Cap'n?' he said breathlessly. 'What'll it be?'

Captain Kempe, gazing through his telescope, seemed unconcerned by the turn of events. While his crew crumbled around him, he stood firm. Calm, unruffled, handsome as ever. But cold, cold fear had gripped him. He could feel it turning in his belly like a living thing.

'*Cap'n?*' The First Mate watched a tiny muscle, tick-tick-ticking on the captain's neck.

Captain Kempe gazed on. The pirate ship was a

brig. They couldn't outrace her. But they could try.

He snapped the telescope shut. 'Let's show them what we're made of,' he said. 'All the speed we can muster, Flynn, straight away.'

'Aye aye, Cap'n.'

'And, Flynn – prepare the cannon. Just in case.'

'Aye, sir,' said Flynn, with the ghost of a smile. Both men knew the *Hope* was doomed.

Captain Kempe turned back to the ocean. The pirate ship was speeding towards them, riding the waves like a storm demon. With a sigh, he stroked the sword that hung, cold and deadly, from his belt.

He reopened his telescope. The ship was nearly upon them. So close, he could see the pirate flag, black silk fluttering in the ocean breeze, and the pirates, calmly going about their business. How different from his own men, with their wide eyes and praying mouths, running backwards and forwards, pale with panic, pulling, heaving, positioning the cannon, trying to believe that firepower alone would save them.

BOOOOM! The pirate ship opened fire. The *Hope* lurched violently as the first cannonball struck her.

'RETURN FIRE!' yelled the Captain.

BOOOOM! The *Hope* replied with a thunderous volley. The pirate ship reeled under its impact and Captain Kempe punched the air triumphantly. Down below, in a fug of smoke and sweat and powder, his men raced to prepare a second round.

But the crew of the pirate ship, the *Mermaid*, was doing exactly the same. And there, in the dark and the dust, they heaved a massive cannonball into place and – *tsss!* – torched the powder and – *BOOOOM!* – the cannonball was spat from the gunport. It tore through the air, racing its own shadow across the waves, faster, faster, faster. A death-bringing, wood-smashing, hope-crushing globe of destruction. Faster, faster, faster. CRAOWOOPOOOM!

The mighty cannonball smashed through the *Hope*'s hull planks and careered into the hold. Here there were crates, dozens of them, full of wooden eggs. *Crrooom!* Half were smashed to smithereens; the eggs tumbled out on to the floor. A flickering lantern, swinging from a roof beam, fell from its hook and – *vooomf!* – the flame ignited the spilt oil and a fire began.

It spat and clawed like a flaming tomcat. It pounced on the shattered crates. Mauled the decking. Snapped the bones of the ship. It hissed and growled. Whipped an angry, fiery tail till the hold fizzed with sparks. Then it crept forward on its belly and started licking at the remaining crates.

Inside those crates, a strange thing happened. As the temperature rose, the wooden eggs started to move. They twisted and turned, this way and that, and suddenly – *BANG!* – one of the crates exploded. The eggs were thrown high into the air, and fell back down like apples in a windstorm. And one pale egg, whiter than all the others, rolled away into a quiet corner and lay there, quite still.

But deep inside that egg, things were beginning to change. Cells were dividing, multiplying, replicating. Limbs were forming, straining, pushing. The egg was swelling, bigger, bigger. The wooden shell became leathery, taut. It bulged as a foot pressed here, a nose poked there. Whatever was inside wanted to get out and nothing was going to stop it.

Oof! Out came a leg. A pale wooden leg, with tiny toes. *Oof!* Another, kicking hard. *Ug!* An arm. *Ug!* Another. Fine wooden fingers, feeling, feeling. The baby rocked from side to side, trying to right herself. *BOOM!* Another cannonball screamed into the hold and toppled a tower of crates. They fell so hard, the baby was bounced into the air – *wheeeeeeee!* – and landed on all fours like a headless cat. Her hands reached for the empty space between her shoulders. She took hold of her hair and pulled – but her head wouldn't come out. She pulled again, harder now, and – *pop!* – out it came. It wobbled on her neck like a loose button. And there she sat, bare-bottom naked, goose-grey eyes blinking. A strange, pale wooden baby with just one thing on her mind.

2

FOOD! The desire for it knotted the baby's belly. Sharpened her senses. Kicked her into moving. And she wasn't alone. All around, babies just like her were crawling, searching, screaming for food. But the pale baby was silent, concentrating. She considered the light: the sparkling, leaping light across the way. She turned and peered into the shadows behind her. She frowned. Blinked. Chose the dark and started crawling. Soon she found a piece of rope. She picked it up and sniffed it. Bit into it with her sharp wooden teeth and chewed steadily. *Na!* She spat it out and moved on, sniffing, sniffing. *Uh?* A rusty nail. She licked it. *Na!* A broken lantern. A ball of string. An iron bar. *Na! Na! Na!* She crawled on.

Aaah! A faint rotting smell tickled her nose. Somewhere in the smoke, in the fire, in the filth . . . *Ha!* She pounced on the upturned bucket, threw it aside and seized the rat. It was cold and old. Wet with maggots. But the baby quivered with excitement and stuffed it into her mouth. She crunched and chewed, and down it went – fur, flesh, bones – until the tail was hanging from her lips like a question mark. With a final flick of her tongue, that disappeared too.

The baby sat there, looking puzzled. But not for long. She burped so violently, the force of it toppled her over backwards. But she picked herself up, smiled vacantly and crawled on.

Flames were dancing in every corner now. A grey octopus of smoke spread its deadly tentacles into every nook and cranny of the hold. And the baby felt a strong, primal instinct stirring deep within her. *Get out.*

Miraculously, the steps leading to the deck were still intact. She crawled over and began the long climb up, pushing on, claiming her space in a wedge of babies. Onwards, upwards, into the light – and into the battle.

The deck was a forest of legs: boots and shoes and blue tattoos, flat feet, bare feet, socks and sandals. Stomping, stamping, whirling, twirling, sword and cutlass, dagger hurling. Clash of silver, splash of blood; grunt and moan and fall and – *thud!* – a sailor hit the deck. His teeth shot out like ten white mice. The baby ignored him and crawled on.

She could smell . . . chickens! Three of them, dead in a crate. She smashed her fist through the wooden slats, dragged one out and ate it, feathers, feet and all. And she was just about to pull out the second when another baby reached over and grabbed it. She whipped round. It was a boy, with an odd eye and a smile as big as a banana. He was stronger than her. Much stronger. She let him have the chicken. There was still one left. She pulled it out and ate it all.

Time went by. One hour, two hours. The battle was over, the pirates had won, and the pale baby was walking now, strong as a two-year-old human. On she went, sniffing, sniffing, eating anything she could find. A lump of liquorice. A leather shoe. A barrel of fish. A single finger. She was still hungry.

Then she saw it. A firm white leg, right in front of her. Hairy, with torn britches flapping at the knee. Lip-licking, mouth-dripping, fat, fine, juicy.

Aieeee! The pirate howled as her teeth sank into his flesh. He bent down and tried to force her head away. She growled and gripped harder. *Aaargh!* He took hold of her ears and pulled them savagely. *Oooh!* Her teeth sank in deeper. She wrapped herself around the pirate's leg, clinging like a monkey.

'Get her off!' cried the pirate. 'Somebody get her off!'

The baby felt strong hands tugging at her. But the leg was tender and she was hungry. She wouldn't let go.

Then a rich, meaty smell drifted past her nose. *Ah!* Out of the corner of her eye she saw a man. He had something in his hand. Something round and brown. He was offering it to her.

She sniffed at the food. *Oh!* She dropped from the pirate's leg, took the pork pie in her mouth and scuttled away, over the deck and into the rigging. And there she sat, happily munching her prize, while the pirates began their celebrations below.

～❦～

Night fell. In the vastness of the ocean, the *Mermaid* and the *Hope* lay at anchor together, side by side like slippers. The pirates had covered the *Hope*'s rigging with lanterns. Now they sat beneath them, smoking tobacco and swigging rum. Both tasted sweeter tonight.

Scar Arm, the pirate who had been bitten earlier, emerged from the shadows and walked an unsteady line across the deck, zigzagging to avoid the countless wooden babies that still crawled free.

'These blasted tiddlins!' he said. 'They're getting under my feet something rotten. I reckon we should throw 'em overboard. They're no use to anyone now.'

'But they're so cute!' said another, Dog Ear, who was cradling one of the babies in his arms. 'Look at this one here. She is the sweetest thing! I'm gonna call her Mouse, 'cause her eyes are the softest brown – just like a little brown mouse.'

'Well, if you're gonna call her Mouse, I'm gonna call that one Blackeye,' said his mate, Squid. He pointed at the baby who had eaten the second chicken. 'You can't see it from here, but he has the most incredible eye. You know the bit where it's blue or brown? On him, it's black. And if you look really close, there's a ring of silver around the edge. It's weird! I don't know if he can see through it, it's so dark.'

'You can't go giving 'em all names!' cried Scar Arm, throwing up his hands in despair. 'Not if we're going to toss 'em overboard!'

'Who says we're doin' that?' said Dog Ear. 'Not I!'

'Nor I,' said Squid. 'Oh, come on now, Scar Arm! You'll bust a gut the way you're goin' on.'

He offered the pirate a glass of rum. Scar Arm took it, grunted and settled himself on a nearby sack of beans.

'What about that one?' said Dog Ear, nodding at something in the rigging.

The others looked up. There was the pale baby, still clinging to the masthead.

'She's very skinny,' said Squid. 'How about . . . Boneybum?'

'Nah.'

'She should be Fang,' said Scar Arm grumpily. 'She's vicious, that one.'

'Nah,' said Dog Ear again. 'She's not vicious, just hungry. They all are. But she is a fighter, though.'

'You're not wrong there. In a scrap, she'd be the last one standing.'

'Aye. She'd be there, long after everyone else had gone.'

'*Wait*,' said Squid urgently. Inspiration had seized him. His eyes widened. His brain whirred . . . and a single word fell from his mouth: 'Snowbone.'

'*Eh!*' breathed Dog Ear. 'That's genius, is that!'

'I know!' said Squid. His grin was so wide, it tickled his ears.

High in the rigging, the baby heard the name. She didn't know why it was clever, but she liked it. She repeated it slowly, rolling it off her tongue: '*Snowbone*.' Sounded good to her. 'Want it,' she said to the night and stars. 'Mine.' She smiled. Now she had something no one could ever take away from her.

The following day, the *Hope* was stripped of her valuables. Soon nothing remained but an old, lumbering hulk, no use to anyone. So the pirates sank her, right there in the middle of the ocean, and the *Mermaid* headed for home.

Home for the pirates was Puffin Island. It was a small island, busy with birds, which lay off the north-west coast of the much larger Ashenpeake Island. Puffin Island had sheltered beaches, rich land and plenty of fresh water. It lay low on the horizon, like a basking turtle, and its deep-water bays were big enough to hide any ship. All things considered, it was the perfect place for a secret pirate hideaway.

The voyage to Puffin Island took seven days and, during that time, the tiddlins grew at an astonishing rate. The pirates watched and wondered. Whispered about *unnatural magic* and *things beyond our understanding*. Some said the wooden babies were wiser than they ought to be and would bring bad luck. *We'll never see home again*, they lamented. *There'll be a storm or a fire or a terrible sickness.* But there never was. Day after day, the ship sailed safely on, and the tiddlins thrived.

By the sixth day, the tiddlins were as big as five-year-old humans. They could talk with confidence, their personalities had emerged and a curious thing had happened: Snowbone had become their leader. No one knew how or when it began, but suddenly Snowbone was the one the tiddlins looked to when they were challenged. She had the answers. She knew what to do.

Snowbone had noticed the tiddlins' respect for her and was pleased. But she had also noticed something else. She might be the most capable tiddlin in the gang – and she was certainly the most determined – but she wasn't the most popular. That was Blackeye.

Everyone adored Blackeye. He was so warm and friendly and entertaining. Even the pirates loved him. Griddle, the ship's cook, gave him special tidbits. Lord Fox, the pirate captain, stood him on a box so he could take a turn on the wheel. He was everyone's favourite.

Blackeye had a special game he called *dive-bombing*. He would climb up the *Mermaid*'s rigging and throw himself off: *wheeeeeeeeeee!* When he hit the deck, he would bounce, pick himself up and laugh at the sheer exhilaration of it all. Then he'd climb back up and do it all again – especially if Mouse was watching, which she usually was. She watched him endlessly, adoringly, with her soft brown eyes.

Snowbone sat on the deck, watching Blackeye dive from the rigging for the umpteenth time. She listened to the cheers that greeted his landing and couldn't help feeling envious. Blackeye seemed to live in a bright bubble of love and laughter. Her bit of the world seemed dark and lonely by comparison. 'If I could dive-bomb,' she said to herself, 'would people like me more? I wonder . . .'

Late that night, when the tiddlins were asleep in the hold and the pirates were snoring in their hammocks, Snowbone returned to the deck. There was no one around except the night watch and he was at the far end of the ship. She started to climb. Up, up, up she went, climbing the rigging like a ladder to the moon. Higher and higher. Finally she stopped and looked down. *Oh!* Did Blackeye come this high? *Yes. Higher, knowing him.* It seemed such a long way down. But Blackeye did it all the time. He never hurt himself.

Snowbone took a deep breath, closed her eyes and jumped. *Whoo!* She fell like a conker, so fast she heard the wind whistling past her ears, and – *DUUD!* – she hit the deck.

She didn't bounce like Blackeye. She didn't hear laughter or applause. She didn't pick herself up and wave gaily. She just lay there, shaken to her very core. She wasn't hurt; she wasn't broken. But she felt . . . wrong. As if some part of her, deep inside, had been shaken out of place. And there was a pain. A dull ache in her head, across her eyes.

Slowly, very slowly, she sat up. She drew in her knees and wrapped her arms around them. Hugged herself close while the sky blushed peachy-pink at the sun's first kisses. And that was how Griddle, the ship's cook, found her when he arrived on deck for his early-morning stroll.

He knew it was Snowbone, and knew she wouldn't want to be seen like this: lost, shaken, tight as a pine cone. But he couldn't leave her there.

'It's not like you to be up at dawn,' he said as he sat down beside her.

Snowbone lifted her head. 'I'm not hurt.'

'No. Neither is a pigeon when he falls from a nest. He's a bit wobbly, though.'

'I'm not wobbly.'

'No.' Griddle saw her proud little face, trying to be brave. He had to smile.

'I was trying to dive-bomb.'

'Aye. Well, I'd leave that to them that are daft enough to do it. You let well alone, that's my advice. Stick to what you're good at.'

'I don't know what that is.'

'Well, you've not been long in the world, have you? Happen you'll find out one day. Now me – I'm good at cooking. And I know there's a frying pan down in the galley right now, crying: *Griddle! Griddle! Come and make pancakes!* And since you're not hurt, or wobbly, or upset, or any of those things, perhaps you could help me. Do you like pancakes?'

'Don't know. Never had one.'

'Oh, then you are in for a treat, little lady! A hot pancake, with a touch o' lemon and a dollop of syrup . . . *Oh!* My mouth's gone all dribbly, just thinking about it. Come on!'

Snowbone had been sitting for so long, her joints had seized up. Getting up wasn't easy. But Griddle turned his back and pretended not to notice her struggle. He didn't offer any help and Snowbone didn't ask for any.

But she did ask for extra syrup on her pancakes, and Griddle was more than happy to give her that.

After seven days at sea, Ashenpeake Island came into sight: a dark land, wrapped in sea mist, with the great, snow-capped cone of Ashenpeake Mountain rising above it all.

This was where the tiddlins would soon be setting up home. Lord Fox, the pirate captain, had made the decision. He didn't dislike the tiddlins, but he had no use for them. They were too young to go to sea and too many to stay at the pirates' hideaway.

'They're such hungry little beggars,' he said. 'They'll eat all we have. No, they must go elsewhere.'

Lord Fox decided to settle them at the north end of Ashenpeake Island. They would be safe there: the land was heavily forested and sparsely populated. The pirate captain had no doubt they would survive. They would be well provisioned and there would be time for them to learn survival skills before they were taken to their new home. Snowbone was a strong, capable leader and the group wasn't over-large. Of the hundreds of babies born during the attack on the *Hope*, just twenty-eight remained. Many had died in the fire and most of the survivors had jumped overboard in search of adventure. They had drifted away on the waves, bobbing like driftwood, laughing and waving and wriggling their toes.

'It's a perfect plan,' Lord Fox told himself. 'They'll *adore* Ashenpeake. They'll build a camp and make it cosy. It'll soon feel like home.'

In truth, Ashenpeake Island really *was* the tiddlins' home. They were Ashenpeakers. They belonged to the oldest race of people in the world.

Ashenpeakers were proud, hard-working, steadfast folk. Their wooden bodies made them immensely strong and virtually indestructible. But this blessing became a curse when someone, somewhere, realized that Ashenpeakers would make perfect slaves.

From that single thought, a worldwide slave trade had grown and flourished. Over the years, thousands of eggs had left Ashenpeake Island, bound for the Nova Land, Candalia, Tuva – wherever cheap labour was needed. The eggs were stored until they were wanted, then thrown into fires, triggering an incredible process that catapulted them from birth to work within a month, full of strength and empty of memory. Perfect slaves, with no past happiness to disturb their dreams or trouble their minds.

Snowbone learned these things from Barkbelly, the galley boy from the *Hope*.

Barkbelly was special. All the other sailors on the

Hope – those who hadn't been killed in the fighting – had been taken prisoner. They were down below, safely secured in the *Mermaid*'s hold. But Barkbelly and Griddle, the *Hope*'s cook, had been treated differently. Griddle was now the pirates' cook, and Barkbelly was allowed to roam freely about the pirate ship. Snowbone wondered why. She also wondered about the *Hope*. Where had it been going when the pirates attacked it? And why was it carrying hundreds of wooden eggs, packed away in crates?

Barkbelly had been the only Ashenpeaker on board the *Hope*. He wasn't very old, but he was a big, brawny lad, with an honest, friendly face. And Snowbone had realized that, young as he was, Barkbelly had knowledge. He had seen something of the world.

And so she had asked him what he knew, and Barkbelly had told her. It wasn't much. He hadn't grown up on Ashenpeake, so he couldn't tell her about that. And until the tiddlins were born, he had never even *seen* another Ashenpeaker, so he couldn't tell her how a wooden body worked. But, based on his own experience, he could tell her two important things. If a bit was chopped off – a hand, say – it would grow back, good as new. But if it were *burned* off – no. It wouldn't grow back. He showed her the stump of a missing finger to prove it.

'Fire is deadly,' he said. 'It brings us to life, but it can kill us, I know it can. Keep away from it, Snowbone. Keep away.'

Then he told her what he knew of the *Hope*. She had been heading for Farrago, a sea port on the east coast of the Nova Land. The Nova Land was a newly discovered country, far across the Indigo Ocean. The eggs would have been sold as slaves.

Snowbone was outraged. 'Why is slavery allowed?' she stormed. 'Why has no one done anything to stop it? Doesn't anyone care?'

'I care,' said Barkbelly, 'but I don't know what's to be done.' And he shook his head sadly and said no more.

5

The pirates sailed north, along the coast of Ashenpeake to Puffin Island. When they arrived, the beach was clamorous with wives and children, and any thought of unloading the ship was abandoned. A safe return, a ship full of booty – it was time to celebrate! So it wasn't until the following morning that the tiddlins began their lessons.

'Lessons? What lessons?' said Snowbone. 'I don't understand. I thought we were unloading the ship today.'

'No,' said Lord Fox, elegantly wagging his finger at her. 'The *men* are unloading the ship. *You* are having lessons. I may be the cruellest pirate ever to sail the seven seas, but even I would not be so heartless as to abandon infants without some instruction. No! You must learn how to take care of yourselves, and these lovely people –' he indicated the pirates' families – 'will be teaching you. You have just *one day* to learn these things, so use it well. Tomorrow, armed with your knowledge and boatloads of provisions, my men will take you over to the main island . . . and leave you there.' He smiled devilishly. 'Alone! Abandoned! Marooned! Oh, you poor things!'

And so the lessons began. The pirate boys showed the tiddlins how to whittle an arrow, fire a bow, throw a knife, track a deer, set a trap. The girls taught them how to spear fish, make fires, grow vegetables, find fresh water. The elderly men, excused lifting and carrying because of old wounds and bad backs, energetically demonstrated how to make shelters and build defensive fortifications. The wives showed them how to cook and make clothes.

'We don't need clothes,' protested Snowbone when it was her turn to learn sewing. 'You're human. You wear them to protect your skin and keep warm. But we're wooden. We don't need them.'

The women smiled indulgently.

'There are many reasons why people wear clothes,' said Squid's wife. 'Ashenpeake is a civilized island where people go about their business properly dressed, whether they are wooden or not. If you won't wear clothes, what will you wear?'

'Smiles,' said Blackeye.

'You'll need clothes!' insisted Squid's wife. 'Blackeye, you can't run around town with no pants on.'

Blackeye grinned. The other tiddlins began to giggle.

'*Sssh!*' hissed Snowbone. 'You're being very rude.

23

This lady is trying to turn us into proper Ashenpeakers, and all you can think about is bare bottoms.' She turned to the wives. 'I'm listening,' she said, picking up her needle and smiling prettily. 'You can begin. And *you*,' she added, looking at Blackeye, 'can behave.' With that, she winked, and the lesson began.

By sundown, the tiddlins had learned many vital skills. They had also been given everything they would need and much, much more; Lord Fox had been extremely generous. But then, unexpectedly, the pirate captain sauntered over to Snowbone and said, 'There's just one more thing. Pick a couple of chums, there's a good girl, and then we can go.'

Snowbone's eyes narrowed. She wasn't sure she liked this *good girl* business. But she did as she was told. She summoned Blackeye and then Fudge. Fudge was a tall tiddlin with no visible wood grain on his body. He had some faint swirls on the palms of his hands, but other than that he was a solid block of buttery brown.

To the tiddlins' surprise, Lord Fox gave them each a lantern and an empty sack. Then he led them along the beach till they came to a cave mouth set deep within the cliffs.

'Come,' he said, and he lifted his lantern high and entered.

The tiddlins followed. On and on they went, stumbling down a long, dark tunnel, wondering where it would end, when suddenly they emerged into an enormous cave – and it was stuffed to the roof with weaponry. Knives, crossbows, cutlasses, spears, shields, slings, daggers, swords . . . Guns too, though the pirates didn't use them much, preferring the polished elegance of a blade.

'*Whoa!*' said Blackeye, speaking for them all. 'Where did you get all this?'

'We plunder several ships a year,' said Lord Fox, 'so we always have more weapons than we can possibly use. Help yourselves.' And with a flourish, he stepped aside.

The tiddlins wavered. There was so much to choose from! The hoard even included cannon, though how the pirates had managed to drag them from the beach was anyone's guess.

But then, in the glow of the lanterns, Snowbone spotted a jewelled dagger . . . a carved bow . . . a pistol small enough to fit her hand . . . and that was it. She pounced on the pile like a dog on a molehill. Dig, dig, dig, she went, deeper and deeper into the hoard, until nothing could be seen but a little wooden bottom, wiggling in excitement, while Blackeye and Fudge burrowed beside her, determined to find the best gun, the brightest sword, the sharpest blade.

All too soon the sacks were filled. It was time to go. But the tiddlins didn't mind. They had treasure!

As they quick-marched back along the beach, with their booty slung over their shoulders, their grins were brighter than their lanterns. They were real pirates now.

6

The next morning, the weather was appalling. Rain fell endlessly from a sodden sky and a bitter wind whipped across the beach, harrying the tiddlins as they packed boxes and bundles into the longboats, ready for their journey to Ashenpeake. Snowbone couldn't believe their adventure was starting so miserably. She had hoped for a gorgeous day, with the pirate families standing on the beach waving them farewell. Instead, there was nothing but a squally, fling-'em-in-anyhow mess of a departure, with no one venturing out into the rain to say goodbye.

Snowbone sighed and clambered into one of the longboats. She had Mouse beside her and a boy with sticky-out teeth. Looking across at one of the other boats, she saw Blackeye, wedged in tightly beside Barkbelly. She waved.

Then the boats were pushed on to the water, the pirates pulled on the oars and they were off, heading over the sea to Ashenpeake. Snowbone thought she would burst with excitement. What an adventure this was! Her thoughts were noisy as gulls, flapping round inside her head. *We have so much to do once we get there. Setting up camp. Getting organized. But we can do it. I can do it. First we have to . . . and then we must . . . and after that . . .*

Snowbone was so lost in thought, the journey passed without her noticing. But suddenly she realized the rain had stopped. The clouds had cleared. She sat up straight and peered ahead. The island was close now. It looked a cold place. A bit hilly. Covered in forest, as far as she could see. Empty beaches. Black sand.

Snowbone felt an unfamiliar thumping in her chest. Her heart! Ten days old and this was the first time she'd been aware of it. Thump, thump, thump. What did it mean? Was she scared? *No.* Sick? *No.* What, then? She was already wide awake, so why did she feel she was waking up? Why did she feel such longing for a piece of land? And why, oh why, the tear in her eye?

'What's going on?' she wondered. 'Why do I feel like this? Is there some kind of magic at work here?'

There were no answers. Not yet. But when the boat reached the beach and Snowbone felt the sand beneath her bare toes, she did discover something. Ashenpeake felt like home.

7

Snowbone had made her plans long before she set foot on the beach. Lord Fox had given them tarpaulins and timber, and she wanted to build a camp. But Snowbone realized she couldn't personally oversee twenty-seven tiddlins. She would need assistants – captains – trustworthy individuals who would accept her orders and organize small groups on her behalf.

She had intended to ask Barkbelly, but he left almost as soon as they arrived. He said he wanted to find his family and disappeared into the forest. No one was expecting him to return.

And so, with Barkbelly gone, Snowbone picked just five captains. Blackeye and Fudge were obvious choices. Mouse was a surprise: she was so quiet. But Snowbone had been watching her and knew she was bright and popular. Two Teeth and Tigermane completed the team. Two Teeth was a bit of a joker, but hard-working and capable. Tigermane was a tall, intelligent girl. Strong, calm, practical . . . everyone admired her. But the most remarkable thing about Tigermane was her hair. It was magnificent – long and lustrous, like a lion's mane, but tiger-striped in black and amber.

With the captains chosen, a camp was soon constructed. Fudge organized a working party and built the beach huts: six of them, right at the edge of the forest, facing the sea. Two Teeth supervised the digging of a vegetable plot. Tigermane sorted the provisions and moved everything to the safety of store caves. Blackeye constructed a lookout post, right at the top of the tallest tree. Mouse created a meeting circle, a place where the tiddlins could assemble to discuss matters of importance. It was marked out with twenty-eight stones – one for each tiddlin to sit on – with a long, curly horn in the middle. One blow upon the horn summoned the entire company.

At the end of the first week, Snowbone sat on the beach, alone with her thoughts. She gazed at the camp and the tiddlins going about their daily business, and felt so proud. So happy. So amazed! They had achieved more than she had dreamed possible. The camp was comfortable and secure. The tiddlins were cheerful, well fed, clean and clothed. They were proper Ashenpeakers now.

As for Black Sand Bay . . . *Oh!* Snowbone had fallen completely under its spell. It probably wasn't the most beautiful place in the world, she realized that, but it was wild and wonderful and she loved it.

Here, the sea met the sky, and the wind met the water, and they all danced together, rising and falling to the rhythm of the seasons.

And though the winter was coming and they might be safer moving into the forest, Snowbone wanted to stay on the beach, where she could see her beloved ocean. Here she felt free. Nobody's slave.

At Black Sand Bay, the tiddlins would weather the storms together, and grow taller, stronger, wiser. In time, they would move on. She didn't know when. She didn't know why. But she did know one thing. When that time came, they would be ready.

8

The year turned. First it was winter and the land was lost, hidden beneath a mantle of snow. Then came spring and the forest edge was peppered with primroses. Then came summer and dolphins sang in the bay. And then came autumn and the birds flew south, ahead of the winter winds.

Snowbone had grown and so had the members of her gang. Blackeye and Two Teeth were as tall as ten-year-old humans. Fudge was a head taller. Tigermane was the biggest girl; Mouse was the smallest. Snowbone was middling, like most of the others. All were healthy and strong, with boundless energy. Together they made a formidable team.

Snowbone was feeling restless. She might be strong, but she was ignorant. She knew nothing of the Ashenpeakers and her body was a mystery. She knew that fire was dangerous, but other than that, nothing. How long would she live? Would she grow any taller?

Her head was full of questions and she was

determined to find answers. The tiddlins had explored some way into the forest, but it was immense. They had found no sign of habitation. Yet Snowbone was sure there were people out there. If she wanted to find them, they would have to widen the search. And so one crisp, windy day, she sent for Blackeye.

He ran to her instantly, at full speed. 'What?'

'You're going away for a few days,' said Snowbone. 'Into the forest.'

'*Yes!*' cried Blackeye, punching the air. 'Why?'

'There must be someone out there,' said Snowbone. 'We're just not going far enough. I want you to stay out until you find something.'

'OK.'

'I want three of you to go. Who do you want?'

Blackeye thought for a second. 'Two Teeth, 'cause he makes me laugh, and Fudge.'

'Not Mouse?'

'No!'

'I thought you were friends,' said Snowbone mischievously.

'Not specially.' Blackeye couldn't blush, but he was definitely glowing.

'Your decision,' said Snowbone.

And so the three boys shouldered their backpacks, filled their water flasks and were off, slipping between the trees like deer.

Snowbone watched them go. She had every

confidence in Blackeye. He was a good captain and a born adventurer. She knew he wouldn't return until he had found something.

And she was right. He didn't.

9

Blackeye, Fudge and Two Teeth walked on through the forest, fighting the urge to fool around. It wasn't easy. There were branches to swing from and pine cones to shove down shirts. Pools to splash in and mud to squelch through. This was their second day of walking and they hadn't found anything. They needed some amusement. But they were also further into the forest than they had ever been before. They needed to look and listen.

'Snowbone's right,' said Blackeye. 'There must be people somewhere. Even if we have to walk right out of the forest, we must –'

'*Ssh!*' Fudge stopped, a finger to his lips and a hand in the air. '*Listen.*'

Dum. A dull thud, somewhere to their right. And more: a low shushing sound. And a voice, calling.

The boys nodded at each other. Cautiously, silently, they moved towards the sounds. The light was failing; a mist was rising, curling round their feet like serpents. The forest suddenly seemed strange,

35

otherworldly. And then, through the mist, they saw shadows. Shapes. Men, moving silently. Working with axes and saws.

'*Woodcutters*,' whispered Blackeye.

They crept as close as they dared, then hid themselves behind a tangle of brambles. For some reason, they didn't feel like introducing themselves. Not yet. Better to watch awhile.

There were a dozen men, working in teams of two. A constant, savage ripping of timber cut through the forest. One after another, trees fell sighing to the ground.

Suddenly, the boys heard a shout: 'Tarn! There's one here with a face and fingers. What do you want us to do?'

'Hold on,' came the reply. 'I'm coming.' Peaty footsteps thudded on the forest floor and a woman appeared through the veils of mist. 'Where are you, Kilim?'

'Over here.'

The boys crouched lower. The woodcutter who'd shouted – a tall man with sleek black hair – was close by. Suddenly the woman was heading right for them. But thankfully she stopped before she saw anything.

'He's still Moving On,' said the man, pointing at a tree.

'Take him anyway,' said Tarn. 'He's in the way of the wagon.'

'You're the boss.' The black-haired man picked up

his axe and swung it at the tree. *Thuud.* The blade sliced into the wood.

Thuud. A second axe was swung, by a muscular lad with striking blue eyes. The blade landed square on the wound, opening it further. *Thuud.* The man swung again, setting up an easy rhythm.

Blackeye turned to his friends and silently pointed over his shoulder. Two Teeth shook his head and held up his hand. No. Wait. It's not safe.

They were on the other side of the tree now – the black-haired man and the blue-eyed lad – opening a second wound with a cross-cut saw. Splinters flew through the air and littered the forest floor. The tree was starting to topple. The men stood back, breathing heavily. The tree fell. And as the trunk crashed down, a shimmering blue light, no bigger than a plum, came out of the earth. It burrowed out of the soil like a mole, hovered briefly over the fallen tree, then darted away into the mist.

The boys' eyes nearly fell out of their heads. *What was that?* They turned to each other, slack-jawed, dying to say something. Then Fudge glanced back at the woodcutters and a look of complete bafflement came over his face. *What now?* The others turned to see.

The black-haired man had a hand-drill with an enormously long metal bit. He crouched down and inserted it into the cut end of the tree. He turned the handle and the drill bit screwed its way in. Deeper and deeper it went, the metal tunnelling like a silver worm, until a strange, white sap began to ooze. Then the man pulled out the drill and inserted a long rubber tube. He pushed it into the hole as far as it would go and then sucked on the free end, starting the siphon. As the sap began to flow down the tube, he put the free end into a limp leather flagon. He held it there until every last drop of sap had been drained from the tree and the flagon was fat and full. Then he stuck a bung into the flagon and pulled out the tube, coiling it in his hands like a snake.

'Stand back,' said the blue-eyed lad suddenly. 'Wagon's coming.'

From out of the mist came a team of five-horned oxen, their long blue tongues licking the air as they dragged the wagon behind them. In it sat the rest of the men, a rough-looking lot. The black-haired man climbed up on to the wagon as it passed and threw his flagon into a crate. The blue-eyed lad clambered up behind him.

'Well done, lads,' said Tarn, who was riding up front. 'That was a good day's work.'

The men grunted. They were too tired for compliments.

With the crack of a whip, the oxen lumbered off deeper into the forest. The mist closed in behind, wrapping itself around the fallen trees like a shroud. And soon nothing could be heard except the cry of a returning bird and the drip-drip-dripping of the leaves.

'They weren't woodcutters,' said Two Teeth, finally daring to speak. 'They didn't take any wood.'

'No, just that sappy stuff,' said Blackeye.

'What was that blue thing?' said Fudge.

'I've no idea!' said Blackeye. 'But eh, lads – haven't we got a tale to tell!'

10

The boys spent a restless night curled up together on a bed of leaves, tight as mice. They had left the logging site well behind, walking through the darkness for another hour until they felt safe enough to rest. But even then they couldn't sleep. They were listening out for the rumble of a returning wagon, the thud of an axe, the slash of a saw. Those woodcutters weren't to be trusted – they were sure of that.

And so, the next morning, it was a tired and grumpy bunch that marched through the forest. They were taking a different route home. That seemed sensible. But the forest looked the same as it ever did: silent, endless, friendless.

Towards midday, they noticed the trees were thinning ahead, and Fudge's sharp ears heard the sound of whistling on the wind. And so, for a second time, they crept forward – and found a house. A strange little place, with a tin roof and a chimney and dozens of pots and pans dangling from the eaves.

The boys crept closer and hid themselves behind a holly bush. They peered over cautiously. It was a homely scene, quiet and peaceful.

Suddenly the door to the house opened and a man came out carrying a knife and a bucket. He sat down on the porch, reached into the bucket and pulled out a potato. He started to peel it. When he'd finished, he pulled out another and then another. That was it. Nothing exciting, but nothing scary either.

And Blackeye was just wondering whether he should show himself or say something when, beside him, Two Teeth started to fidget. He rubbed his eye. He rubbed the other. Then he put his hand to his nose and stared panic-stricken at Blackeye as he felt the first tickle of a sneeze. He pinched his nostrils together. His eyes grew bigger and rounder and whiter, till they bulged like baby mushrooms. His shoulders started to heave, his lungs filled to bursting and *at – choooo!*

Leaves were blown from the bush. Birds were thrown into the air. Snot and dribble fell like summer rain. And as the man outside the house dropped his knife and jumped to his feet, Two Teeth leapt out of the bush and ran off into the forest, as fast as his legs would carry him, with Blackeye and Fudge haring after him, and they didn't stop running until the house was far, far behind.

Snowbone was sitting on the beach, staring out at the waves, thinking about the boys and wondering just how big the forest could be when she heard it.

WOOOAAAA! WOOOAAAA!

And there was Blackeye, standing in the meeting circle, blowing the horn, with tiddlins running in from every direction to hear his news.

'So?' said Snowbone when they were all seated and listening. 'Did you find anything?'

'We did,' said Blackeye. He told them about the woodcutters and the strange blue light, the siphon tube and the sticky white sap.

'Well!' said Snowbone. 'I didn't know what you'd find, but I wasn't expecting that. These people . . . were they wooden?'

'No,' said Fudge. 'At least, the ones we saw up close weren't. They were human.'

Snowbone frowned. 'Did you see anything else?'

'Yes!' said Blackeye. 'A house, set in a sunny glade, with a man sitting outside.'

'Was *he* wooden?'

The boys looked at each other and shook their heads.

'Don't know,' said Blackeye.

'Oh!' cried Snowbone, throwing up her hands in frustration. 'That was the kind of thing you were supposed to be looking for!'

'I know,' said Blackeye, 'but we didn't manage to get close before he saw us.'

'He saw you?'

Blackeye nodded. 'We were doing fine until Two Teeth sneezed.'

'Sorry,' said Two Teeth. 'I don't know what made me do it.' He flashed Snowbone a toothy grin but she wasn't amused.

'How far is this place?' she said.

'It depends which way you go,' said Fudge. 'It took us three days to get there, but we made it back in under two hours.'

Snowbone smiled. 'Well done, lads. This is good news. The man you saw at the house . . . did he look friendly?'

They nodded.

'I'd like to talk to him.'

'We'll show you the house,' said Blackeye.

'No,' said Snowbone with a sly smile. 'You'll show me the *path*. I'll go alone. Tomorrow. Early.'

11

The next morning, Snowbone headed into the forest, following the track Blackeye had found. When the freckled sunlight became stronger, she knew she was nearing the glade. Once she was there, she took cover behind a bramble thicket and peered over the top.

There was the house, just as Blackeye had described it. And there was the man, pegging out his washing. Two shirts, a vest and a big pair of pants. He looked friendly enough.

Snowbone made up her mind and walked out into the clearing. And the man must have seen her coming, because he turned around and smiled.

'It never ceases to amaze me,' he said. 'Here I am, living in the middle of a forest, with only squirrels and rabbits for company. And yet people drop by just as I am thinking of putting the kettle on.'

Snowbone stared at him, tongue-tied. She had rehearsed a dozen opening lines, but none of them would answer that.

'Are you hungry?' said the man.

She nodded.

'Good. Because I am famished, and food tastes better when it's shared. Go on in. I'll clean myself up and be with you in no time.'

Snowbone went into the house and noted the simple furnishings. Absorbed every new sound and smell. Soon the man entered, grinning broadly and smelling of soap.

'I haven't introduced myself,' he said. 'I'm Figgis.' He held out his hand.

Snowbone looked at it. It was wooden. But wooden or flesh, it made no difference. She didn't like touching people.

Figgis saw her discomfort and smiled. He'd stand there all day if he had to.

Snowbone grabbed his hand, shook it and dropped it like a wet fish. 'Snowbone,' she murmured, unconsciously wiping her hands on her britches.

'I'm very pleased to meet you, Snowbone,' said Figgis, grinning now. He began to busy himself in the kitchen. 'I bet you're wondering what I'm doing out here, on my own, in the middle of the forest?'

Snowbone nodded.

'I'm a tinker. I mend pots and pans, and anything else I can find on my travels. Not that I travel far, mind. Just into town now and then, and round and about the villages.' He took a loaf from a cupboard and began to cut it. 'I saw your friends yesterday. I assume they *are* your friends?'

'Yes.'

'So why aren't they with you today?'

Snowbone shrugged. 'Didn't need them.'

'I can believe that,' said Figgis, glancing at her determined little face. 'But you do need something, or else you wouldn't be here.' He handed her a plate of sandwiches.

Snowbone nodded. 'Information.'

Figgis returned with the tea and found the sandwiches were gone. 'I like a girl with an appetite,' he said. 'More?'

Snowbone nodded eagerly.

'What do you want to know?'

'Everything,' said Snowbone.

Figgis handed her a second plate of sandwiches and eased himself into an armchair. 'You're one of the tiddlins from Black Sand Bay, aren't you?'

'How do you know that?' said Snowbone, instantly on her guard.

'Oh, people pass by and tell me things,' said Figgis. 'Do you want to know how to find your family?'

'No,' said Snowbone, with a puzzled frown. 'I'm not interested in that. I want to know about Ashenpeakers. You're the first grown-up I've seen. I want to know how we live, how we grow, how we die.'

'I can tell you that,' said Figgis.

'And I want to know about the slave trade.'

'Do you now? And why might that be?'

Snowbone's eyes hardened. She held up a stubby

46

finger and thumb, and squeezed them close, like a crab's claw. 'Because I came *this close* to being one myself,' she said. 'And if it takes me the rest of my life, I will find the people who did that to me. And they will be sorry.'

Snowbone fell silent and Figgis, studying her face, knew she would show no mercy. And, in that moment, the tinker had a vision of slavery – no hope, no happiness, no memory of home or family, just toil and torment in a foreign land – and he rejoiced that this strange, pale girl was in the world. 'I have so much to tell you,' he said. 'If I begin now, will you come back for more at another time?'

'Absolutely,' said Snowbone. 'I'll come back tomorrow, and the day after that, and the day after that, as long as it takes. If you will tell, I will listen.'

'Then listen now,' said Figgis. 'And learn.'

12

Snowbone took one look at the turbulent sky the next morning and cancelled her plans for the day. *Oh, spits and spats and hairy cats!* Why did there have to be a storm today? She desperately wanted to learn more from Figgis. Already he had told her how the Ashenpeakers were descended from nine magical beings called the Ancients. Today, he would explain their life cycle, from birth to death – except she wasn't going to be there. She couldn't leave the camp with a storm coming. There was too much to do.

Thick, anxious clouds were piling in from the north. Hundreds of seabirds were abandoning the waves and flying inland. They swooped and dived beneath the lowering clouds and slashed the sky with ragged calls. The wind was rising. The trees at the forest fringe were starting to sway and the sand eddied about her feet as she walked down the beach to the sea. Mouse was already there, sniffing the wind.

'Is it bad?' said Snowbone.

'Very bad,' said Mouse. 'Worse than any storm we've seen so far.'

Snowbone frowned. They had seen several storms, some of them severe. If this one was worse . . . She marched to the meeting circle, picked up the horn and blew it.

'Secure the shelters,' she said when everyone had assembled. 'Everything movable should be taken to the store cave. Tigermane, set up beds in the cave. We'll spend the night there. Fudge, we'll need a supply of fresh water.'

She waved them away and gazed again at the rolling waves. Much as she loved the sea, right now she was glad to be on land.

By midday, the sky was swollen and bruised. A strange, shadowy twilight played across the land and the wind had worsened. It tormented the tide. It bullied the birds. It stalked the forest like a troll, snapping any tree that refused to bend.

Snowbone and her gang sat on the beach, watching the waves. The air was thick with salt and spray and wind-whistle. Then suddenly the sky blackened and the rain began: a torrent of water cascading down, sluicing the beach, rattling the shingle. And the tiddlins, instantly soaked, leapt to their feet and started to dance. A wild, primeval dance as the earth met the sky and the sky met the sea. Open to the elements, they spun and whirled, powered by an energy they couldn't understand. It charged their feet and urged them on in a glorious, abandoned celebration of life. They laughed and danced like demons, and still the rain came down in a grey, grey blessing.

But in the middle of it all, Blackeye stopped dancing and stared out to sea.

'A ship,' he said, though no one was listening. He walked to the water's edge and peered through the curtains of rain. '*SHIP!*'

Snowbone was instantly by his side. 'Where?'

'There,' he said, pointing into the teeth of the storm.

The dancers were breaking their circle now, running to join them.

Snowbone followed the line of Blackeye's finger and screwed up her eyes, but she couldn't see anything. Just greys and whites and blues and blacks, colliding, riding, striding the storm.

'Yes!' said Fudge, his head bobbing up and down in excitement. 'I can see it.'

Snowbone cursed her stupid eyes and squinted harder.

'It's a brig,' said Two Teeth. 'You don't think it's the *Mermaid*?'

'No,' said Blackeye. 'She's too big.'

Snowbone glared at them and cursed again. She still couldn't see it.

'Whoever it is,' said Two Teeth, 'they are in big trouble.'

Snowbone was nearly in the water now. From the tip of her nose to the tip of her toes, she was taut with frustration. Was she the only one who couldn't see the blessed thing? Well, if she was, she wasn't about to let anyone know. 'There's nothing we can do,' she said, turning away.

'We can watch for survivors,' said Tigermane. 'She'll go down. She won't stand a buffeting like that.'

'She's heading for the Red Rock!' cried Blackeye.

Necks stretched and eyes narrowed as everyone strained to see. The Red Rock was a jagged tooth of volcanic stone that lay off the coast of the island. The tiddlins had seen it when the pirates rowed them ashore and knew how deadly it was. The peak could slice through timber like a knife through an apple. A ship could go down in minutes, and take her crew with her. Why was the rock red? Because it was stained with the blood of all the sailors who had died there . . .

'*Oh!*' cried Mouse. '*Oh!*'

Snowbone knew the worst had happened. She could tell by looking at the faces around her. The ship had reached the rock and, with a great shudder, it had toppled as the deadly peak ripped through its timbers.

'She's a goner,' said Fudge.

No one spoke. The tragedy unfolded on the savage stage of the sea, and the tiddlins could only watch, horrified yet fascinated. And they were so wrapped up in the storm and the sorrow that none of them noticed the wind. It was howling like a dragon, soaring up and down the beach, swooping over the forest, tearing trees out by their roots, hurling driftwood into the air like dandelion seeds. And then, with a vengeful wail, it rushed upon the group and Mouse was taken, tossed through the air and spat into the hungry sea.

'*MOUSE!*' cried Blackeye. He ran to the water's edge. '*MOUSE!*'

'She won't drown, she'll float,' said Two Teeth hopefully.

'That's not the point!' snapped Snowbone. 'She could drift for miles. Fudge, get a rope. Take one off a shelter.' She stared at the raging ocean, trying to see where Mouse was heading.

Blackeye waded into the water. '*Mouse!*' he cried. '*Mouse!*' He scanned the waves, looking for any sign of life.

'*There!*' shouted Tigermane. '*She's there!*'

A hand was reaching for the sky. Wooden fingers, panic-palmed. Below it, a terrified face with a mouth like a black button. Calling, calling, but the words were lost to the shouting storm.

'*Hold on!*' shouted Blackeye. '*Mouse! Hold on! I'm coming! Aargh . . .!*'

Snowbone pulled him back so hard, he fell over his own feet. 'What are you doing?' he cried, flapping on the sand like an angry octopus.

'Wait for Fudge!' said Snowbone. 'I've already lost one captain. I don't want to lose two. Look, he's coming.'

Fudge was sprinting over the sand with a heavy rope.

Blackeye grabbed it from him and tied one end around his middle. 'You'll have to hold me, buddy,' he said.

Fudge nodded and tied the other end around himself. Soon more hands were on the rope. Everyone wanted to help with the pulling.

Blackeye waded into the water and started to swim. Further and further he went, battling against the waves, swimming towards Mouse. He could feel the water seeping into his wooden flesh. He was growing heavier by the minute. He swam on, turning his head from side to side as he looked for her. But every stroke was an effort. The salt water stung his eyes and it was dark now. So dark.

But there she was. Floating on the water. Limp and lifeless. A piece of flotsam. Driftwood. Deadwood. *Mouse.*

Blackeye swam to her, threw himself high above the waves and seized her. 'Pull!' he shouted, and the rope tightened as the tiddlins hauled them in.

Shooosh! Blackeye bounced over the waves backwards, with Mouse held tightly in his arms. He didn't let go till they were back on the beach, sprawled on the sand like a pair of starfish. Only when the tiddlins took her from him did he close his eyes and allow himself to relax.

But not for long. As Fudge began untying the rope, Blackeye opened his eyes, sat up and looked for Mouse. The tiddlins were crouched around her. She wasn't moving.

Blackeye crawled over, pushed his way into the circle and took Mouse's body in his arms. 'Mouse,' he said. 'Mouse. Can you hear me?'

Nothing. But suddenly her eyelids were flickering . . . opening . . . and Blackeye was looking into her warm, loving eyes.

Mouse nodded, very gently, and smiled up at him. And in that moment Blackeye thought her smile was the brightest point in a dark, dark world. Carefully, he helped her to her feet, but Mouse was so wet she couldn't walk. So he picked her up and carried her up the beach, out of the storm and into the safety of the store caves.

The tiddlins followed, noisily wondering at Blackeye's bravery. The ship was forgotten; nothing could be done anyway. They would have to see what the morning would bring.

Only Snowbone remained on the beach. She watched the tiddlins dancing over the black sand. 'It's like a walking wedding,' she said and, with a smile, she followed on behind.

13

By morning, the storm had passed. The tiddlins emerged from the store cave and found a warm, welcoming day. The air was tangy with the taste of the sea. The birds had reclaimed the sky. Everything seemed right with the world.

But down on the beach, it was another story. A scene of complete and utter devastation greeted the tiddlins when they returned to camp. The black sand was strewn with all kinds of debris thrown up by the sea. Mounds of seaweed, scuttling with crabs. Dead birds. Driftwood. Endless wreckage from the stricken ship: barrels, timbers, ropes, sailcloth, furniture, tools, bodies. So many dead bodies. Goats, chickens, rats. Sailors. Dozens of drowned sailors. Some on the beach, some in the water. The gulls were feasting.

The tiddlins walked among them, anxiously searching for familiar faces from the *Mermaid*. But these men didn't look like pirates. Then Fudge found the ship's nameplate, *Tamberlory*, and the wondering was over.

'We can't leave them lying here like this,' said Tigermane. 'The birds are pecking them to bits.'

Snowbone thought for a moment. 'I don't want to burn them,' she said. 'The smoke might attract attention. We'll have to bury them. Blackeye, find some shovels and spades. Organize some diggers. We'll bury them over there, behind the rocks. Tigermane, check the shelters. See if they need repairing. The rest of you can comb the beach. Anything worth salvaging can go to the store cave.'

The tiddlins went about their work and Snowbone turned her attention to the wreckage. A waistcoat, with shiny buttons. A bent spoon. A broken mop handle. Nothing of use except –

What was happening? Such a commotion further down the beach! Ten, twenty tiddlins were standing around something, jostling each other, talking all at once. As Snowbone ran towards them, she could hear Fudge's voice above the rest: 'Bring a crowbar!' And suddenly Two Teeth was dashing to fetch something.

'What is it?' said Snowbone, elbowing her way forward.

It was a wooden chest. A fine-looking thing, made from dark, polished wood with a hinged lid.

'It's a treasure chest!' said Fudge, unable to contain his excitement. 'It's locked but it's heavy. It is *soooo* heavy.'

Snowbone knelt down and examined it closely.

There were two golden padlocks on the front, holding the lid firmly down.

'He's back!' cried a voice, and the crowd parted to let Two Teeth through. He handed Snowbone the crowbar; she handed it to Fudge. She would look a right fool if she couldn't force the locks. Fudge was stronger. Let him try.

Fudge was only too willing. There was treasure in that chest and nothing was going to stop him having it. He attacked the locks like a gorilla, with a grunt and a heave, and – *POING! POING!* – the padlocks snapped right off. Fudge threw open the lid – and there was no treasure. There was a boy. A black human boy, quite naked except for a piece of cloth tied round his loins. He was packed in so tightly, he couldn't move if he wanted to. But more than this, he was bound. His hands and feet had been tied together with lengths of silver cord.

And with a supreme effort, the boy turned his head, looked straight at Snowbone and whispered two words: 'Help me.'

14

While Snowbone was standing on the beach, gazing down at the bound boy, Figgis the tinker was repairing a broken window. In the night, the storm had ripped a fence post out of the ground and hurled it at the house like a spear. The post had smashed through the window and fallen at Figgis's feet.

'It's lucky you slowed it down,' said Figgis to the window as he knocked out the broken glass. 'If you hadn't, I'd have been skewered like a sausage on a barbecue.'

He held the new glass up to the frame to see if it would fit. As he did, he saw something out of the corner of his eye. One of the bushes was moving.

'Who's that?' he asked himself. 'Snowbone? She's mighty shy this morning.'

He put down the glass and looked around. The forest was quiet, basking in the late-autumn sunshine. But suddenly there was a mad flutter of wings and a pheasant cluckered off into the trees.

'Come out!' called Figgis. 'I know you're there.'

Nothing moved. But Figgis could feel a decision was being made somewhere among the trees. Then the bushes slowly parted and out came . . . a lad. A tall human lad with extraordinarily blue eyes. And behind him a black-haired man. Figgis started to suspect there might be others still hiding.

'Mornin',' said the blue-eyed lad, with a curt nod.

'So it is,' returned Figgis.

'We were just passing,' said the lad.

Scouting more like, thought Figgis. *These are slave traders. No question about it.*

'Do you have any water?' said the black-haired man.

Figgis nodded and pointed to a barrel at the side of the house. The man walked over to it, cupped his hands and drank. Figgis noticed the man had a water flask attached to his belt, but he didn't refill it.

'We'll be on our way, then,' said the man, wiping his wet hands on the seat of his britches.

'Right,' said Figgis. 'Safe journey.'

The man nodded and headed off into the forest, trailed by the lad. Figgis stood where he was, waiting to see if any more men would show themselves. They didn't.

But when he went inside, he watched from the window and, within a minute, four more traders emerged from the undergrowth and followed on behind.

'What can they want?' said Figgis as he set the

59

kettle on the stove. 'They're not likely to find eggs out here. *Ah!* Are they looking for the kids?'

Figgis glanced out of the window again. Hopefully, Snowbone would turn up soon. He needed to warn her. The slavers would return.

15

Back at the beach, Snowbone tipped up the chest and threw the boy out on to the black sand.

'Snowbone!' cried Mouse. 'Be careful!'

'How else did you think we'd get him out?' said Snowbone. 'He was as tight as a fat man's sock.'

Mouse still wasn't happy. 'You didn't have to be quite so rough,' she said. 'You'll cover him in bruises.'

'He has those already,' said Blackeye, looking at the thin body sprawled on the sand. He reached into his pocket, took out a knife and began to cut the silver cords.

'He's so tall,' said Tigermane. 'How did they get him in there?'

No one answered. They were too busy wondering *why* he was in there.

Once the ropes were cut, the boy tried to stretch out his legs. But he had been in the chest so long, his muscles had completely seized up. He groaned and his face puckered with pain.

'This is going to take some time,' said Snowbone.

'We'll carry him up to the shelters. Tigermane, run to the store cave and fetch some blankets. Blackeye, take his legs. Two Teeth, take his body.'

And so the boy was carried up the beach to the shelters. There he was laid upon a bed and given water. He drank deeply, then wet his hands and wiped them over his face. He whispered his thanks and smiled weakly. Then he closed his eyes and slept – a deep, safe sleep – while the tiddlins watched and waited and wondered. Who? What? Why?

The sun was setting by the time the strange boy awoke. He was feeling much better. His limbs ached but he could move them. He was ravenously hungry and readily devoured three bowls of soup. Mouse was thrilled – she had spent the whole afternoon making it. The boy didn't know how honoured he was; Mouse had never made soup before. The pirate wives had taught her how, but the tiddlins were so wary of fire, they still ate everything raw.

But the boy was human. Mouse had realized that when night came, he would be cold. He would need warm clothing and nourishing food. So she had rummaged in the store cave for a bundle of clothes, and gathered armfuls of vegetables. Tigermane had collected wood and together, very carefully, they had built a fire in the middle of the meeting circle. And that evening, as the boy sat by the fire, snug in a woollen jacket and britches, his fingers cradling another bowl of soup, the tiddlins gathered round and he told his story.

'I am Manu, High Prince of Balaa,' he said proudly. 'I am fourteen years old, and right now, I should be sitting in a palace —'

'You should be dead,' said Snowbone.

Manu stared at her, completely taken by surprise. Then he smiled. 'You're right,' he said. 'You saved my life. I couldn't have lasted much longer.'

'Why were you in the chest?' said Snowbone.

'It's a long story,' said Manu.

'Shorten it,' said Snowbone.

'Yes, Your Majesty,' said Manu, clearly amused. He finished his soup and settled himself. 'My story begins on the island of Balaa, where I was born. My father was Meru, King of Balaa. My mother was Arcana, his queen. I was their only child and they doted on me — especially my mother, I believe. But she died when I was one year old, and my father chose to remarry.

'His new wife was beautiful but ambitious. In the beginning, she tolerated me. But when I was eight years old, she gave birth to a boy, Jobi, and things began to change. My father was growing old, and my stepmother wanted Jobi to be king after him. But I was the heir to the throne. I was the firstborn. If Jobi were to be king, she would have to kill me first.'

'No!' gasped Mouse.

'Yes!' said Manu. 'She had a servant, Enkola – a spiteful man – who had served her faithfully for years. He would do anything for her. *Anything*. So she told him to kill me. She didn't care how he did it. He could cut my throat, drown me in the river – anything, as long as I was out of the way.'

'No!' said Mouse again.

Snowbone dug her in the ribs. 'Shut up!' she hissed. 'We'll be here all night.'

'Enkola was a superstitious man,' said Manu, picking up the thread of the tale. 'A very clever man. He studied the stars. He believed in omens. He believed in the eternal power of kings and he believed in destiny. And when Enkola looked to the stars for guidance that night, he saw a red moon. And he decided, there and then, that it was wrong to kill me. I was a prince. He had no right to determine my fate.

'And so he chose both to *obey* and to *disobey* the queen. In the dead of night, he stole into my bedchamber, as she had commanded, and put a wet cloth against my face. I awoke. I struggled and fought, kicked like a rabbit, but the cloth made me drowsy. Enkola carried me down to the beach. But he didn't kill me.

'He bound my hands and feet with cords and put me into the chest. All the while he gabbled on about omens and moons, till I was quite dizzy. Then he slammed down the lid, fastened the padlocks and left me to my destiny. The tide carried me away . . . I drifted on the waves. For how long, I do not know. And then the storm carried me here.'

'You're making this up,' said Snowbone. 'Kings. Wicked stepmothers. How stupid do you think we are? This is a fairy tale.'

'No,' said Manu. 'It's true. I swear on my father's life.'

'Prove it,' said Snowbone.

Manu stared at her. 'Why should I? I know it to be true.'

'So you have no proof?'

'I have this chain,' said Manu. He showed her a fine golden chain round his neck.

'Give it here,' said Snowbone.

'I can't,' said Manu.

'What do you mean, you can't?' said Snowbone. 'Take it off and give it here.'

'I can't,' said Manu. 'That's the whole point.'

He leaned towards her, too close for her liking. She felt his breath on her face and squirmed.

'Look,' said Manu, holding up the necklace. 'There's no fastening.'

Snowbone looked closer and found it was true. She slid the slender chain through her fingers. It was exquisite. But there was no clasp – just a single, unbroken length of gold. 'How did you get it on?' she said.

'I was born wearing it,' said Manu. 'Only a prince

of Balaa would be born with such a gift. This is my proof. Whether you choose to believe it or not is entirely up to you.'

Snowbone said no more.

'Have you ever tried to cut it?' said Blackeye.

'Enkola tried, before he put me in the box,' said Manu. 'He had wire cutters, but they wouldn't cut through.'

'But it's so delicate!' said Mouse. 'There's nothing of it!'

'I know,' said Manu proudly.

'Manu,' said Tigermane, 'there's something I don't understand. Where does the *Tamberlory* fit in?'

Manu shook his head. 'Now *I* don't understand!' he laughed. 'What is the *Tamberlory*?'

'It's a ship,' said Mouse. 'It went down last night in the storm and the wreckage was washed up on the beach. We thought you were part of that.'

'No,' said Manu. 'I was never aboard a ship! I was on my own out there, believe me.'

And they did believe him. Except Snowbone. She wanted to believe him, but she couldn't help feeling that Manu, like the weather, wasn't to be trusted.

16

Early the next morning, while the tiddlins were still fussing over Manu like a new puppy, Snowbone slipped out of camp unnoticed. She bounded through the forest. It was a glorious day. Sunlight was filtering through the leaf canopy, strewing her path with golden pennies of light. She felt rich indeed.

When she reached the glade, she saw Figgis digging in the vegetable patch. As she approached, he spun round, holding the spade like a weapon. But when he saw who it was, the anger and fear fell away from his face and, with a sigh, he lowered it.

'Who were you expecting?' said Snowbone.

'No one,' said Figgis wearily. He scanned the forest. 'Are you on your own again?'

Snowbone nodded.

'You want to be careful,' said Figgis.

'I'm not afraid,' said Snowbone.

'I can see that,' said Figgis. Snowbone stood no taller than his middle, but she gazed fixedly at him, her hands on her hips, completely assured. He smiled. 'Let's go in. I'll fix us something to eat.'

'I didn't believe you, you know,' said Snowbone as she followed him. 'When you said you weren't expecting anyone. You looked scared.'

'I had visitors yesterday. Slave traders.'

'Really? How do you know they were traders?'

Figgis shrugged. 'They were human. A bit rough. Mean-looking.'

'Yes, but the sap-collectors look like that.'

'Sap-collectors?' said Figgis. 'Who are they?'

'I don't really know,' said Snowbone. 'Blackeye saw them. There was a gang of them, cutting down trees. But it was a bit strange, because they didn't take the timber. They had these long siphon things and they drilled into the wood. Then they drained off some white stuff into a flagon. They had hundreds of flagons, in crates. Oh, and there was this blue thing that came out of the earth and whizzed – Figgis, are you all right?'

The tinker looked as if he were going to be sick. He swayed on his feet, then gripped the back of the chair for support.

'*Figgis?*'

'They're not trees,' he said heavily. 'They're Ancestors.'

'Sit down,' said Snowbone in confusion. 'I'll put the kettle on.'

'Snowbone, you have no idea what you've just told me! It's unbelievable. A nightmare.'

'I don't understand.'

'No, you wouldn't, because I hadn't got round to telling you. Forget the kettle – I want to show you something. Come on.'

Figgis took her outside, across the glade and into the forest. There he stopped beside an enormous tree with a trunk so massive Snowbone couldn't walk round it in fewer than twenty steps.

'Now *this*,' said Figgis, 'might look like a normal tree, but it's not. It's an ashen tree. It didn't grow from a seed, like an oak or a sycamore. This was once a man. A living, breathing Ashenpeaker.'

Snowbone stared at him. '*What?*'

'This is what I was planning to tell you today. You wanted to know how Ashenpeakers die? Well, we don't die. Not like humans. When our time comes, we Move On. It's a strange process. It takes several weeks, but basically we turn into trees. Ashen trees.'

Snowbone was still staring – shocked, horrified, but desperately wanting to know more.

'I know it's hard to take in,' said Figgis with a smile. 'But it's true.'

'Does it hurt?'

'No, it doesn't hurt. You see this feller here?' He slapped the tree beside him. 'This is my great-great-great-grandfather Burdock Figgis. One day, more than a hundred years ago, he felt his time had come. And so he came here, to this part of the forest, and slowly, peacefully, he Moved On. And this here –'

he touched another vast ashen tree – 'is his wife, my great-great-great-grandmother. And this is my grandfather. This is my mother. This is my great-uncle. This is my brother, who Moved On at the age of eight. This one here is my father. So you see –' his face suddenly hardened – 'those men weren't cutting down trees, they were cutting down people.'

'*This one has a face and fingers*,' said Snowbone.

'What?'

'Something the traders said. I've just remembered. Oh! This is outrageous!' She started to pace up and down angrily. 'Why are they doing this?'

'Now that I don't know,' admitted Figgis. 'Ashen sap is strong stuff, for sure. It has the power to heal. But why they'd want it in any great quantity is beyond me.'

'And what was the blue light?'

'Ah, *that*,' said Figgis. 'That was the soul of the Ancestor, leaving the body.'

'Where was it going?'

'I don't know. But I do know this: it won't ever come back.'

And Snowbone looked at Figgis and saw such bleak despair in his face, she shuddered. Despite the sunshine, the day had suddenly turned very, very dark.

17

Night had fallen by the time Snowbone left Figgis. He had talked all day, while she soaked up the words like a sponge. Given the darkness outside, Figgis had suggested she stay the night, but Snowbone had declined the offer. She said she would return the next day and, with that, she had disappeared into the shadows, heading for Black Sand Bay.

Now Figgis sat quietly in his house, mending a hole in his working shirt. Except for the occasional creaking of his chair and the wind rustling in the trees outside, there was no sound. Nothing unusual. But Figgis couldn't help feeling there was something wrong.

He put down his mending, eased open the front door and slipped outside. It was too dark to see anything: the moon was tucked up in a blanket of cloud. But the tinker's ears were attuned to the night. To the snuffles and rustles of the forest creatures. And whatever it was, moving out there, it wasn't furred or feathered.

Then he saw a glow: a horn lantern, shining between the trees and *thuud*. The first axe struck home.

And now Figgis was running towards the amber glow. Running, running, running faster than he had in years. *Thuud*. Tearing through brambles, stumbling over roots, hurtling towards the sound of slaughter. *Thuud*. And there they were: the black-haired man and another he hadn't seen before – a towering giant of a man, with hands so monstrously huge, his axe looked like a toy.

Thuud. Figgis saw his Ancestor standing between them, with a great gaping wound in his trunk. Saw the giant raise his axe a fifth time. Saw the smirk on the face of the black-haired man. And Figgis lunged forward, crashing into the circle of light.

And that was when everything seemed to go into slow motion.

As Figgis hurled himself at the giant:

The axe was thrown from the monstrous hand
And flew through the air like a silver owl,
Fell at the feet of the black-haired man,
Who raised it high and brought it down: *shoooo*.

Figgis saw his severed arm,
Falling to the sodden ground,
And with his remaining hand,
Fumbled for his faithful knife.

Then he thrust the silver blade
In the belly of the giant.
Blood fell down like ruby rain
And the giant groaned in pain: *ohhh.*

The black-haired man, the bleeding giant,
Stumbled off in shadow flight.
Figgis closed his heavy eyes,
Tumbled into darkest night.

18

Another morning, another march through the forest. But Snowbone wasn't her usual self. She hadn't slept. Now she was tired and grouchy. Her eyes were fixed on the ground and her shoulders sagged. Knowledge was a heavy burden.

Eventually she reached Figgis's house and found the front door closed. *Strange*, she thought. *On a day like this, Figgis would have it open.* She moved closer, wary now. There was a lantern burning inside. *In the middle of the morning?*

Snowbone felt her heart leap in her chest. She crept forward and peered through the window. The room looked empty. She opened the door and went in. No one there.

She went outside again and scanned the trees. Nothing moving. She sniffed the air, momentarily wishing that Mouse was with her. She had a keener nose.

She decided to search the forest fringe. She walked through the trees, looked under bushes, found nothing. Then she saw the knife. Figgis's knife. He had polished it yesterday while he talked. Now its blade was crusty with blood.

A few footsteps further and she found the sleeve of Figgis's jacket. It was empty.

Next, a leather flagon.

Snowbone inched forward, reading the scene with every sense. She felt no fear, just a calm, controlled thrill.

And suddenly there he was. Lying in a crumpled heap, face down, quite still.

Snowbone touched him with the toe of her boot. Nothing. She rocked him with her foot. Still nothing. She kicked him. Figgis moaned and slowly rolled over.

'I thought you were dead,' said Snowbone.

'So did I, for a minute,' said Figgis. 'Storm and thunder, my head is banging like a drum.'

'What happened to your arm?'

'Cut off with an axe.'

'But where is it? I just saw your sleeve. It was empty.'

'Yes, well, it would be. When bits get cut off, they vanish into thin air. Don't ask me why. I don't know.'

'Will your arm grow back?'

'It will,' said Figgis wearily. 'But at my age, it takes time. A week. Maybe longer. Will you help me up?'

Snowbone helped the tinker to his feet and supported him as he walked to the house. There he lay on the bed while she made tea.

'*Oh!*' sighed Figgis as he drank the first of several cups. 'I have never needed that more.'

75

'Tell me,' said Snowbone.

'Yes, m'lady,' said Figgis. He eased himself into a more comfortable position. 'They came back last night. One I'd seen before and another – a giant of a man. I felt there was something wrong, you know? So I went outside, and they were there, with their axes. They were cutting down my brother. Can you believe that? Snowbone, hand on heart, I tell you: I don't know what to do. This is not just another part of the forest. This is a sacred grove. For hundreds of years my family has been coming here to Move On, and there has always been a Figgis here to watch over them. A guardian, if you like. But they have never needed guarding until now. And I *will* guard them. To the last breath in my body, I will fight for my family. I will not let the slavers have them.'

'The slavers will return,' said Snowbone.

'Aye, they will,' said Figgis, 'and they'll be angry. I cut one of them last night. Stuck him like a pig. But he won't be dead. Not a man his size.'

'You can't fight them on your own,' said Snowbone.

'I don't have an alternative.'

'You do,' said Snowbone. 'I'll bring my gang. We'll face them together.'

And when Figgis looked in her granite-grey eyes and saw that she meant it, he felt weak with relief.

'I'll be back,' said Snowbone. And with that, she stormed out of the house.

19

Snowbone ran through the forest back to Black Sand Bay. Her mind was awash with thoughts, but one loomed larger than all the others. 'Why did I insist on seeing Figgis on my own?' she asked herself over and over again. 'If Blackeye was with me, he could fetch the others and I could stay guard.' Because of her pig-headedness, Figgis was alone. 'There's no need,' she muttered angrily. 'No need at all.'

Snowbone arrived back at camp to find a flurry of activity. Two Teeth had led a successful hunting expedition; now he was skinning a deer. Blackeye and Fudge were building a tree house. Tigermane and Mouse were weaving rush mats. Everywhere Snowbone looked, someone seemed to be mending or building, cleaning or digging. It seemed a shame to leave it all behind. But this day was always going to come. It had just come sooner than any of them had imagined.

Snowbone strode to the meeting circle, picked up the horn and blew it.

'Gather your belongings!' she cried as the tiddlins came running. 'We're leaving. I want everything packed and ready to go within the hour.'

'Leaving?' said Mouse. 'Why? Where are we going?'

'South,' said Snowbone. 'There's another storm coming.'

Mouse sniffed the air. 'I can't smell anything.'

'It's not that kind of storm,' said Snowbone. 'Fudge, bring the weapons. Tigermane, food – everything we have. Blackeye, water. Two Teeth, ropes.'

The captains ran to obey.

'If there is a storm coming,' persisted Mouse, 'why are we striking camp? Surely it's better to bed down here? We survived the last one.'

'And we shall survive this.'

'But –'

'If you don't want to come, stay here.'

'No!' said Mouse, in a sudden panic. 'I was just saying –'

'Well, don't,' said Snowbone. 'Just *do*.'

Mouse's eyes filled with tears. She bit her lip to stop them falling and hurried away.

Snowbone turned to Manu, who was sitting on one of the meeting stones, looking lost.

'Don't just sit there,' she said, prodding him hard. 'Do something. Pack the tarpaulins.'

Manu stared at her. 'Am I coming with you?'

'Of course you are,' said Snowbone. 'You're one of us.'

Manu beamed at her and sprinted away.

Snowbone walked to the tideline and gazed out to sea. She took a deep breath of salty air . . . held it . . . sighed it away. This was where she belonged. Black Sand Bay was the only life she had known. The great bowl of the sky above, the blue below. The wind on her face, the taste of salt on her tongue. She had absorbed the ocean into her body. The salt had seeped into her wooden limbs. The grain on her skin was the swirling of sand. Her eyes were the grey of gull wings. Her hair was the silvery spinning of foam. Her heart was a pirate ship, set to plunder.

She loved this place. She didn't want to leave it. But she had no choice. 'I shall return,' she promised, and the wind snatched her words and tossed them into the waves.

Within the hour, the camp was dismantled, packed and shouldered. With a nod from Snowbone, suddenly they were off, with their bundles on their backs, like a trail of snails. South into the forest, with Snowbone explaining about Figgis, Ancestors and the slavers as they went.

By late afternoon, the light was already failing and, though no one could feel it except Manu, the temperature was dropping. Winter was definitely on its way.

'I can smell smoke,' said Mouse suddenly.

Snowbone stopped and sniffed. Nothing.

'Are you sure?'

'Yes,' said Mouse.

Snowbone didn't doubt her.

'Close?'

'No,' said Mouse. 'It's faint. Half an hour away. Maybe more.'

Snowbone frowned and they marched on, faster now.

Pfoooow.

A gunshot. Sharp, clear, unmistakable.

Snowbone threw off her backpack. '*Leave the stuff!*' she hissed. '*Where's Fudge? Fudge, weapons. Now.*' With her pirate dagger held tight in her wooden fingers, she ran on.

The house wasn't far; they were soon there. Snowbone stopped running and signalled to the others to creep forward. The air was thick and dark. Heavy with woodsmoke. Snowbone listened for any sound of slavers, but there was nothing. Just a strange, still silence broken by an occasional thump and the soft crackling of flames.

Snowbone stepped into the glade and stared, horrified, at what she found. The house was gone. Nothing remained but a gutted, smouldering ruin, black with soot, hot with embers.

All around, there was nothing but wanton destruction. The water barrel had been overturned. Winter vegetables had been torn out of the ground. Clean washing had been trampled into the dirt.

And in the sacred glade, every ashen tree had been cut down.

Snowbone fell to her knees and stared at the fallen Ancestors. A tight knot of anger twisted her belly. Stole her breath. Her brain battled through pain and disbelief, trying to make sense of things. *Who had done this? Why?*

Unconsciously, her hand reached for an ashen tree.

She felt the stickiness of the sap on her fingers. But there was something wrong. Alert again, Snowbone looked closely at the trunk. There was no drill hole. She looked at another, and another. They were all intact. Why? Sap was rare and precious. Why had the slavers disappeared without taking it?

Oh! Snowbone took a deep breath to calm herself. She knew why. This hadn't been business. This was an act of revenge. Cold, calculated revenge. The slavers had no intention of harvesting the trees. They had been felled for one reason only – to punish Figgis. He had dared to defy them. This had been his reward.

But where was Figgis?

Snowbone approached the burning house, warily watching for sparks. Fire was her deadliest foe; she wouldn't take chances. She could make out shapes among the fallen timbers. A blackened kettle . . . a charred chair . . . sooty pots and pans . . . a twisted bed frame . . . *a pair of boots*. Snowbone felt an unfamiliar tightening in her chest as she saw them. She could imagine the scene. Figgis had been inside. The slavers had surprised him. Beaten him until he fell unconscious to the floor. It was possible, even with a wooden head, if the blows were hard enough.

Snowbone turned away and saw the tiddlins had gathered, waiting for her words.

'These are dark deeds,' she said. 'Murder . . . massacre . . . These things must be avenged. For the sake of the Figgis clan. For the sake of us all. I swear to you now, I will find the men who did this. I will make them pay for what they have done. And though I will travel alone if need be, I hope that you will all go with me.'

A murmur of agreement spread through the gang.

'It will be a dangerous mission,' Snowbone went on, 'and it won't be easy. We have no idea who these men are, or what they look like.'

'Yes, we do,' said Mouse. 'Blackeye, Fudge and Two Teeth saw them, cutting down trees.'

Snowbone shook her head. 'We don't know it was them. There could be more than one gang.'

'And even if it was them,' said Fudge, 'that was ages ago. I can't remember what they looked like.'

'One has raven-black hair,' said a cracked voice behind them. 'One is a lad with the bluest eyes you have ever seen. Find these and you will find them all.'

It was Figgis.

21

'I thought you were dead!' said Snowbone. 'There's a burned pair of boots in the house.'

'They were my old ones,' said Figgis, shakily walking towards them. 'Luckily, I was wearing my new. It must be Fate. She wants me well shod for the journey ahead.'

'Journey?' said Snowbone.

Figgis smiled at her. 'Did you think I'd let you go without me?'

'You said you'd never leave this place.'

'I did, I know. I said this place was a sacred grove, and it was. But look at it now. It's a killing ground. They've slaughtered them all. Seventy-three ashen trees. An entire Figgis family – gone.'

'Will they regrow?' said Mouse.

'No, they won't,' said Figgis. 'They're dead.' He looked across at his fallen Ancestors and his eyes hardened. 'They would have gone on for another two, three, four hundred years. But now . . .' He said no more.

'We heard a gunshot,' said Manu.

'I shot one of the slavers,' said Figgis. 'He's dead. Over there.' He pointed into the trees behind the house. 'That was right at the beginning. I was hit on the head soon after. You can feel it.'

He leaned down towards Snowbone. She backed away. Two Teeth stepped forward and felt the tinker's head instead.

'Cor!' he said. 'There's a ruddy great dent! Did it hurt?'

'No,' said Figgis, 'but it did knock me out cold. So I didn't see the felling, or them setting the house alight.'

'Why didn't they kill you?' said Tigermane.

'I don't know,' said Figgis. 'They'll wish they had when I find them.'

'We'll leave in the morning,' said Snowbone.

'Why not now?' said Blackeye. 'They can't be far ahead. We could lose them by tomorrow.'

'No,' said Snowbone firmly. 'We'll make camp here tonight. We need to damp down the house. One strong wind and the whole forest will be up in flames.'

'What about the ashen trees?' said Mouse. 'It seems wrong to leave them just lying there. Is there anything we can do for them, Mister Figgis?'

'If there is,' said the tinker, 'I can't think of it. I don't know what to do, and that's the truth. I don't like to see them lying there, but we can't bury them. I'd float them down the river into the sea, except there's no river. I can't burn them. I just *can't*, even though they're dead. And besides, it's too risky. We're damping down the house because of sparks. How can we burn seventy-three ashen trees? I can't believe I'm saying it, but I think we'll have to leave them. They won't be there forever. The wind and the rain and the beetles and the worms will do their work in time. That's the way of the world.'

'Could we move them closer together?' said Tigermane. 'Into groups? They might like that.'

Figgis thought for a moment. 'That's not a bad idea,' he said at last. 'I'm sure my mother would like to be lying next to my father. And we could put my brother alongside.'

And so they got to work. Wives were carried to husbands, children were returned to parents and laid to rest under a sullen sky. Figgis cursed the loss of his arm. He had to watch helplessly while others toiled, and it grieved him. But it was soon done, and the band ate a hearty meal and abandoned themselves to sleep.

Blackeye dreamed of adventure. Manu dreamed of home. Figgis dreamed of a giant. Snowbone dreamed of the sea.

And somewhere in the night, the guilty slept too, dreaming of gold.

22

When they awoke at dawn, the tiddlins found themselves rimed with the first frost of winter. All around them, the forest was silver-chilled, diamond-dusted.

Soon the camp was packed and loaded, and the tiddlins stood ready to go. Snowbone looked at them and felt a surge of excitement, much stronger than anything she had experienced before. This was it! The real adventure was beginning. Life was beginning! Now she knew what she had to do. She had to find the slavers Figgis had described and make them pay for their actions. But that was just the beginning. There were other slavers out there – on Ashenpeake, in the Nova Land, in the world. She would find them all. Punish them all.

And she wouldn't be travelling alone. Her gang would follow her anywhere. That was the best feeling in the world.

'Ready?' said Figgis.

'Absolutely,' said Snowbone, and she hoisted her backpack higher on her shoulders and started walking.

PART TWO

23

In the middle of one of Ashenpeake's many forests there was a log cabin. In the cabin there was a table. On the table there was a notebook, and in the notebook there was a figure: 732.

'Seven hundred and thirty-two flagons, Kilim!' said Tarn, the slaver boss, as she put down her pen. 'In less than two weeks! That's quite some haul. And there's been no opposition.'

'There was that bloke two days ago,' replied the black-haired man.

'Yes, I know,' said Tarn. 'But it was nothing you couldn't handle. You were just a bit careless, weren't you, Buttress?'

The giant, slumped in the corner, heard the mocking tone and grunted. His hand moved protectively to his wounded stomach.

'We shouldn't be working like that,' said Kilim. 'On our own, without back-up. Word's spreading. We won't get away with it forever. They'll come after us.'

'Who will?' said Tarn with a sneer.

'Someone,' said Kilim.

'*Who?* The people here are such primitives! There's no army and barely a constabulary. Blue Boy, can you think of anyone?'

The blue-eyed lad shook his head. Then he settled himself more comfortably in his bunk and closed his extraordinary eyes.

'See?' said Tarn. 'Even Blue Boy can't think of anyone. Kilim, this is Ashenpeake. These people have allowed a slave trade to flourish on their island for more years than I can remember. They have accepted our money and turned a blind eye. And do you know why? Because they are meek, dull creatures. They might have a reputation for fighting, but I've never seen proof. A cornered cat has more spirit! They won't wage war over their Ancestors, however precious they are. They don't fight for the future – they certainly won't fight for the past.'

'Someone will come,' said Kilim quietly. 'I feel it in my bones.'

'You'll feel *this*!' said Tarn, and – *sssss!* – a knife sliced through the air and embedded itself into the wall behind him.

Kilim slowly opened his eyes, hardly daring to move in case Tarn threw a second.

But she didn't. She just smiled, stretched and ran her fingers through her long, long hair. 'Sometimes, Kilim,' she purred, 'you speak too much.'

24

Snowbone's army travelled south, guided by Figgis. Wherever they went, they asked the local people if they had seen the slavers, but the Ashenpeakers shook their heads and the tiddlins marched on.

Every night the party made camp and Figgis made a fire. The tiddlins were still wary of flames, but Figgis said life on the road was hard enough without forgoing tea. And the tiddlins had to admit that sitting round the fire while Figgis told late-night tales was an undeniable pleasure. Figgis told them many things, and Snowbone would listen spellbound, her grey eyes never leaving the tinker's face. Afterwards, she would repeat the important facts over and over again before she fell asleep.

The snow arrived at the end of the first week. Fat flakes fell from the bulging sky and soon the countryside was transformed into a shimmering, crystalline world. The temperature plummeted, but the tiddlins were unaware of it. They marched on merrily, eager to find the slavers. But Manu suffered badly. Mouse had made him a thick, fur jacket, but still the winter chilled his bones. He had never known such weather – Balaa was a tropical island, never cold. As a young boy, he had read about snow in his storybooks and longed to see it. He dreamed of snowflakes and icicles and frost-frozen ponds. But now, trudging through the slush with the cold biting his nose and nipping his ears, he was sorry that snow had ever been invented.

Surprisingly, Figgis felt the cold too. He knew that was impossible – he was wooden. But still he shivered and coughed. By day, he walked with a blanket draped round his shoulders. At night, he slept like a hedgehog, curled up in a tight ball. But his biggest concern was his arm. It wasn't growing back as it should. Every morning he looked for signs of growth and was disappointed. Figgis said nothing, but everyone could see the worry, whittling at his face like a penknife.

Snowbone realized it was a problem. Not just for Figgis but for all of them. 'I need a sign,' she said to herself. 'Something that will tell me what to do.'

And, two days later, there *was* a sign. It was tall, wooden and standing by the crossroads at Wimberry Tump.

It was late afternoon. The sun had slipped from the sky. Snow white was fading to shadow grey, and the travellers were looking for somewhere to spend the night. Anywhere dry would do. But there was nothing to be seen except a man on an ox cart, coming down the lane towards them.

'Excuse me, sir,' said Tigermane as it drew near. 'We're looking for somewhere to stay for the night. A barn? An outbuilding?'

The carter gazed down and Tigermane couldn't help smiling. His great, round face was such a curious caramel colour, his head looked like an enormous pickled onion.

'There's a farm further on down the road,' he said without stopping. 'They'll help you.'

'Just one more thing!' said Tigermane. 'We're trying to find some slavers. A black-haired man? A blue-eyed lad?'

The carter's lip curled. 'They came this way a couple of days ago,' he said. 'Ten, maybe twelve men and a woman. Nasty creature she was, for all her fine looks. Very rude. They had a wagon.'

'Which way did they go?' said Tigermane.

'On to Wimberry Tump,' he said, waving his arm in the direction he'd come from. 'Then left at the cross-roads to Puddle.' With a curt nod, the carter clicked his reins and continued on his way.

'This is fantastic news!' said Snowbone. 'Good work, Tigermane.'

They marched on to Wimberry Tump. Any thought of shelter for the night had gone, squished like the snow beneath their boots. Soon they saw the crossroads with its wooden sign: Puddle, Hayricks, Bogey Bridge, Pennyfold.

'Left!' cried Snowbone, and, like a flock of birds wheeling in the air, the entire party turned left on to the Puddle road.

But something made Mouse look behind and there, still standing by the signpost, was Figgis.

'Wait!' she cried in her loudest voice. She ran back. 'Figgis? What's the matter?'

Figgis looked down into Mouse's concerned little face and smiled. If there was a nicer tiddlin than this one, he'd like to meet it. He pointed at the sign with his remaining hand. 'You see that? Bogey Bridge? My aunt lives there.'

'That's nice,' said Mouse. She didn't know what else to say.

Luckily, the others returned and Snowbone took over.

'What's the matter?'

'It's Figgis's aunt,' said Mouse. 'She lives in Bogey Bridge.'

'So?'

'I have to go to her,' said Figgis, unconsciously cradling the stump of his arm.

'You can't,' said Snowbone. 'Not now. We're getting close.'

'I must,' said Figgis. 'My arm isn't right. *I'm* not right.'

Snowbone wavered. 'I know. I can see that. But

I don't want to lose them. Figgis, we *can't* lose them now.'

Figgis heard the despair in her voice. And when he looked into her eyes, he saw tears. Sharp, unwanted tears, just for a moment.

'I'm sorry,' he said.

'We won't lose the slavers,' said Manu. 'If we can find them once, we can find them again. And Figgis isn't the only one who would benefit from a hot meal and a dry bed.'

It had gone very quiet. Everyone was watching Snowbone, waiting for her decision. She felt pulled. Split like the crossroads sign. Head going one way, heart going another, feet going nowhere.

'We'll go to Bogey Bridge,' she said at last. 'Lead the way, Figgis.'

Figgis nodded and started down the road, with Mouse beside him. The tiddlins followed, noisily wondering what Figgis's aunt might have for supper. Snowbone trudged on in silence, thinking.

'You did the right thing,' said Manu, joining her. 'They're happy now. And when they're happy, they'll follow you anywhere.'

Snowbone smiled. 'That's worth remembering,' she said. 'I can't win this fight on my own.'

'No,' said Manu, 'you can't.' And they walked on together, while the snow fell like feathers all around.

25

Night had fallen by the time the travellers reached
Bogey Bridge, but the village lights were warm and
welcoming, and they easily found the right house. It
was beside the bridge and so smothered in snow, it
looked part of the same structure, as if the bridge
builder had finished going up and down the arches
and finished with a flourish, sweeping the stone
upwards into the peak of a roof and the tilt of a
chimney.

Figgis knocked on the front door. While they
waited for an answer, he turned to the company.
'She's a little sharp,' he said, 'but don't let it fool
you. She has a heart of gold.'

The door opened with a tumble of snow and there,
with her hands on hips, stood Figgis's aunt Butterbur
Baxter-Figgis. She arched an eyebrow. 'Well now,'
she said. 'Figgis Hurley-Figgis! I thought you'd
forgotten me.' Her face relaxed into a half-smile.
'Come in. All of you.'

The tiddlins didn't know how they all managed to

fit inside Butterbur's sitting room, but they did. The room seemed to expand to fit them. And curiously, Butterbur seemed to possess endless crockery and an inexhaustible supply of blueberry muffins. She went back and forth, from kitchen to sitting room, so many times that Snowbone thought she would wear a hole in the carpet. But eventually she poured herself a cup of tea and claimed the one remaining armchair.

'A merry band,' she said, scanning the tiddlins over the rim of her teacup. 'You're not well,' she added, looking at Figgis.

The tinker shook his head.

'I'll see to you when I've finished my tea,' said Butterbur. 'You'll stay a few days?'

'If we may,' said Figgis.

'Of course you may,' said Butterbur. You are my sister's boy and these are your friends. Do you expect me to turn you out into the snow?'

'No,' said Figgis, smiling.

'Of course not,' said Butterbur. Suddenly she pointed at someone across the room. 'You there, with the teeth.'

Two Teeth leapt to his feet as if he had been stung in the pants.

'Pull that rope beside you.'

Two Teeth pulled the bell rope. Nothing seemed to happen, but seconds later a young girl appeared, wearing a starched white apron.

'We have guests, Fern,' said Butterbur. 'Show them to their rooms, there's a good girl.'

The maid bobbed and held the door open wide. 'Follow me,' she said prettily, and the tiddlins filed out of the room. Only Figgis remained.

'Come,' said Butterbur.

Suddenly Snowbone appeared from behind the sofa.

'Not you,' she added.

Snowbone smiled. 'Where he goes, I go,' she said.

'Not in my house, you don't,' said Butterbur. 'Go on! Join the others upstairs.'

'No.'

Butterbur drew in a dangerous breath. '*Go on,*' she said again.

'No.'

Tall and small, they faced each other like cats on a barn roof. Figgis could feel the air crackling between them.

'I don't think there's any real need for this,' he said carefully. 'I know this is your house, Aunt B., and your word is law. But Snowbone is curious. She wants to see you at work, that's all.'

Butterbur considered his words. 'Just this once,' she said to Snowbone, wagging a warning finger. And she marched out of the room and down the hall.

Snowbone and Figgis followed, hurrying to keep up. Butterbur was striding away like a pair of scissors. And it was strange: from the outside, the house had looked modest, but the hall seemed endless. On and on they went, passing room after room. Then Butterbur stopped at a closed door with a small brass sign:

SURGERY
Knock. Wait. Enter.

'In here,' she said. And she opened the door and went in.

26

Butterbur's surgery was a spacious, low-ceilinged room. Oil lights flickered against chaffinch-pink walls. Bottles and jars jostled for space on the shelves. Pots and pestles gleamed on the worktops and, in the middle of the room, a polished wooden table stood square and dogged, with a fat, leather-bound book lying enticingly open upon it.

But the most curious thing about the surgery was its scent. It didn't smell of disinfectant, soap or polish. It smelt of flowers, herbs and spices. And beneath that, Snowbone caught the warm, musky scent of animals and hay. Soon she discovered why. There was a stable door at the far end of the room, and when she looked over it, she found an animal hospital.

'*Oh!*' she said. '*Oh!*'

She turned to Butterbur, and Figgis couldn't help but notice the expression on her face. Snowbone, hard little Snowbone, had gone soft. Gooey soft. With her wide eyes and wondering mouth, she looked as if she'd seen the fairies.

'Can I go in?' said Snowbone.

To Figgis's surprise, his aunt smiled. In that moment, Butterbur had seen herself in Snowbone. Many moons ago, she had been just the same: a guarded, prickly little girl whose heart was open only to animals. She nodded.

Snowbone stepped through the stable door into ankle-deep hay and started exploring. She immediately noticed the patients weren't penned. They were mingling in perfect harmony. A bandaged pig was dozing beside a mule with saddle sores. A cow with hoof rot was sharing a hay-bag with an itchy goat. On a beam above sat a cat with an amputated tail. On a cushion in the corner sprawled a dog with bellyache.

Snowbone went to each in turn, noting the strange-smelling ointments smeared on every wound. And when she returned to the surgery, she found Butterbur was mixing up something similar to treat Figgis. A small stove had been lit, and Butterbur was adding handfuls of this and sprinklings of that to a bubbling pot.

'This is nearly ready,' said Butterbur. 'Take off your shirt and sit down.'

Figgis obeyed.

Butterbur took a large, triangular piece of muslin and spooned the mixture on to it, then tied it round Figgis's body so the poultice was lying against the troublesome stump of his arm. 'All done!' she said. 'Now, I think it's time we joined the others for dinner.'

And what a dinner it was! Wildwood pie, roast potatoes, carrots and gravy, with toffee-baked apples and cream to follow. The travellers feasted like kings and talked till midnight. Finally, they retired to their rooms, and if they found it strange that such a modest house should contain dozens of bedrooms, they didn't say so. They just clambered into their beds and, with the snow piling up outside, fell asleep wishing they could stay till spring.

Time passed. The house grew colder. Nothing could be heard except the ticking of a clock, the scratching of a mouse . . . and a bedroom door, slowly being opened. Footsteps padded across the floorboards. A hand reached out. A sleeper awoke.

'Blackeye,' whispered Butterbur. 'Come with me. Now.'

27

Butterbur took Blackeye to the surgery. The oil lamps were burning low; the animals were sleeping; the scent of the poultice lingered in the air.

Butterbur pulled a stool out from under the table and sat Blackeye upon it. Then she took his face into her hands and turned it so his left eye – the black one – was facing her.

'Tell me,' she said, examining it closely. 'How good is your eyesight?'

'Pretty good,' said Blackeye.

'Just pretty good? No better than anyone else's?'

Blackeye thought for a moment. 'You're right,' he said. 'It *is* better, now I think about it. When we were back at the beach, a ship went down in the storm and I saw it long before anyone else. I don't think Snowbone *ever* saw it, though she pretended she did. Her eyes are rubbish.'

'This black eye of yours is very beautiful,' said Butterbur. 'And very special.'

'Would my parents have black eyes too?' said Blackeye.

'No,' said Butterbur. 'It's extremely rare. Maybe one in a million.'

'You're kidding!' said Blackeye. 'I thought it would be common.'

'Oh, no,' said Butterbur. 'Definitely not. Tell me, do you ever have . . . funny feelings? Like feeling that something's going to happen before it does? Or feeling like you're in two places at once?'

'No!' said Blackeye, laughing.

Butterbur smiled. 'Well,' she said, 'you're still young.'

She pulled out a stool for herself, while Blackeye wondered what on earth she meant.

'Long ago,' said Butterbur, 'in some parts of the world, people believed that a man's soul lived in his left eye. So when they went into battle, they gathered the bodies of the warriors they had killed, cut out their eyes and ate them.'

'Urgh!' said Blackeye.

'I agree!' said Butterbur. 'But they thought it would make them strong. It would double their souls. Double their power.'

'Does my black eye mean something?'

'Oh, yes,' said Butterbur. 'It means you have the ability to see beyond this world.'

Blackeye was mystified. He stared at Butterbur. In the pink half-light of the room, her eyes were red as holly berries.

'There are two worlds,' she said. 'There's this world – and there's the Otherworld. That is the home of the Ancients.'

'Where is this Otherworld?' said Blackeye.

'Under our feet!' said Butterbur. 'But if I took a shovel now and started to dig, I wouldn't find it. The Otherworld is real but it's hidden in a different dimension. I can't see it. But *you* can. You have special sight. *Shadow-sight.* You can go to the Otherworld. For you, it will be real.'

'I don't want to go to the Otherworld.'

'Oh, but you must!' said Butterbur. 'The Ancients have given you this gift. You must use it.'

'But how?' said Blackeye. 'You say the Otherworld is real, but how do I find it? Do I have to dig a hole?'

'No!' laughed Butterbur. 'If you are to travel into the Otherworld, you must leave your body behind. Your soul must do the journey alone. I can give you a potion that will help you the first time. So – what do you say? Are you ready to go?'

Blackeye didn't know what to say. He couldn't help thinking it was all a dream. Soon he'd wake up, Manu would be snoring in the other bed and the smell of breakfast would be drifting up from the kitchen.

But it wasn't a dream. It was very, very real.

Butterbur was standing in the corner of the surgery now.

She was kicking aside a rug.

Pulling on a heavy ring set into the floor.

Opening a secret trapdoor.

And Blackeye heard himself saying, 'Yes. I'm ready to go.'

28

Butterbur unhooked a lantern from the wall and led the way, down, down, down into a dark cave quite different from the surgery above. Here everything was damp and dingy. The bottles and jars crouched like spiders in the shadows, clinging to rough shelves hewn in the rock walls.

Butterbur hung the lantern from a hook in the middle of the ceiling and Blackeye saw a low couch.

'Lie down.'

Blackeye obeyed. Butterbur went to one of the shelves and returned with a small bottle containing a clear, amber liquid.

'Drink this,' she said.

'What will it do?' said Blackeye.

'Relax your mind,' said Butterbur. 'I will watch over your body and be here when you return.'

Blackeye took the bottle and drank it down.

'Close your eyes,' said Butterbur. 'Concentrate on your breathing. In, out. In, out. Nice and slow. In, out.'

Blackeye breathed slowly, deeply, in, out, and waited for something to happen. Eventually he noticed a heaviness creeping up his body from his toes. Soon he couldn't move, even if he wanted to. He felt so heavy, he thought the couch would collapse under him.

Then he seemed to be sinking. Down through the couch, down into the earth. He was leaving his body behind! The journey was beginning.

He opened his eyes but there was nothing to see. Everything was black. And still the sensation went on – the gentle falling, down, down, down. Almost like falling into a deep, delicious sleep. He closed his eyes and journeyed on.

Oh! Suddenly, he wasn't moving any more. Was he there? He lay quite still, not daring to move. He took a deep breath. The air was moist and smelt of soil. He opened his eyes.

First, he looked at himself. He was all there, but he was shadowy. Transparent. He could see and smell and presumably hear, but it seemed he couldn't touch anything. He tried to feel the ground but his fingers disappeared into it, like smoke.

Next, he looked at his surroundings. He was in a tunnel, with earth all around him and a thick tangle of tree roots above.

Blackeye cautiously stood up. He was clearly deep underground, but there was a strange twilight, enough to see by. He started down the tunnel. It twisted and turned, taking him deeper, and he couldn't help feeling he was in an enormous rabbit warren. Then he saw a mysterious blue glow ahead and, as he emerged into a sizeable chamber, he discovered its source. There were blue flames flickering among the tree roots overhead, tumbling, climbing, chasing each other like squirrels.

Blackeye had never seen anything so breathtakingly beautiful. He felt he could watch for hours. But he moved on. Tunnel after tunnel, chamber after chamber, all of them shimmering and shining, bathed in the same cool, celestial blue light, and all of them deserted.

Blackeye drifted on, but the light was fading. Now the chambers were deathly dark. No roots, no fingers of flame. The air was thickening. A heavy muskiness permeated the burrow system. And the ground was moving.

Blackeye hardly noticed it at first: it was no more than a faint trembling. But soon it became a rumble. The whole tunnel was shaking and he knew why. *There was something coming.*

Blackeye froze. He could feel his heart pounding in his chest. His legs seemed rooted to the ground. A wind battered his face as it rushed ahead of the horror. A beast-howl bark snapped at his ears. *It was coming.*

Blackeye turned and started to run. Faster, faster, boot and brain: *think-think-think-think-think-think-think!*

He didn't know where he was going. The Beast did, and it was getting closer. There was no way out, no escape, and the Beast was getting closer. He had no knife, no gun, no sword. The Beast had teeth and claws and it was getting closer.

STOP! Blackeye skidded to a halt. 'This isn't my body!' he said. He patted his thighs, his belly, his head. His hands passed right though. 'This is just a projection! The Beast can't kill me . . . can it? *Can it?* Oh! Oh! *OHHHH!*'

A great black paw swiped round the bend in the tunnel. Cleaver claws sliced the air where Blackeye had been. But Blackeye was floating. Up, up, up through the blackness, up through the couch, back into his body. And when he dared to open his eyes, all he saw was the moon of Butterbur's face, golden in the gleam of the lantern.

29

Blackeye told Butterbur all he had seen. She nodded her head.

'I have read this in the old books,' she said. 'The roots are the roots of ashen trees and the flickering blue flames are the souls of the Ancestors. As long as the trees live, the souls remain tethered and the Ancestors thrive.'

'And what about the Beast?' said Blackeye with a shudder.

'Ah, the Beast!' she said. 'That is the Spirit of the Land. The Spirit of Ashenpeake. Did you see what it looked like?'

'No.'

'That's a shame! I'd like to know, and the books never mention it.'

'Why did it attack me?'

'It was protecting the island, I imagine. Or the Ancients – the Otherworld is their home, remember. Anyway, young man, it's time you were in bed. So come!'

They climbed the stone stairs back to the surgery.

'I would like you to do this every night while you're here,' said Butterbur, concealing the trapdoor with the rug. 'If you develop your skills, you can shadow-fly wherever you want. There are many things I can teach you. Will you come?'

Blackeye nodded.

'Good lad. But promise me this: you won't tell anyone what you're doing.'

Mouse. Blackeye told her everything. There were no secrets between them. They were the best of friends. No, they were more than that. One day, they would be married. They both knew it.

'You must promise me,' said Butterbur sternly. 'Your friends will learn about it in time, but until then –' She put her finger to her lips.

Blackeye promised. Then, with a yawn, he crept up the stairs to his room, carefully opened the door and slid into bed. Soon he was fast asleep, with Mouse and the soul-lights dancing through his dreams, fleet as the frost outside.

30

The tiddlins stayed with Butterbur while the snow fell ever deeper. Every day Butterbur applied a fresh poultice to Figgis's arm, which, to his immense relief, started to regrow. Snowbone worked in the animal hospital, learning how to fold bandages and mix medicines. The tiddlins built snowmen and threw themselves downhill on sledges and tea trays.

Every night, Blackeye flew.

He was a perfect pupil. He remembered everything Butterbur told him and practised hard. Soon he was able to shadow-fly wherever he wanted, and he didn't need the amber potion. He simply had to concentrate on his breathing until he felt himself slipping out of his body and then he was away.

Blackeye didn't return to the Otherworld. He had no desire to meet the Spirit of Ashenpeake again, and there were far more interesting places to go. On the second night, Butterbur had suggested flying to Black Sand Bay.

'Can I?' he said. 'Really? I thought I could only visit the Otherworld.'

'No!' laughed Butterbur. 'You can go wherever you want. Up or down.'

And so, night after night, Blackeye had explored the island. He had looped-the-loop over Black Sand Bay, soared over the summit of Ashenpeake Mountain, drooled at the aroma of fish and chips over Kessel harbour, and raced dolphins by moonlight off the southern peninsula.

He kept his promise to Butterbur. He didn't tell anyone his secret, not even Mouse. And though he was tired and stumbly after his lessons, he always managed to return to bed without disturbing anyone.

But on the fifth night, someone was watching. Someone who had noticed his tired eyes and faraway look. Someone who now stood, pale and silent, in the shadows at the end of the corridor.

Snowbone.

31

'What's going on?'

It was the following morning. Butterbur had called a special meeting in the dining room and Snowbone had decided to ambush Blackeye before he could get there.

'I don't know what you're talking about,' said Blackeye.

'I think you do,' said Snowbone. She squared up to Blackeye, hands on hips, eyes bright. 'I saw you last night, sneaking back to bed when you thought no one was looking. I've seen you whispering with Butterbur in the surgery.'

'So?' Blackeye grinned. 'It's nothing.'

He slipped by her and headed for the dining-room door, but Snowbone was there first, barring his way.

'Tell me,' said Snowbone.

'No.'

'Tell me!'

'No!' said Blackeye, and he flashed his usual carefree smile.

Snowbone felt like thumping him. 'I bet you've told *her*.'

'Told me what?' Mouse had appeared out of nowhere.

'Where he goes when the rest of us are in bed,' said Snowbone.

'No, he hasn't,' said Mouse, and, to Blackeye's dismay, her beautiful eyes clouded over.

'It's nothing to worry about,' said Blackeye, taking her hand.

'So there *is* something!' cried Snowbone triumphantly.

'Yes, but I can't tell you.'

'Why?' demanded Snowbone.

'Because I told him not to!' said Butterbur. She had been in the dining room all the time. 'And that's the way it's going to stay. Back off, Snowbone! You don't need to know everything. There are things in this world that simply don't concern you. Now get out of the way. You're blocking the door, and Blackeye is trying to come in for a good reason. And it's no use scowling at me, young lady, I won't change my mind. Mouse, welcome. Take a seat. Figgis, Manu and Tigermane are already here.'

Snowbone stomped into the dining room and found a seat. Butterbur took her place at the head of the table and smiled at the gathering.

'Figgis has been telling me your plans,' she said. 'I'd like to help. That's why I've summoned you all here. I've brought some maps along. I think they'll make things clearer.' She unrolled one of the maps. 'This is Ashenpeake Island,' she said. 'We are here at Bogey Bridge. As for the traders you're after, the man at Wimberry Tump said they'd taken the Puddle road. Well, that makes sense to me, because I suspect they're heading *here*.' She pointed at a place on the east coast. 'Spittel Point. It's a port, very popular with slavers.'

'Why would they go there?' asked Tigermane.

'That's where all the deals are done,' said Butterbur. 'They can find a ship that will carry the sap to the Nova Land.' She unrolled another map. 'This is a map of the world. We are here, on Ashenpeake. This –' she traced a route west, across a vast expanse of ocean – 'is the Nova Land, the "new world". It's a vast place. Most of it is still unexplored. All the towns are here, on the east coast. Farrago is the biggest – and the roughest. It's growing so fast, no one can really control it. It's wild and dangerous, and that's why the sap will be going there.'

'I don't understand,' said Mouse.

'The slave trade is changing,' said Butterbur. 'When people first moved to the Nova Land, the demand for slaves was enormous. Traders shipped thousands of eggs across and fortunes were made. Now the market is starting to collapse. The Nova Landers are breeding their own slaves. Suddenly there's no need to buy in eggs from abroad. So the traders are dealing in something that the Nova Land doesn't have – ashen sap.'

'What exactly is ashen sap?' said Manu.

'Ashen sap is what Ashenpeakers have instead of blood,' said Butterbur. 'If you cut us deep enough, it comes out. It's a sticky white stuff and it has extraordinary healing powers. It can heal any wound – even a flesh-and-blood wound – and that's why the traders are so interested in it. The Nova Land is a dangerous place. People are having all kinds of accidents, and traders who can supply ashen sap will be rich.

'There's just one problem. How do they get hold of it in the kind of quantities they need? They can't harvest it off living people. If you cut an Ashenpeaker, the sap seeps out very slowly.'

'That's true,' said Figgis. 'When my arm was cut off, I didn't lose more than a cupful of the stuff.'

'Exactly,' said Butterbur. 'But inside every Ashenpeaker, there is a reservoir of sap. It's like a well, right here in our middles. That's why we have a bit of a belly on us! We've got this extra piece of baggage that humans don't carry. Even when we Move On, the well remains. In fact, it gets larger over time and the sap becomes more potent. So the traders have realized that this island is covered with thousands of sap wells – inside the ashen trees. That's what this rogue band of slavers is doing. They're harvesting sap, and killing our Ancestors in the process.'

'It's horrible,' said Mouse.

'It's the truth,' said Figgis. 'That's why we must find those slavers. We must make them pay. My arm will be good as new by the end of the week. We can get after them then.'

Snowbone frowned. 'You're well enough to travel now, aren't you?'

'The end of the week will suit everybody better,' said Butterbur firmly.

And Snowbone knew that by *everybody* Butterbur meant Blackeye. What on earth were they up to?

32

Leaving Butterbur's house, the tiddlins travelled south. By day, they marched relentlessly, beetling down the high-hedged lanes. At night, they slept – in barns, in sheds, in snow-canopied woodland – anywhere they could find a dry floor. The tiddlins didn't feel the cold, but they did suffer from the constant damp. The snow penetrated their clothing and sank into their wooden limbs. After hours of tramping, their legs would feel heavy and tight round the joints. Without those few, precious hours under cover every night, they wouldn't have been able to go on, no matter how high their spirits.

They travelled on. To the west they saw the huge bulk of Ashenpeake Mountain, brooding on the horizon like a sulky giant, snow-capped, immovable, timeless. To the east, endless forests. Broad-leaves and pines, evergreens and ashen trees, cold and close in troubled times, snow falling from their heavy boughs in a symphony of sighs.

And then, one day, the tiddlins caught a familiar

scent on the wind. *Salt*. Soon there were gulls screaming overhead. A fresh breeze was singing in from the south. And when they climbed a slippery ridge, they found the sea.

Snowbone closed her eyes and took a deep breath. The air was cold, charged, tingling with the energy of the ocean. And with that single, pure breath, all the grime of the journey was washed away. She sighed happily.

'There's a path,' said Blackeye.

Snowbone opened her eyes.

He was pointing along the cliff. 'See? Leading down to the beach.'

'So what are we waiting for?' said Snowbone. '*RUN!*'

And off she went, haring along the cliff top, with the others scrabbling and screaming behind her. But suddenly – *whoosh!* – Manu overtook her so fast, he was nothing but a blur. Snowbone stopped running. She wanted to watch. Manu was running at an incredible speed, with apparently no effort. He was down the path faster than a greyhound, running towards the sea while the tiddlins were still on the cliff. And when he reached the waves, he somersaulted, turned a cartwheel, kicked off his shoes and started paddling.

'That boy can run!' said Figgis.

Snowbone simply nodded. She was too stunned to speak.

The tiddlins made camp on the beach, and that night, as they gathered round a fire to talk, it almost felt like home.

Figgis had drawn a map of Ashenpeake Island in the sand. 'I reckon we're about here,' he said, marking a spot on the coast. 'The southern peninsula is here and Spittel Point is right down here, at the tip. So if we follow the coast all the way, we can't miss it. Two or three days and we should be there.'

'What will we do when we get there?' said Two Teeth.

'Start looking for the slavers,' said Snowbone.

'Where?' said Fudge.

'In the taverns,' said Figgis. 'That's where they meet. I imagine there'll be a bit of a harbour, with taverns all along the seafront. You won't be able to come with me – it's no place for tiddlins. And before you tear my tongue out, Snowbone, that's not me talking! It's the landlords. They won't let you in, believe me. And anyway, we don't want to draw attention to ourselves.'

'Won't they recognize you?' said Manu.

'I doubt it,' said Figgis. 'Why would a tinker from the north be drinking in Spittel Point? Besides, they left me for dead.'

'But won't it look strange – your being in a bar when you're not a trader?' said Mouse.

'No,' said Figgis. 'I'm sure strangers turn up all the time. Sailors looking for work, people like that. And besides, it's a regular port. They're not all rogues. Some of them are dealing in honest cargo. But it's out of the way and the slavers like that. If they used Kessel, on the west coast, everyone would see their business.'

'What will we do if we find the slavers?' said Tigermane.

'There's no *if* about it,' said Snowbone. 'We'll stay there until we do.'

'And what then?' said Mouse.

Snowbone said nothing. But a smile passed over her lips, cold as the waves beyond.

33

When the tiddlins awoke the next morning, they found a thaw had begun. Icicles were melting. Water was running in rivulets down to the sea. The clouds had disappeared and the sun was lazing in the sky like a comfy cat. Even Manu had to admit it was a glorious day.

By mid-morning, the snow had almost completely disappeared. All that remained were long, thin fingers of white, lurking in the shadows beneath the bushes.

'D'you see them?' said Figgis, pointing them out to Snowbone. 'Do you know what they're called?'

Snowbone shook her head.

'They're called *snowbones*. They hold on, clinging to the land, defying the sun, even when the rest of the snow has long gone. And that reminds me of someone I know. What do you think?'

Snowbone said nothing, but she couldn't hide her smile. For once, it was warmer than the winter sun. And, deep in her heart, she thanked the sailor who had given her such a brilliant name.

On the third day, the path began to rise, still following the contours of the coast. Jutting out into the sea ahead was a sharp promontory with ferocious cliffs that fell away beneath.

'Spittel Point must be on the far side,' said Figgis. 'We can cut across land. No need to go all the way round.'

Snowbone agreed, but she could see it would still be a long, arduous climb.

They laboured on under the midday sun. Higher and higher they went, seeing nothing ahead of them but sky. And they were just nearing the summit when they heard something: a low rumble that seemed to set the earth quivering. Then it became a rush and a roar, and the tiddlins fell to their knees and covered their heads as a dragon soared up over the cliffs and screamed away over the land. Snowbone felt the downbeat of its wings. Heard the screech of its tongue. Felt the tip of its tail sweep by. Like the other tiddlins, she stayed curled up in a ball until she was sure it had gone. Dragons meant just one thing: *fire!*

But when she dared to open her eyes, she saw Figgis calmly sitting beside her, gazing to the north with a smile on his face.

'Wasn't that grand!' he said. 'I've never seen a flying machine so close!'

Snowbone followed his gaze and saw it wasn't a

dragon at all. It was a man-made travelling machine. Like a flying ship with rigging, but instead of sails it had something spinning round and round, high above the deck.

Blackeye was already on his feet. 'It's trailing a mooring line!' he laughed, still able to see the machine in detail, though it was powering away. 'I felt something brush by and I thought it was a scaly tail!' He pounced on Mouse and she squealed.

'Where did it come from?' said Snowbone.

'I don't know,' said Figgis. 'But I think we'll soon find out.'

The tiddlins scrambled to the top of the slope and stopped just in time. The ground ahead fell away into a great sweeping basin of a bay. Directly below was a shelf of land, covered in grass, and on it – flying machines. Ten or more, tethered like goats. The grass was criss-crossed with mooring lines. The machines hummed tunelessly as the wind whistled through their rigging, while the sun glistened on their feather blades.

To the left of the airfield, a wide sloping road led down to the town. Spittel Point was a jumble of houses locked between the cliffs and the sea. Every house was a different colour: paintbox pink and custard cream, downy peach and daisy green; blue and lilac, red and yellow, cool and calming, warm and mellow. The houses jostled against each other, nudging their neighbours closer to the harbour, where a dozen sailing ships waited for cargoes, crews, tides.

Snowbone was buzzing like one of the flying machines. The thrill of the hunt, the view of the sea: *oh!* It was a heady brew. They were close now. So close.

She turned to Figgis. 'You'll go in tonight?'

Figgis nodded. 'I will. And wherever those scummy dogs are hiding, I'll find them.'

34

It seemed the gods were protecting the slavers. Night after night, Figgis and Manu went into Spittel Point, but they couldn't find them. A black-haired man, a blue-eyed lad . . . Hour after hour, Figgis sat in smoky taverns, waiting for them to enter. Hour after hour, Manu watched the street outside, waiting for them to walk by. But they never did.

A week passed. The tiddlins were staying in a deserted barn outside the town. Every morning, Figgis and Manu reported back to Snowbone. She would hear them coming up the path and, just by listening to the drag of their boots, she could tell it had been another fruitless night. Snowbone was in a frenzy of frustration, but nothing more could be done. Figgis and Manu had to watch, she had to wait. It was as simple as that.

It was a cold night. A gibbous moon hung low in the sky, silvering the rigging of the silent ships.

Figgis sat on the quay, smoking his pipe.

'It's getting late,' said Manu, appearing from the shadows as if by magic.

Figgis nodded. He was tired. He longed for his bed in the barn. 'One more,' he said. 'One more, then we're off.' He tapped out the embers of his pipe, slipped it into his pocket and they started walking.

Along the seafront, the tavern signs were hanging limp as lettuce. The Whistling Dog? Figgis had been in there earlier. The Three Cockles? Too rough this time of night. The Galley Boy? Figgis peered in through the window. No one there. They walked on.

Suddenly they heard laughter. In one of the side alleys, a door had opened, splashing golden light on to the cobbles. A sailor stumbled out. He saluted to his friends still inside. Swayed. Turned. Walked unsteadily towards them, his forehead corrugating in concentration. When he reached them he stopped, while his brain worked out how to get past.

'Evenin',' said the sailor.

He burped, and the stink that escaped was so savoury, Figgis could taste it: a rich, wet stew of tobacco and spit and spice and ale. It went up Figgis's nose and slid down his throat like an oyster.

'Evenin',' said Figgis.

He stepped round the sailor and headed for the light. It came from a tavern Figgis hadn't noticed before, the Hangman's Hood. The sign showed a fearsome individual leering through a black hood.

Behind the terrifying eyeholes, the orbs were blood red, and a noose dangled from his fingers.

Figgis went in.

The bar was crowded, but not so busy that he couldn't see everyone. The slavers weren't there. Figgis ordered a glass of beer, found a table in a far corner and sat down.

Time passed. His glass was half emptied. A sailor at the bar was getting rowdy. His mates were trying to calm him, but he was violently drunk. Beads of sweat glistened on his bald, fleshy head.

Figgis fished in his pocket for his pipe. 'Where is it?' he muttered, and then, as he bent to look, the room exploded around him.

Fists and feet and flying sailors! The drunken sailor was throwing people across the room. *Hweeeeee!* One of them flew through the air and landed square on Figgis's table: *oof!* He lay there, sprawled on a bed of splinters where the table used to be. *Hweeeeee!* The sailor was throwing someone else. *Doof!* The unfortunate man smacked into the bar wall and slid to the ground.

Figgis retreated further into the corner. It seemed the sailor had a wooden leg. He had unstrapped it and now he was braced up against the bar, holding the leg like a run-round bat and threatening anyone who dared come near.

But the landlord was having none of it. He came out from behind the bar brandishing a bottle, and

he swung it high in the air and brought it down —
boof! — on the bald head. The drunken sailor fell to
the floor like a bag of coconuts.

'Get him out of here,' growled the landlord.

The sailor's mates scrabbled to obey. The landlord
was only a little man, but if he was short on body,
he was big on temper.

As Figgis watched, the sailors hurriedly strapped
the wooden leg back on and hauled the troublemaker
to his feet. Figgis couldn't help smiling. The sailor's
leg was on the wrong way round, with the boot
pointing backwards. But the sailors didn't care. They
just wanted to get out.

Grunting and cursing, they dragged their
companion to the door. But before they could reach
it, the door was opened and a cold blast of wind
ushered in two new customers.

The smile froze on Figgis's lips.

They were a black-haired man and a blue-eyed
lad.

PART THREE

35

'Shut the door, love! We're trying to keep it cosy in here.'

The black-haired man and the blue-eyed lad strolled to the bar of the Hangman's Hood, ignoring the woman who had spoken. She shook her head and turned back to her friends.

'Slavers,' she whined. 'Act like they own the place.'

Figgis, watching from the corner of the room, felt the world had stopped turning. He couldn't move. He couldn't breathe. He could only watch.

As the black-haired man ordered drinks, the lad turned and studied the room. His cool gaze travelled from table to table, from face to face. And it seemed to Figgis that when it reached him, it lingered . . . but then it moved on.

'Blue Boy,' said the man.

The lad turned, took the offered tankard of alc, sidled over to a bar stool and eased himself on. The man joined him. Soon they were deep in conversation.

Figgis remained at the table but his thoughts had

flown away, back to the glade and his murdered family. And now, looking at the smug backs of the slavers, he wanted to stab them. He reached for the knife on his belt.

No. Good sense stopped him just in time. 'Not now,' he told himself. 'Not here.'

He drained his glass and put on his jacket. Walked to the door and stepped out into the alley. Headed for the shadows. Fast, urgent footsteps. Manu appeared from a doorway. Figgis pounced on him like a dog on a bacon bone.

'They're in there!' he panted. 'The man and the lad. Tell Snowbone. I'll follow them. See where they're hiding.'

The tavern door opened again. Figgis pushed Manu back against the wall. But it wasn't the slavers. It was the mouthy woman. She paused and reached into her bag. Swayed slightly. Unwrapped a chocolate caramel and slid it between her purple lips. Departed on unsteady heels.

'Go,' said Figgis, and Manu went.

Figgis stepped into the doorway and waited. An hour passed. Longer. People came and went, but not the ones Figgis wanted to see. And then, just as he was wondering whether the tavern had a back door, they emerged. Man and lad walked down the alley to the seafront, turned left and strode on.

Figgis followed, flitting from shadow to shadow. Through the streets, up the steps, twisting, turning,

higher, higher. Out of town, over the headland –
Figgis hoping and praying they wouldn't turn round,
because there was nowhere to hide – and into a
wildwood. The sun was rising; the trees were yellow
with birdsong. But Figgis had no time to enjoy the
dawn. He had to find the slavers' camp. Nothing else
mattered.

And when, at last, he found it, Figgis studied the
camp carefully. He counted the men as they emerged,
yawning and gritty-eyed, from a bunkhouse. He noted
every door, every window – everything he could see.
Then he raced back to Snowbone and the others,
fierce, jubilant, sure he had all the information they
would need to plan a perfect raid.

But he didn't see the traps hidden in the long grass.
Didn't see the pit beyond the bunkhouse. Didn't see
the arsenal of axes in the woodshed.

By the time he did, it was too late.

36

Snowbone screwed up her eyes and studied the map Figgis was scratching into the dirt of the barn floor.

'So this is the cabin here,' said Figgis, 'with the bunkhouse behind. There's a shed here and an outhouse here – and I reckon that's the latrines, because the path to it was getting a right old hammering this morning.'

'*Thrrrrr!*' said Two Teeth, holding his nose and fanning the air. 'Farty pants!'

The tiddlins giggled.

'He's right,' laughed Figgis. 'The stink will knock you off your feet at twenty paces, so be careful! Especially you, Mouse!'

Mouse smiled, but Figgis could see she was worried. 'It'll be all right,' he assured her. 'Really, it will.'

Blackeye put his arm round Mouse and hugged her. 'When do we hit them?'

'Tomorrow,' said Snowbone. 'At dawn. They'll be sleeping. Won't see us coming.'

'We could go tonight,' said Fudge.

Snowbone shook her head. She was thinking about her eyesight. How shapes became blurry in the dark. 'No,' she said. 'We want to see what we're doing. It'll all be over in an hour. Back in time for breakfast!' She grinned. 'We mustn't forget to raid their stores. Two Teeth, you can be in charge of that.'

Two Teeth saluted her. Snowbone's grin was as wide as a slice of melon.

'Tomorrow will be a great day,' she said, rising to her full height. 'Friends, remember who we are fighting and why. Remember the fate that awaited us in the Nova Land. Remember our brothers and sisters, sold into slavery. Remember the ashen trees, toppled by axe and saw. Remember this moment. Remember we are right, and know this: because we are right, the Ancients will protect us.'

She punched her fist in the air and the tiddlins roared till the roof beams rattled.

'A cheer for Snowbone!' shouted Tigermane. 'Hip hip –'

'*HOORAY!*'

Snowbone was swept from her feet and bounced around the barn on strong wooden shoulders. Everyone was delirious with excitement. Waiting, marching, searching: all these things were over. Tomorrow would bring revenge. Sweet, sweet revenge.

No one noticed Mouse slipping outside. She

walked across the grass to a bench and sat down. *Why am I finding this so hard?* she thought. *Snowbone's right. Slavers bring nothing but death and misery to our people. So why do I feel so bad about tomorrow?*

She gazed back at the barn and thought of Blackeye. *If anything happens to him . . . No! I won't think that way.*

Then Mouse noticed something. The grass was freckled with tiny white flowers. They were so small, she hadn't seen them when she walked to the bench and she had crushed them underfoot. Dozens of broken petals marked her path.

Mouse, pained beyond measure, hung her head and cried.

37

Dawn, the next day.

Snowbone crouched behind an oak tree and assessed the situation. To her left, Blackeye. To her right, Figgis. Beyond them, the other tiddlins – Mouse included – watching, waiting.

Snowbone was holding a long rush torch, soaked in oil. She turned to Blackeye and nodded. He reached into his bag and pulled out a metal pot. Carefully, he placed it on the ground before her and lifted the lid. Inside lay smouldering embers, red as dragon's eyes. Snowbone thrust the torch into the embers and instantly it was ablaze. She winced. Working with fire was terrifying, but it had to be done.

Figgis too had an oil-soaked torch. Snowbone used her own to light it and then Figgis passed the flame on. Down the line it went, until thirty torches had been lit. Then Snowbone raised her hand high in the air and the raid began.

Snowbone ran to the cabin and threw her torch on to the thatched roof. It landed with a dull thud and instantly began its work. Following her lead, tiddlins were all over the camp now, hurling torches, running for cover, taking up firing positions. The cabin roof was blazing. The bunkhouse roof was smouldering. The air was surrendering to smoke.

Then someone started ringing a bell. Shouts tumbled through the morning. The cabin door opened and – *poom!* – Snowbone's pistol exploded. The blue-eyed lad fell against the door frame, blood pouring from a wound in his arm. He staggered back inside. Slammed the door hard behind him.

Snowbone whooped in triumph. Figgis saw her eyes: wild, ferocious, cat-bright.

The cabin door opened again. A hand threw something out. *Boof!* Choking yellow smoke poured from an exploded smoke bomb. The tiddlins couldn't see a thing. *Boof!* A second bomb. Green smoke joined the yellow. The camp was disappearing.

The tiddlins were thrown into confusion. They looked for Snowbone, Blackeye, Figgis. But they had vanished in the smoke, and the tiddlins were lost, trapped in their own private terror. Listening to the boots of the slavers as they came running, armed with axes.

Snowbone felt the earth move beneath her. Saw the smoke eddy in the oncoming wind of an attacker. Heard the bellow of anger as the giant came out of nowhere, swung his axe and – *shooo!* – the blade thudded into the ground beside her. She dropped her pistol in fright. *Shoo!* The blade struck her arm, slicing her like cheese. She scrabbled for her pistol, fingers fishing in the wet earth. *Shoo!* The blade fell a third time, taking her foot clean off. Snowbone felt her whole body reel under the impact. She fell on her face, floundered like a fish, fought for breath. But her fingers found the pistol and, as the giant raised his axe again, she flipped on to her back and fired: *poom.*

The giant dropped like a dead elephant. Blood and bone met earth and stone, and the mountainous man breathed no more.

Snowbone looked around. The camouflage smoke had cleared, revealing a desperate struggle. The ground was littered with bodies: slavers and tiddlins, tangled together. Figgis was pulling someone out of the burning bunkhouse. Fudge and Tigermane were trapped in a tree net. Blackeye was over by the cabin, defiantly trading blows with the black-haired man. But Snowbone could see he was tiring and, as she watched, the blue-eyed lad came up behind him, dangling an axe from his one good arm.

'*BLACKEYE!*' she yelled. '*BEHIND YOU!*'

But it was too late. The axe scythed through the air and Blackeye's legs collapsed under him.

Help us.

Voices. Desperate wooden voices, crying for help, somewhere in the camp.

Snowbone heard them and tried to get up. Then

she remembered her foot. Her boot was lying close by. It was empty; the foot had vanished into thin air. She inspected the stump of her leg. It was sticky with sap and seemed to be vibrating – so fast, she couldn't see the movement itself, just the shimmer it made. And she could feel a strange tingle. Her body seemed tense, as if it were waiting for something.

And then it began. Effortlessly, painlessly, miraculously, a new foot emerged from the stump of the old. Snowbone saw it happen, *felt* it happen, but still couldn't believe it. A new foot? In less than a minute? She tried wriggling her toes. They worked. Everything was perfect. Just perfect.

Help us.

The voices! Snowbone suddenly remembered what was happening. She pulled on her boot, scrambled to her feet and started running. Past Blackeye, unconscious by the cabin. Past Two Teeth, sprawled in the mud. Past Mouse, wide-eyed, wandering, covered in blood. Past the well, round the back of the bunkhouse, through the long grass and – *ssssoop!* – a wire noose tightened around her ankle and she was thrown high into the air. She bounced once, twice, savagely, then found herself upside down, high above ground, dangling on the wire like a yo-yo.

The cries were louder now. Snowbone jerked until the wire turned and she could see the camp again. Beyond the bunkhouse stood the slaver woman, her long hair streaming like lava. In her hands she held a bucket. She was splashing liquid on to the ground. No, not the ground. There was a pit, though Snowbone couldn't see into it.

The woman threw the bucket aside and walked over to the bunkhouse. She drew out a burning piece of timber, returned to the pit and looked down. Then she smiled, said something and tossed in the timber.

The cries became screams as the pit erupted into flames. Snowbone stared in horror. There was nothing she could do.

The woman raised a hand in greeting – the black-haired man and the blue-eyed lad were approaching. The lad looked badly hurt. He was muttering, stumbling, his face contorted with pain. But the man was unharmed. He began a conversation with the woman. Snowbone writhed in anger. Heart-rending screams were rising from the pit beside them, but they were chatting like wives on market day.

'Damn you, Ancients!' she cried. 'Where are you now? Help us! *Help us!* Do you not see this happening? Will you not do something?'

And then, to Snowbone's astonishment, something did happen. *Pfooow!* A single gunshot cut through the hazy air – and the black-haired man fell lifeless to the ground. *Pfooow!* A second shot – and the blue-eyed lad clutched his chest, staggered and fell backwards into the burning pit.

And as the gunman appeared through a veil of smoke, the woman, panicking, turned and ran across the camp to a paddock. There she leapt upon a horn horse, jumped the fence and thundered off into the wildwood.

But Snowbone, watching from the wire, knew the battle wasn't over yet. No matter how fast that horse could run, the gunman could run faster.

'Manu!' she cried. 'Follow her!'

And Manu threw down his gun and started running.

38

Manu ran faster than he had ever run in his life, out of the woods and on to the downs beyond. He could outrun a horn horse, he knew he could, but not today. Not after the fighting he'd done back at the camp. Not when the horse had such a head start. It had disappeared already, dropping down below the hilly ground.

Manu pumped harder with his arms. Faster, faster he went, following the chalky track until he saw the horse again. The woman was low in the saddle, her hair streaming out behind her. She was heading for Spittel Point.

But, strangely, when she reached the road that led down into town, she didn't take it. Instead, she urged her horse over the headland. And it was here that she glanced back over her shoulder and saw Manu sprinting behind her. She spurred the horse on. Its blue hoofs raised a cloud of dust behind it like a legion of ghosts.

Suddenly she turned left, and Manu realized she

was heading for the airfield. Sure enough, when he turned he could see her way below, galloping towards one of the flying machines. When she reached it, she leapt out of the saddle and ran up the boarding ramp.

Manu pushed himself so hard, he thought he was going to die. 'I've got to catch her,' he told himself, over and over and over and over again. 'I've got to catch her!'

He skidded round the end of a fence and ran into the airfield. He ducked under mooring lines, darted round machines, searching, searching for the woman. From above, everything had looked so orderly. Now he was here, it was a maze. Manu raced on and – *oof!* – he slammed into the abandoned horse. It was wild-eyed, shivering, black with sweat. Manu knew how it felt. He pushed it aside and sped on, desperate now – he could hear the sound of an engine firing. A heavy thud as the boarding ramp was discarded. And suddenly the air was roaring around him. The mooring lines were humming like hornets. Everything was rattling, including his teeth. And Manu threw himself to the ground just as the flying machine soared into the sky above him and accelerated away.

Manu lay in the dust and cursed. What could he tell Snowbone now?

He staggered to his feet and shook the chalk dust from his clothes. Now the running was over, his body was beginning to ache. He felt he'd been kicked all over. And he had to get back to the camp somehow. Perhaps he could ride the horn horse? No. It had done enough for one day. He would walk.

The dust clouds were settling. Manu looked around, momentarily interested. He had seen flying machines before, but never so close. Then he noticed a boy dragging something across the turf.

Manu walked towards him and saw a strip of clear ground with a circle of mooring rings set into it. The boy was heaving the boarding ramp clear.

'That machine,' said Manu. 'Where was it going?'

The boy stopped what he was doing and tapped the side of his nose. 'That 'ud be tellin',' he said.

'Then tell,' said Manu.

'Nope!' said the boy. He grinned and Manu saw two rows of rotting teeth. 'Star sailors have secrets!'

'You're no star sailor,' said Manu. 'You're just a lackey. You clear the mess they leave behind.'

The terrible grin crumbled. For a second, Manu thought the boy might cry, but he didn't. He sulked.

'Tell me,' said Manu.

'Won't.'

'Give me strength,' muttered Manu. It was like talking to a toddler. 'Tell me. Where was it going?'

The boy shook his head defiantly.

Manu grabbed hold of him by his elbows. 'Where was it going?'

Nothing.

'*Where was it going?* If you don't tell me, I swear I

will tie you to a mooring ring and the next machine in can land on your fat head.'

The boy's eyes widened in horror.

Manu threw him aside and walked away. 'You don't even know.'

'Do.'

Manu carried on walking.

'*Do!*' shouted the boy after him. '*Do!* I overheard them!'

Manu paused. 'Then tell me! Or I won't believe you.'

The boy wavered. He wanted to be believed so much.

'*Where?*'

The boy tried to decide what to do. He flopped his head sideways. Screwed up his face. Stuck out his tongue. Then he began to smile.

'Farrago!' he said proudly. 'It's going to Farrago!'

Snowbone was sitting outside the barn when Manu arrived. 'So?' she said. 'What news?'

'I didn't catch her,' said Manu. He sat down heavily. 'She escaped in a flying machine. But I know where she's going – Farrago.'

Snowbone frowned. 'We have to follow her,' she said darkly.

Manu nodded. 'How are things here?'

'Bad. Of the thirty we began with, twelve are dead, burned. Ten are . . . Oh, I don't know what they are! They're alive, but they're not right. Figgis thinks they're Moving On.'

'*Moving On?*' said Manu. 'At their age?'

'They were badly wounded,' said Snowbone. 'The wounds have healed but Figgis reckons it's the shock. They're withdrawing into themselves.'

'Are they here?'

'Yes. They're round the back.'

'What about the rest?'

'Tigermane and Fudge came off best,' said

Snowbone. 'They were caught in a tree net early on. Blackeye was felled, but he's OK now. Two Teeth is fine, as is Figgis.'

'Mouse?'

'Ah, Mouse,' said Snowbone. 'She's here, but . . . She got blood on her hands, see? During the raid. She washed it away, but she reckons the stains are still there. So she keeps washing her hands, over and over again. She's obsessed. And she's talking to herself all the time. She's in the barn now with Blackeye.'

Manu leaned back against the wall and closed his eyes. He'd heard enough.

But Snowbone went on. 'We found a wagon, loaded with ashen sap. Figgis reckons That Woman is responsible for the murder of *hundreds* of Ancestors. Can you believe that? We've decided the sap should go to Butterbur. She might be able to use it. Two Teeth and Fudge are taking it.'

'What's the plan?' said Manu, looking at her again.

Snowbone shrugged. 'After what's happened, I can only speak for myself. But I want to go on. I'll go to the airfield and find a machine to take me to Farrago.'

'I'd like to come with you,' said Manu.

Snowbone looked at him in surprise. 'Would you? Well, that makes two.'

'Three.' Figgis had come out of the barn.

'Four,' said Blackeye, behind him.

'Five,' said Tigermane. 'I'm coming too.'

Snowbone smiled. If Mouse joined them, that would make a perfect six.

'I don't believe it!' cried Mouse. 'After everything that's happened, you're still going on?'

The tiddlins were sitting in the barn, deciding what to do.

Mouse stared wildly at the group. 'Have you forgotten what it was like?'

'No,' said Snowbone.

'Blackeye?' said Mouse. 'They cut your legs from under you!'

'They've grown back,' said Blackeye. 'I'm fine!' He slapped his thighs. 'I'm the same as I was before.'

'Are you?' said Mouse quietly. She started to wring her hands, over and over again. 'We lost twenty-two friends.'

'They lost more,' said Snowbone.

'And that makes you proud?' said Mouse. 'Because it makes me sick. Sick to my stomach. *I killed a man.* I have his blood on my hands right now, and it will never, *ever* wash away.'

'If you hadn't killed him, he would have killed you,' said Snowbone.

'Only because I was there, attacking him,' said Mouse. 'I was doing wrong.'

'*Wrong?*' gasped Snowbone. '*You* were wrong? You forget who those people were! They were slave traders. The lowest of the low. They peddled misery. They stole freedom. They bargained with the lives of our people. And you say that *you* were wrong?'

'They had to be stopped, Mouse,' said Figgis. 'If we hadn't done something, they would be out there now, taking more and more trees. Sweetheart, you don't know how that feels. When your loved ones are cut down in front of your eyes . . . You don't have a family –'

'And whose fault is that?' growled Snowbone.

'If you did,' Figgis went on, 'you would understand.'

'I see that something has to be done,' said Mouse. 'It isn't fair – it isn't right – that such things are allowed to happen. There must be laws. Justice! But what we did – what you want to carry on doing – isn't justice. It's revenge. Wild, bloody revenge.' She started pacing up and down. 'When you take a life, you lose a bit of yourself. War isn't the answer. Love will save the world.'

Snowbone shook her head. 'I can't believe I'm hearing this.'

'Well, you are,' said Mouse, 'and you'd better listen,

because I'm telling you the truth. You can take That Woman out of this world, but you won't stop slavery.'

'I can try,' said Snowbone.

'You can *die*,' said Mouse. 'Is that what you want? To die in a strange land? Because I want to live – here, in a quiet country – and when my time comes, I want to Move On.'

'And when you Move On,' said Snowbone, 'do you want someone to come with an axe and cut you down? Steal your sap and leave you to die?'

'No,' said Mouse. 'Of course I don't.'

'So?' said Snowbone. 'How do you plan to stop it happening?'

Mouse said nothing.

'You see?' said Snowbone. 'Mouse, we're fighting for *you*.'

41

'I reckon you'd want the Paradise Bar for that,' said the road sweeper. 'All the star sailors hang out there. Go along this road, turn left into Fortune Lane, then look for Goose Alley. It's down there. You can't miss it.'

Figgis nodded his thanks and trudged on through the wet streets of Spittel Point. Another day, another mission. Now he was looking for a flight to Farrago, and that wouldn't be easy with no money to pay for it.

He turned into Goose Alley and found the tavern. It looked just like all the others he'd visited in the town. Grubby windows, peeling paint on the front door, a tatty sign swaying in the sea breeze . . . As Figgis stepped in, glad to be out of the rain, he was completely unprepared for the surprise awaiting him.

'Well, bless my bendy fingers!' he laughed. 'What merriness is this?'

The tavern was decorated to look like a tropical island. The floor was yellow and sprinkled with sand.

The roof was supported with palm trees (not real, but very convincing), while the bar was a long beach hut, with a palm roof and a painted vista of the sea on the wall behind. The ceiling was peacock blue and covered with tiny silver lanterns. Even the air was exotic, rich with rum and coconuts.

Figgis drifted over to the bar and ordered a beer. But no sooner had the barman served him than there came the rumble of distant thunder. And when Figgis looked at the ceiling, the star lanterns were disappearing beneath a thick covering of cloud. Then came a flash of lightning and a crack of thunder and suddenly the whole place was trembling. Figgis felt the floorboards shaking beneath his feet. His beer glass was rattling on the bar top. Then came a second flash and another rumble, louder than the first. But curiously, none of the star sailors seemed concerned. They resumed their conversations as the thunder died away, and soon the storm clouds cleared and the stars shone as before.

Figgis gulped down his beer and ordered another to steady his nerves. He looked around and saw two star sailors, Ashenpeakers, sitting together at the far end of the bar. He drank the second beer, then sidled over.

'I wonder if you can help me?' he said. 'I'm looking to fly to Farrago.'

'You've come to the right place,' said the first sailor. 'But I can't take you. I'm flying to Pomona at the end of the week. How 'bout you, Pen?'

The second shook his head. 'No, I'm heading east. What about Moontar?'

Figgis followed the sailor's gaze and saw a man studying a map. He was so absorbed in his work, he seemed blissfully unaware of the enormous purple parrot that dangled above his head, shredding one of the palm trees.

'No,' said the first sailor. 'Moontar can't do it. I was speaking to him earlier and he's off to the Geld Gardens tomorrow.'

'Is he really?' said the second. 'Blimey!'

'That's what I thought!' said the first. He turned back to Figgis. 'You could try Skua,' he said, pointing to a distant corner of the room. 'He's been up to his elbows in repairs this past month, but he might be sorted now. Tall feller. Human. Big ears.' He pointed again.

Figgis thanked the sailors and headed over. The room became darker; the air was smoky and close. The tables were empty. But then a figure loomed out of the shadows: a great bull of a man, with a shaved head and diamond ear studs. He sat alone at a table, with a whisky bottle before him.

'I'm looking for a flight to Farrago,' said Figgis. 'I hear you might be able to help.'

'I might,' said Skua. 'Sit down.'

Figgis pulled up a chair.

'What's the cargo?'

'Just me and a few youngsters.'

'Is that right?' A lazy smile broke through the star sailor's stubble. 'Like I said, I might be able to help. It depends how much you can pay.'

Figgis shifted in his seat. Skua leaned forward, suspicious now. 'Did I say somethin' wrong?'

'We don't have any money,' said Figgis. 'We were hoping to work our way across.'

'Then you're talkin' to the wrong guy,' snorted Skua. 'You need a first mate, not a star sailor. Go down to the harbour. Find a ship.'

'We can't,' said Figgis. 'It's a question of time. We're trying to find someone.'

'You're tryin' to *catch* someone,' said Skua.

Figgis said nothing.

'It's not hard to guess,' said Skua. 'Everyone in here knows the *Esmerelda* flew out this mornin' with no cargo except a good-lookin' woman. And she was goin' to . . . ? Oh, yes. *Farrago*.' He leaned back in his chair and rubbed his eyes wearily. 'I can't help you.'

Figgis sighed. All the star sailors in the bar would say the same thing. Skua was just the first of many. He scraped back his chair.

'Wait,' said Skua. 'You said you were takin' youngsters. Ashenpeakers?'

Figgis nodded. 'Four of them. And a Balaan.'

'Is that so?' Skua poured himself another drink, buying time to think. 'Sit down, er . . .'

'Figgis.'

'Right. Listen, Figgis. I'll make a deal. I'll take you and your friends to Farrago – for free – but you must do somethin' for me in return.'

'What?'

'I can't tell you now,' said Skua. 'It's complicated. It'd take time, and that's somethin' you don't have. I'll explain later, when we're airborne. So, what do you say? Do we have a deal?'

Figgis wavered.

'Do you really think anyone else in this room will carry you for free?' Skua held out his hand.

'No,' said Figgis finally. He shook the star sailor's hand. 'We have a deal.'

'Good!' said Skua. 'Meet you at the airfield at sunrise tomorrow. It's the *Stormrunner* you're lookin' for. She has red riggin'.'

Figgis rose to go. 'Would you know where the washroom is?'

'Down that passage.'

'Thanks.'

Figgis nodded farewell to the star sailor and started across the room. As he did, he heard another low rumble of thunder. Soon the ceiling was clouding again and, by the time he reached the passage, the storm was raging.

Figgis walked on, looking for the washroom. There were no signs. He opened a door: mops and brooms. He opened another: beer barrels. He opened a third: monkeys! Five of them! These were the storm-makers.

Two were pumping bellows, creating the clouds in the bar. Two were rotating enormous metal drums to make the thunder. One was working the lights by flicking a switch up and down, but the switch was so stiff the tiny creature needed both paws to manage it.

Eventually the storm was over. The monkeys fell back against the apparatus, panting heavily. Figgis saw one fingering the collar round its neck where it was chafing. All the monkeys were chained to their workstations.

Figgis looked up and saw a small skylight set into the ceiling. He smiled, reached into one of his many pockets and drew out a small pair of pliers. Soon his nimble tinker's fingers had cut every chain and opened every collar. Then he clambered on to a chair and opened the skylight, and, with a flash of fur, the monkeys were gone, bounding across the rooftops of the town.

And Figgis slipped out of a back door and disappeared into the drizzle.

42

The *Stormrunner* was easily found. It was a striking machine, built like a sailing ship with red rigging and black feather blades. The boy with the terrible teeth was standing beside it, expertly coiling ropes. He grinned at Manu as the travellers arrived.

The tiddlins paused at the foot of the boarding ramp and waited for Skua to appear. But it wasn't Skua who came down it to meet them. It was a young man whose long blond plaits and pale skin suggested that he came from the Loki Islands.

'I am Stellan,' he said, with a broad smile. 'Come on up.'

The tiddlins reshouldered their bags and began to board. But Mouse hesitated . . . climbed halfway up the ramp . . . stopped . . . and went back down.

'What's the matter?' said Blackeye, following her.

'I can't go,' said Mouse. She began pacing up and down, wringing her hands over and over again.

'I thought we'd sorted this,' said Blackeye.

Mouse shook her head. She wouldn't even look at him.

Blackeye took her hands into his own. 'Mouse, I don't want to leave you.'

'Then don't go!'

'I must,' he said. 'There are things we have to do.'

'Let Snowbone do them,' said Mouse. 'She enjoys killing.'

'That's not fair,' said Blackeye. 'Please, Mouse. *Please.*' He held her head gently in his hands and looked down into her sweet, anxious face. 'Come with us. Come with me.'

Mouse wavered.

'I want you to be there. Please?'

Mouse gazed long at him. Eventually she sighed and nodded, and Blackeye led her up the ramp.

'Everyone on?' said Skua. He went to the rail. 'Ramp away! Moorin' lines to go!'

Down below, with a flash of his terrible teeth, the boy scrabbled to obey.

Stellan had disappeared. He was elsewhere, firing the engines. Suddenly there was an almighty roar as they kicked in, and the whole machine shuddered.

'Sit down, all of you!' hollered Skua above the din. He pointed at two narrow wooden benches set into the stern.

Snowbone led the way as the massive feather blades began to rotate: *voomf – voomf – voomf – voomf.* She threw herself down, breathless with excitement.

She could feel the machine beginning to lift. It was straining against the mooring lines. So many cracks and groans and roars and rushes! Bumps and grinds and moans and shushes!

Snowbone glanced at the faces of her friends. They were open-mouthed, wide-eyed, panting, laughing, *loving* it! Except Mouse. She looked as if she were going to be sick. She was rocking backwards and forwards. Wringing her damn hands again! Would she never stop?

Voomf – voomf – voomf. Faster now, faster. Skua was at the wheel, checking things. 'We're away!' he shouted.

And they were. Snowbone felt the sudden surge upwards as the last mooring line was untied. '*Y-E-E-E-E-AH!*' she cried, unable to stop herself. '*W-O-O-O-O!*' She punched the air wildly.

But Mouse . . . Mouse was on her feet. Mouse was running. Mouse was across the deck and climbing over the rail before anyone realized what was happening.

'No!' shouted Blackeye, suddenly tearing after her. 'Mouse!'

'I can't go with you,' said Mouse. She was clinging to the outside of the flying machine. 'It's wrong. I can't do it.' Tears were streaming down her face.

Blackeye was nearly there. He was reaching out to her. Looking into her soft brown eyes. 'Mouse –'

'Goodbye, Blackeye,' she said. 'I love you.' And, with the softest of smiles, she let go.

'*NO-O-O-O-O!*'

Blackeye threw himself against the rail and looked down. Mouse was falling. Down . . . down . . . down . . . *Ah!* She hit the ground.

'Where is she?' said Snowbone, pushing the others out of the way. She looked over the rail and cursed her eyes as usual. 'Where is she? Can you see her?'

Blackeye *could* see her and, unbelievably, Mouse was staggering to her feet. And as the *Stormrunner* wheeled in the sky, splintering the sunlight, Blackeye saw her look up, searching for him.

His tears fell down towards her like drops of summer rain.

She was waving at him. Goodbye. Goodbye. Goodbye.

43

The flying machine hurtled north, with the island unfolding beneath it like a fan. Wildwoods and forests . . . fields and farms . . . pebblestone villages . . . towns with towers. Snowbone studied it all, storing the images carefully away in her memory in case she shouldn't return.

In the distance loomed Ashenpeake Mountain: a brooding mass of impenetrable rock, pine-clad and proud. The *Stormrunner* was heading right for it – a fact that didn't bother Snowbone until they were flying over its foothills and *still* they were heading right for it.

The star sailors were arguing at the wheel. Stellan was urging Skua to do something. What it was, Snowbone couldn't hear, but she could see Stellan starting to panic. Suddenly he ran off in the direction of the engine room and Skua, swearing, carried on without him.

'What is it?' said Snowbone.

'Nothin',' snapped Skua.

'*What is it?*'

She sounded so menacing, the star sailor told her. 'It's a problem with the steerin'. I thought we'd fixed it.'

Snowbone looked ahead. The mountain was coming closer. 'You have to do something!' she urged.

'I'm tryin', ain't I?' said Skua.

But the mountain was coming closer. Suddenly there was a scraping sound and the machine lurched to one side as the keel razored the treetops.

'Try harder!' cried Snowbone.

The mountain was so close, it filled the horizon. She could see nothing but green and, above that, the winter-white summit.

'Flamin' ferrets!' cursed Skua. The *Stormrunner* was rocking violently from side to side like a boy in a hammock. 'What is he doin' down there? *STELLAN!*'

And now the air was filled with fluttering as hundreds of birds were shaken from their roosts. Pine needles showered down on to the deck and still the mountain was coming closer.

The tiddlins were rolling around the deck like marbles, desperately trying to grab hold of anything that was bolted down.

'WHOA!' cried Snowbone, but it was too late. They were going to crash. She closed her eyes and braced herself for the impact.

But it never came. With one final wrench on the wheel from Skua, and a metallic *taaang* from somewhere below decks, the *Stormrunner* banked at an impossibly steep angle and turned towards the sea. And when Snowbone stumbled over to the rail and dared to look down, all she could see was Kessel town: the terracotta rooftops, the serpentine streets, the smiling curve of the harbour and the beckoning bay beyond.

'That was close,' said Figgis beside her. 'I swear my heart is still somewhere on that mountain. I felt it go. It jumped out of my mouth just before we turned. I tell you, it's back there, running around screaming. And the people will say: what's that wet, lumpy thing that runs through the forest at night, wailing like a ghostie? And they'll say: it's a heart, bless it. Poor wee lost lamb.'

'No,' said Snowbone. 'You haven't lost it. I can still hear it thumping.'

Figgis put his hand to his chest. 'So you can. I thought that was yours I could hear.'

'That Skua!' spat Snowbone. 'When you made the deal, did he tell you his machine wasn't airworthy?'

'Well, I did hear that he'd done some repairs, but Skua didn't say anything – no.'

'He should have told you,' said Snowbone angrily.

So angrily, that Figgis decided it was no time to tell her what the deal really was. 'It'll have to wait,' he said to himself as she stomped off. 'We've plenty of time. And whatever we have to do, I'm sure it won't be much.'

But Figgis was wrong. Skua would call in the favour much earlier than he expected, and it would prove more dangerous than any of them could imagine.

44

The *Stormrunner* flew on through the afternoon, leaving Ashenpeake Island far behind. Now there was nothing but ocean, ocean, ocean. Eventually the sun slid from the sky and a slick of gold burnished the waves. Then came night and the tiddlins slept beneath a blanket of stars. Then came another morning and, looking down, Snowbone could see turtles and tuna, and dolphins that shaved the waves, jewelling the sky with salt-spun diamonds. She breathed in deeply, savouring the briny tang, feeling dizzy with freedom, drunk with happiness.

Then she noticed Blackeye standing forlornly in the bow of the flying machine. He was leaning over the rail, his eyes fixed on the horizon but seeing nothing.

In that moment, Snowbone felt a new emotion – pity – prodding her heart, and somehow the day lost a little of its lustre. She knew the world was dark and dangerous, filled with calculated cruelty. But she liked to feel that her world – the bit that she could see and touch and smell and hear – was as good as it gets, because she worked hard to make it so. Clearly, this corner of her world – Blackeye's corner – was cold and cloudy, even on a glorious day like this. That pained her.

Blackeye stood up front all morning, never moving, never eating. But then, in the afternoon, he called for Manu.

'Yes, my friend!' cried Manu, running over with Snowbone and Tigermane close behind. 'What is it?'

'That machine that flew out of Spittel Point with the woman on board,' said Blackeye. 'Do you remember what it looked like?'

Manu thought for a moment. 'It was blue. Bright blue, like a swallow's wing. Quite fancy. Gilded carvings, golden rigging. Why?'

'I think it's up ahead.'

'Where?' said Snowbone, squinting into the sun.

'There,' said Blackeye, pointing. 'But it's too distant for any of you to see.'

'How can that be?' said Manu. 'They left a full day ahead of us. We haven't been travelling that fast.'

'But we *have* been passing islands,' said Tigermane. 'They could have stopped for fuel or supplies or something. They left in a hurry, remember.'

The tiddlins stared into the distance, eager to see.

'Whatever!' said Snowbone. 'This is fantastic news. *Fantastic!*'

Her excitement spread through the company like measles. Even Blackeye brightened. And when the *Esmerelda* finally came into clear sight, the tiddlins howled like dogs, and grabbed each other, and jumped up and down, and laughed and pointed and marvelled.

'They must be going incredibly slowly for us to be gaining on them like this,' said Figgis. 'Let's be honest, the *Stormrunner* is a creaky old bucket of a machine.'

'Who cares?' said Snowbone. 'We're catching them, and that's all that matters.'

By late afternoon even Snowbone could see the *Esmerelda* clearly. Blackeye was convinced he could see the slaver woman, pacing anxiously up and down the deck. But clouds were gathering. Low, wispy clouds that trailed beneath the *Stormrunner* like mermaids' hair. And suddenly, the *Esmerelda* started to accelerate.

'They've seen us!' cried Tigermane.

'They would have seen us hours ago,' said Snowbone. 'No, someone's starting to panic.'

'Yes,' said Figgis. 'It's me. We can't afford to lose them.'

'Why?' said Tigermane. 'We know where they're going: Farrago.'

'That Woman could change her mind,' said Figgis. 'Go elsewhere. Even if she does land in Farrago, it's

175

a big place. She could disappear, easy. If we're there when she lands, we can follow her.'

'We must go faster,' said Snowbone. 'As fast as we can.'

But no sooner had she said those words than the *Stormrunner* gave a groan that was almost human and everyone felt her braking.

'No!' wailed Snowbone. *'Not now!'* She ran to Stellan at the wheel. 'What's happened?'

'Nothing,' said Stellan. 'I braked.'

'Why?'

'We're beginning the descent.'

'What? You mean – we're going down? Why?'

'Ain't Figgis told you?' said Skua, coming up behind. 'The deal we made? I would take you to Farrago for free if you would do somethin' for me in return. Well, that time has come! See that island down there? That, sweetheart, is Finoa, and that's where we're goin'.' He grinned. 'Take 'er down, Stel.'

Stellan turned the wheel. The *Stormrunner* banked like an albatross and began her descent. Down through the ragged clouds to an immense tropical island, with palm trees, golden sand, rampant jungle and, towering above it all, a volcano, black as beetle wings.

And as the clouds closed over her head, Snowbone cursed Skua and Figgis and the whole rotten world. The *Esmerelda* and her solitary passenger were gone, gone, gone. Flying to Farrago, to freedom and beyond.

PART FOUR

45

And so the island of Finoa appeared, lying on the ocean like a treasure map. Wild, exotic, enticing.

Stellan expertly landed the *Stormrunner* on a sun-baked beach. The feather blades slowly stopped rotating and, with their downdraught gone, Snowbone felt the tremendous heat. Not in a warming of the body, as a human would feel it, but in the density of the atmosphere. She had to breathe more deeply. And she was amazed that such a climate change could exist only two days away from cold Ashenpeake.

'Right,' said Skua. 'Let's get a fire goin', then we can have a barbecue!'

He threw a rope ladder over the side of the machine, climbed down, ran to the water's edge, kicked off his boots, pulled out his gun and waded in. *Poom!* He fired into the water. *Poom! Poom! Poom!* Within minutes, he returned with two-dozen flame fishes.

'These'll do for starters.' He grinned. 'And if we

want more –' he waved his gun wildly – 'we'll go and get 'em!'

Night had fallen by the time the feasting was over. The travellers sat beneath a magical moon, enjoying the tranquil night. Ceaselessly, sighingly, the waves rolled in . . . kissed the beach . . . scattered their sequins . . . and withdrew, leaving nothing but the promise of love. Beyond the throw of the firelight, the helmet crabs scuttled back and forth across the sand, defending their territories. In the palm trees, firebirds paraded their plumage in a passionate display of challenge and courtship. In the air, bats hung like washing, heavy, black and strangely solid. No flitting or fluttering for them, just a languid, deadly downbeat of wings, a sigh over the sea, a moth on the tongue. So quiet, the night might never notice they were there.

Snowbone too was quiet, brooding, her grey eyes full of fire glints. But she couldn't keep the peace for long. She turned to Skua. 'What is it you want us to do?' she said.

Skua lifted a wine flask to his lips and drank. Then he burped and said, 'I want you to fetch me somethin'.'

'What?'

'The Tongue of Torbijn.'

Snowbone stared at him warily. 'The Tongue of Torbijn? What is it? A jewel? A statue?'

'No, it is a tongue,' said Skua. 'It's a relic.'

'What's a relic?' asked Tigermane.

'It's a bit of somethin',' said Skua. 'Somethin' that's magical or holy. In this case, it's a bit of a man. A very special man.'

'Torbijn,' said Snowbone.

'Exactly,' said Skua.

'What was special about him?' asked Blackeye. 'Did he have magical powers?'

'No, he didn't,' said Skua. 'That's what makes it interestin'. He wasn't a wizard or a medicine man or anythin' like that. He was a mapmaker.' He took another glug of wine, savouring the moment and Snowbone's irritation, then continued. 'His maps are still around. I've got a couple on board. Use 'em all the time. Anyway, he came here – let's see, now – two hundred years ago, just doing his job. And, accordin' to the legend, he fell down a pit and died. But the natives found him because his tongue kept talkin'. Torbijn was dead, but still his voice was cryin' out: *Help! Help!* It was a miracle. So the natives cut out his tongue and kept it. Preserved it some'ow. And that was when the real magic began to show itself. Because they discovered that anyone who held the tongue in his hand could make a wish and it would come true. Just one wish, mind! A few people tried to make a second and they disappeared.'

'What do you mean, they disappeared?' said Snowbone.

'Just that. They disappeared. *Pooof!* Vanished into thin air.'

'Who told you all this?' said Manu.

'An old star sailor I met in a bar in Kyrle. He'd tried to find the Tongue himself once.'

'What stopped him?' said Snowbone. 'The natives?'

'No!' laughed Skua. 'The Finoans are long gone. The island is uninhabited.'

'What's your wish?'

Skua spun round, his face strangely savage in the firelight. 'What's that?'

'I was just thinking,' said Figgis. 'If you want this Tongue – and I can clearly see that you do – you must have a wish in mind.'

'If I do,' growled Skua, 'it's none o' your business.' He said no more, but the air crackled between them like an incoming storm.

'Why don't you fetch it yourself?' said Snowbone.

'It's not an easy task for a human,' said Skua. 'You'll see why. But for an Ashenpeaker –' he waved his hand dismissively – 'no problem! You can have it back here in a few hours and we can be on our way.'

Snowbone fell silent. She had a bad feeling about this. Skua wasn't telling them the whole story, she was sure of that. But what alternative did they have? Bad deal or not, Figgis had agreed. If they didn't fetch the Tongue, Skua would abandon them on the island. And all the time they were deciding, the *Esmerelda* and That Woman were getting further and further away.

'Do you know where this Tongue is?' she said at last.

'I do,' said Skua, with a wine-soaked grin. 'I have a map right here.'

46

Snowbone and Blackeye left the beach and entered the jungle, following Skua's map. It was a strange place, quite different from the forests on Ashenpeake. Everything was damp and drooping but full of life. Spiders, snakes, lizards, birds . . . Butterflies of every colour imaginable. And there were bigger beasts, no doubt. Predators, hiding in the undergrowth. Snowbone was convinced they were being followed.

'I can hear something,' she whispered. 'Behind us. Can you see anything?'

'No,' said Blackeye. 'But I can feel something.'

'Keep walking,' said Snowbone, 'then turn round suddenly.'

Blackeye nodded and walked on. Then he whipped round – and something black dived for cover. Blackeye breathed a sigh of relief. 'Come out, Manu.'

Manu emerged from the bushes, with leaves sticking out of his hair. 'That was a rotten trick,' he said. 'Sending me to fill water flasks then sneaking off while I was gone.'

'We knew you'd want to come with us,' said Blackeye. 'But you heard what Skua said.'

'Yes, I did. He said the task wasn't easy for humans. But he didn't say it was impossible. And besides, I'm a Balaan. I'm fast. Acrobatic. You might need me.'

As it turned out, they didn't. But someone else did. And for that person, Manu would mean the difference between life and death.

The day became even hotter. Manu was beaded in sweat. All three drank constantly from their water flasks, which were soon empty.

'There's a pool marked here on the map,' said Snowbone. 'It's a little out of our way but not much. What do you think?'

'I say yes,' said Manu. 'My mouth is as dry as an elephant's ear.'

Blackeye agreed. 'There doesn't seem to be anything nearer. The pool must be beyond that ridge of trees.'

They started to battle through the dense undergrowth. The tiddlins pushed on happily, but Manu began to realize what Skua had meant. Thorns tore at his flesh. Sticky burrs caught in his hair. Insects bit him before he'd even noticed they were there. And he was hot. So hot.

Snowbone reached the trees first.

'Oh!' she said. 'It's gorgeous!'

And so it was. The pool was unbelievably beautiful – deep, azure blue, ringed with a necklace of water lilies. Above it, the air danced with dragonflies; around it, the land was filled with flowers. But what flowers! The blooms weren't on stems, like roses or bluebells. They lay flat against the ground, their gorgeous petals spread out like rugs in a bazaar. There were so many of them, it would be impossible to reach the water without treading on some.

'Sorry, flowers,' said Snowbone. She began to thread her way through the blooms.

Blackeye and Manu swayed after her, delighting in the heady scent and longing for the azure water.

Shlooop! Snowbone heard something behind her. A sound like a toad snatching a fly with its tongue, but louder. Much louder. And when she turned to look, Manu had gone. Where he had been standing there was a towering, trumpet-shaped bloom, red as blood, taller than a man, with something inside it, wriggling.

'Spittin' spiders!' cried Blackeye. 'They're flytraps! Giant flytraps! They'll eat him a—'

Shlooop!

Blackeye said no more. Snowbone stared in horror at the puke-yellow plant that had just snatched him. She didn't dare move in case she was taken too.

'Do something!' she urged herself. 'Do something!' But what? Run? Fetch help? Scream? It was all happening so fast . . . and yet so slow. Time had no meaning any more.

Blackeye was kicking the inside of the flower. Snowbone could see the petals bulging to the shape of his boots, but it wouldn't let him go. Manu was fighting too. His hand punched out of the trumpet – then sank back down. Snowbone heard a muffled cry, then nothing more.

'Oh!' she cried uselessly. 'Oh!' She was hopping from foot to foot, waving her hands in the air, desperately wishing she knew what to do.

Thoooooooooooo – ca – thoo! Without warning, the puke-yellow plant spat out Blackeye. He sailed through the air and landed – *pdoosh!* – in the azure pool.

'What did you do?' Snowbone asked urgently as Blackeye dragged himself out of the water.

'Nothing,' he said. 'I kicked it. Punched it. Nothing special.'

'But Manu's doing that!' said Snowbone. 'Why won't it let him go? *Oh!*' Her hands flew to her face as she realized.

'It's eating him!' cried Blackeye.

'We must do something!'

'I've got a knife,' said Blackeye. 'It's in my bag, over by the trees.'

'So have I!' said Snowbone. 'Oh, why aren't I wearing it?'

'Can you get to them?' said Blackeye. 'You're nearer than I am.'

'I'll try,' said Snowbone.

She began to tiptoe between the plants, her brow furrowing in concentration. She was doing well, so she dared to go faster. But she didn't see the root and suddenly she was falling . . . *Ooof!* She landed so close to one of the flowers she could see its petals curling, as if they were sniffing her out. She hardly dared to breathe.

'Get up,' urged Blackeye from the pool. 'Go on!'

She picked herself up and crept towards the bags. Reached them. Delved inside. Brought out the knives and waved them triumphantly at Blackeye.

'Find a branch!' he shouted. 'See if you can trip the traps!'

Snowbone nodded and picked up a fallen bough. She approached the nearest flower and touched it, right in the middle.

Shlooop! The flower sprang closed.

'It works!' she cried. She went from flower to flower, clearing a path towards Manu. Blackeye gingerly crept in from the opposite direction, and they arrived at the same time.

Snowbone handed him a knife and together they hacked at the base of the blood-red plant. But the petals that looked so soft and velvety were tough as leather. The tiddlins poked and stabbed, but they couldn't be punctured.

'Manu!' cried Snowbone. 'Are you still there?'

'Of course he's still there!' said Blackeye. 'Where else would he be, you daft dollop?'

'You know what I mean,' snapped Snowbone. 'Manu! Are you there?'

'Mmmmm!' The trumpet bulged as Manu kicked frantically inside.

'We're trying to reach you!' shouted Blackeye, beavering away with his knife. 'Hold on!'

And then, scarily, the flytrap began to quiver. It shook uncontrollably, like a pan boiling over on a stove, and, with a cough and spit – *wheeeeeeeeeeeeeeeeee!* – Manu was ejected from the flower. He flew through the air like a football and – *thuud!* – hit the ground hard and lay there, dazed.

'Manu!' cried Snowbone, running over. 'Are you all right?'

Manu slowly sat up. His clothes were soaked and clinging to his body. His legs were sticky with a strange, gooey juice and he stank like a dead dog. 'Yes,' he said. 'I think so.'

'What happened?' asked Blackeye.

'Nothing,' said Manu.

'Nothing?' said Snowbone. 'Something must have happened. One minute it was eating you alive and the next it spat you out.'

'Nothing happened,' said Manu. 'OK?'

'Manu!' said Snowbone. 'Tell us!'

Manu looked at them uncomfortably. 'All right,' he said. 'If I must.' He took a deep breath. 'I was scared in there. Really scared. I couldn't find a way out and the plant started to spray me with something. *Urgh!* It was thick and snotty. And the smell . . .'

'We know about that,' said Blackeye. 'You're pretty whiffy!'

'It's foul, isn't it?' said Manu, pulling a green globule off his legs. 'Like baby cack. Anyway, I was scared – and I wet myself.'

'*You peed on the plant?*' said Snowbone.

Manu nodded and hung his head in shame. 'I don't think it liked the taste.'

It had gone very quiet. Manu dared to look at his friends' faces. Snowbone and Blackeye were convulsed in silent laughter. Tears were rolling down Blackeye's cheeks as he tried to keep it all in.

'I'd drunk a full flask of water,' said Manu. 'There was ever such a lot of it. About a bucketful.' With that, he started to smile, and the tiddlins exploded into giggles.

'It's not funny!' he said, laughing anyway. 'You rotten pair!'

'You're the only rotten thing around here!' said Blackeye. 'I suggest you get in that pool and wash it all off, before the parrots start falling from the trees.'

So Manu bathed, while the tiddlins laughed until their sides were sore.

'Do you think Skua knew about the flytraps?' said Blackeye, when they were walking again.

'Yes!' said Snowbone. 'Of course he did! That's

why he wanted Ashenpeakers to fetch the Tongue. It all makes sense now.'

But Skua hadn't known about the flytraps. He had a very different reason for sending the tiddlins – as they were about to discover.

47

The three friends walked on through the afternoon, following the map. Past the bat cave, over the stepping stones, round the coconut grove.

'That Skua,' grumbled Snowbone for the umpteenth time. 'So much for *You can have it back here in a few hours.* This is taking forever.'

'We have to do it,' said Blackeye. 'If we don't, we'll never get to the Nova Land and we'll never find That Woman.'

'I know, I know,' grumbled Snowbone. 'But I don't have to be happy about it, do I?' She stopped and looked at the map again.

'Where are we?' said Manu.

'Here,' said Snowbone. She traced a line across the parchment. 'We have to cross this bit of open land, then pick up this track here. That will take us round the flank of the volcano and the way in is right there.'

'We're going *inside* the volcano?' said Blackeye. 'Erm, haven't you forgotten something?' He rapped his knuckles on his arm.

'I know,' said Snowbone. 'I said exactly the same thing to Skua when he showed me the route. Wood? Volcano? Fire? No! But he says the volcano is extinct. It's cold.'

'What happens when we get inside?' said Manu.

'We follow the track. There's only one, according to this bit of writing: "Follow the Solitary Way to the Cavern at the Core. To the Crusty Cave and Torbijn's Tongue."'

'Sounds easy enough,' said Manu.

'Hm. A bit *too* easy,' said Snowbone. She drank from her water bottle. 'Let's go. The sooner we're there, the sooner we're back.'

They started across the scrubland. It was strewn with boulders and colonized by ferns. The ground was curiously bumpy, with endless dips and hollows, like a giant's pillow after a restless night.

'These bumps can't be natural,' said Blackeye. 'They must be man-made.'

And Snowbone was just about to say *mines* when the ground gave way beneath their feet.

'*WHOOOOA!*'

They plummeted down in a thunderous shower of stones and earth and fern and rubble.

'*WHOOOOA!*'

And still they fell. Down, down, down the mineshaft into the black gaping yawn of the volcano, while the light above faded fast. Down, down, down and – *doof!* – they fell no further.

193

'Manu,' said Snowbone into the darkness, 'are you all right?'

'*Mmmmm*,' groaned Manu. 'The soil landed first. Cushioned the fall.'

Snowbone picked herself up. 'You there, Blackeye?'

'Yep.'

Snowbone assumed he was still in one piece. She was. 'Can you see anything?'

'No. But I think we're in a tunnel, and it seems brighter that way. Give me your hand.'

Snowbone wavered. Oh, how she hated touching people! Animals, yes. Boys, no.

'Come on,' urged Blackeye, anxious to be off.

Snowbone was glad it was dark; Blackeye couldn't see her face. Every fibre in her body was crying out against touching him, but she had no choice. She inched towards his voice and held out her hand. She felt his fingers brush against her arm. They tapped down its length until they found her hand. His fingers closed round her own. Tight. Solid. Unexpectedly reassuring. Her palm began to tingle. It was quite nice really.

'Manu,' said Blackeye, 'find Snowbone's hand.'

And now Snowbone felt another set of fingers feeling for her. When they found her, there was no tingling, but they felt OK. Snowbone smiled in spite of herself.

Blackeye led them on. Lava had coursed along the tunnel once and now the adventurers stumbled through, their boots banging every bump and lump in the floor. But it was getting lighter. There was a pale, flickering amber glow and, when they reached the end of the tunnel, they found its source.

Lanterns! Ornate, golden lanterns, hundreds of them, with candles burning inside. The volcano was hollow but its sides were riddled with tunnels, just like the one they had come along. The lanterns were set into the walls between the tunnel mouths. They bathed the whole interior with an enchanting, golden, faery glow.

Snowbone wondered at it all. It was so organized. So clever. So well tended.

'Get back!' said Blackeye. He pulled her into the shadows. 'They might see us.'

'Who?'

'I don't know,' said Blackeye, 'but there's definitely someone here.'

'So much for the natives being long gone,' said Snowbone. 'And so much for "Follow the Solitary Way". There are hundreds of tunnels in here. Oh, this stupid map!'

'No, wait,' said Manu. 'There *is* only one way. One path. We're looking at it, see?' He pointed. 'It comes in up there and spirals down. All the other tunnels lead off it.'

'Are we going to bother with the Tongue?' said Blackeye. 'I just want to get out. We should do it now, while there's no one around.'

'I agree,' said Snowbone. 'I think the Tongue will be further down, but we need to go *up* to get out.'

They started walking. As they climbed, they heard sounds coming from the tunnels. The *tink — tink — tink* of pickaxes; the scraping of shovels; the rumble of trucks; the muted voices of miners.

'It's so hot in here,' said Manu. His shirt was sticking to his back. 'I can't believe this volcano is inactive. Skua's wrong.'

'Skua's a liar,' said Snowbone grimly. 'I swear, when I see him again I'll —'

'*Shhh!*' hissed Blackeye. 'They'll hear us.'

Too late. The Finoans had heard them already. How could they not, when Snowbone's boots were scuffing the tunnel floor and Manu's breath was coming in gasps?

They heard, they watched, they waited. Then they pounced.

Granite-grey fingers grab-grab-grabbing! Poking, pulling, pushing, stabbing! The three friends were hauled into the air and carried like coffins, though with rather less dignity. They were bumped and bashed against the tunnel wall, bounced off the ceiling, squeezed and prodded until the tiddlins were chipped as chairs and Manu had bruises on his bruises.

As they were borne along, Snowbone suddenly realized: they were going down. Down the Solitary Way to the Cavern at the Core. To the Crusty Cave and the Tongue of Torbijn.

But then she saw something that made her forget the Tongue in an instant.

They were passing a cave and it was full of bones. Human bones, carelessly tossed into muddled piles. That was why Skua hadn't tried for the Tongue himself. That was why he had sent Ashenpeakers to fetch it.

The Finoans were cannibals.

48

It seemed to Snowbone that they were carried into the very belly of the earth. When they were finally set down, the heat was so overwhelming that Manu ripped off his shirt and threw it to the ground.

'I can hardly breathe!' he said. 'It's like an oven in here!'

But the heat didn't bother Snowbone and Blackeye. They were far more interested in their captors. The Finoans were clearly human, but they were grey. Grey hair. Grey faces. Grey ragged clothes. Thin grey bodies, curiously stringy, like beans that have grown in too little light. Grey eyes: huge, round, owlish, with fat black pupils. And there were so many of them! Snowbone guessed there might be a hundred, but there were more coming out of tunnels: above, below, behind. They were standing in an enormous space, but it was rapidly filling.

'What do you want with us?' demanded Snowbone.

'We want nothing from you,' said a grey man,

stepping forward. 'But *he* is most welcome.' He nodded in the direction of Manu.

'You can't have him,' said Snowbone hotly. 'No way.'

'What do you mean?' said Manu. 'Snowbone? What do you mean?'

Snowbone said nothing. Manu stared at her. Despite the heat, he could feel a cold finger of fear caressing his spine. He turned to the grey man. 'What are you going to do to me?'

'Nothing – until we have the blessing of the king.' The grey man turned to a boy by his side. 'Fetch him!'

Instantly, the boy disappeared into the crowd, and the tiddlins didn't have to wait long before they heard the *boom – boom – boom* of drums reverberating through the volcano. Then there came a horn – a wild, unearthly sound like a terrified horse – and a strange red glow emanated from one of the tunnels. And then the royal procession entered the cavern, and the grey people fell as one to their knees.

First came the torch-bearers, and the walls were a battleground of shadows, brutal and bloody in the unnatural red light of the flames. Next came the drummers, beating strange pyramidal drums, like upended volcanoes. Then came the horn player – a woman, with a terrifying headdress that looked like a mass of worms dangling down over her face. And then – *tiiish!* – to the clash of an unseen cymbal, four bare-chested men strode regally into the cavern. On their shoulders they carried a magnificent silver shield and sitting on top of it was the king.

Snowbone gasped. He was tiny. Tiny! No bigger than a five-year-old human. But surely he was older than that? The shield-bearers carefully lowered the shield and placed it upon a stone dais. Up close, Snowbone saw the king was ten, maybe eleven years old. And he wasn't grey: he was black. As black as Manu.

His skin had been oiled; it shone opulently in the torchlight. And because the king was wearing nothing but a crown, a chain and a loincloth, Snowbone could clearly see his body. It was strangely shortened, with very little neck, stubby arms, and his legs . . . ? They were squashed under him somehow. Instead of feet, he seemed to have flippers. Snowbone couldn't help thinking he looked like a tree stump. His legs were like roots, anchoring him upright.

Snowbone was captivated. Her eyes wandered over his face, his body, his crown. She wanted to memorize every last detail. And then . . . she couldn't be sure whether it was just a trick of the torchlight, but the slender golden chain around the king's neck seemed to be shining more brightly than it had been before. Soon it was glowing. Shimmering in the dark with an incredible intensity.

'Manu!' said Blackeye. '*Manu!*'

Snowbone turned. Blackeye was goggle-eyed. Breathless with excitement.

'*Manu!*' he said again. '*Look at your necklace!*'

It was shining as brightly as the king's.

49

'Where did you get that chain?' said Manu.

Oooof! No sooner had the words left his lips than he was thumped in the back by one of the shield-bearers.

'Fall to your knees, boy!' roared the shield-bearer. 'And do not *dare* speak to the king again!'

'No!' said Manu defiantly. 'I will not fall to my knees! I am High Prince Manu of Balaa, firstborn son of Meru, King of Balaa. It is you who should fall to your knees before me.'

The shield-bearer glared at him.

'Do you not understand?' said Manu menacingly. 'You will fall to your knees.'

The shield-bearer looked to his comrades for support, but found they had already obeyed. He grunted and, with a scowl, sank to his knees before Manu.

Snowbone's jaw was dangling. Was Manu really a prince? She'd always thought it was just a story, but now . . .

Manu approached the dais. He bowed elegantly and then sank to one knee – not out of deference, but out of choice. He wanted to meet the eyes of this king. 'Where did you get that chain?' he said again. 'Only a High Prince of Balaa is entitled to wear one.'

The king smiled and shrugged his shoulders. 'In truth, my friend,' he said, 'I do not know. Mine is a strange story and not one to be told here. Come! Bring your friends. We shall retire to my private quarters.'

And with that, the king clapped his hands and the shield-bearers bore him away, with Manu and the tiddlins following behind.

'Make yourselves comfortable,' said the king when they reached the royal bedchamber. He indicated a sea of cushions on the carpeted cave floor. 'Forgive me if I don't join you.' He settled himself on a low couch.

Snowbone looked around the king's cave. It was elaborately furnished, with tapestries hanging on the walls and torches burning in golden sconces. Attendants were offering drinks in silver goblets. A manservant was dressing the king in a magnificent silk coat. And, judging by Manu, the temperature in here was infinitely more acceptable.

'To begin,' said the king, 'my name is Filizar. At least, that is the name the Finoans have given me.

They found me on the beach when I was a very young baby. I was in a wooden chest, with no letter of explanation, no belongings – nothing! Just this golden chain round my neck. And I have no idea how it got there. It has no clasp.'

'This is bizarre!' said Snowbone to Filizar. 'It almost makes sense. You and Manu could be brothers. Except Manu has only one brother, and he's much younger. He's six. But you look about ten. I don't see where you fit in.'

'I do,' said Manu. He took a deep breath and sighed it away. 'I thought I'd forgotten but it's still there.' He shook his head, as if he couldn't believe what he was remembering.

'One day,' he said, 'when I was very young – about three years old – my stepmother told me I was going to have a baby brother or sister to play with. I remember I was very excited. My stepmother was definitely carrying a child. Her belly grew big, though at the time I didn't understand why. And then, one morning, she retired to her room and there were cries. The servants ran backwards and forwards all day, with bowls of water and towels. And then there was a scream and it all went quiet.'

Manu fell silent, gathering his thoughts. 'A week or so later, I asked my father when I would be getting the baby brother or sister. He began to cry and said it had gone away.'

'Are you saying that my parents got rid of me?'

said Filizar. 'My own parents? No! I don't believe it. No one could be so cruel.'

'Your mother could,' said Snowbone. 'She did the same to Manu.'

'But why?' said Filizar. 'I was their son. A prince! Why would they do that?'

'Because kings walk tall,' said Manu simply. 'That's the family motto: *Kings walk tall while others crawl*. On Balaa, we pride ourselves on our physicality. Everyone – even the poorest farm worker – is lithe and fast and strong. So the king and the royal family must be like gods. They must be perfect. Tall, healthy, physically beautiful. If they're not . . .' Manu's voice trailed away as he looked at his brother.

'Don't worry,' said Filizar. 'I know what you're thinking. But I can assure you, I'm stronger than I look. I'm strong *here*, in my heart, and *here*, in my head. I don't need your pity. And also I have been *very* lucky.'

He paused and looked around to check that the attendants had gone. Then he leaned forward and said quietly, 'Why? Because of all the islands I could have drifted to, I was washed up here. When I arrived, the Finoans were without a ruler. But there was an old prophecy that talked of a king coming from the sea. So when the waves threw *me* ashore, they welcomed me like a god!'

He gleefully wiggled his fin-like feet. 'Just look at me. Flipper Boy! They thought I'd come from the seals. And I have to confess, I've considered it myself in the past. But now I know the truth, I'm not going to tell them. And please – don't you tell them either. Let them think I'm the King from the Sea. I want to stay. I like it here. I live like . . . well, a king!' And he collapsed into a heap of giggles.

Snowbone smiled. She couldn't help it. Filizar's good humour was infectious.

'Do you know the full prophecy?' asked Blackeye. Filizar nodded. 'It's this:

When winter waves throw the king from the sea
The queen still dreams of ascendancy
And the king upon the gilded throne
Laments what never shall be known
When the sea turns red and the rivers rise
And the storm bird o'er the summit flies
The King of the Sea shall leave this land
And carry death within his hand.'

'It's spooky,' said Snowbone.

'It's hokum!' said Filizar. 'It makes no sense. But it has served me well. Which reminds me – I haven't eaten today.' He reached for a small bell and rang it. When an attendant appeared, Filizar ordered food for his guests. Then he leaned back indulgently on the couch and smiled again. 'Now,' he said, 'let me guess why you're here. In four words: the Tongue of Torbijn.'

The tiddlins exchanged wary glances.

'It's all right,' said Filizar reassuringly. 'I'm not going to burn you! The Tongue is sacred to the Finoans, but –' he lowered his voice again – 'it means nothing to me.'

'So it's real? It's here?' said Snowbone.

'Oh, yes,' said Filizar. 'And you're not the first to come looking for it. I dare say you won't be the last! It's in another cave, on the far side of the Core. You can see it after we've eaten. But now, Manu, my half-brother! Tell me about our homeland.'

And so Manu began to talk, but Snowbone didn't listen. All she could think about was the Tongue of Torbijn, lying no more than a wish away.

50

An hour passed. Manu talked. Filizar listened. Snowbone and Blackeye ate everything that was placed before them. Then Filizar summoned a guide and the friends headed for the Crusty Cave.

'Is it always this hot?' Manu asked the guide as they reached the Core.

'No, it's usually quite cool,' said the guide. 'This heat has been building for a week now.'

Manu wiped the sweat from his forehead and trudged on.

'Manu,' said Snowbone, 'I've been thinking. Balaa must be close. A baby couldn't survive in a chest for more than a day or two.'

'You're right,' said Manu. 'My knowledge of geography is patchy, I must confess. As a prince, I was taught diplomacy and dancing and very little else! But I seem to recall a map and, yes, Balaa is fairly close.'

'Why don't you go back?' said Snowbone. 'Tell your father what happened?'

'I think my father will be dead,' said Manu. 'He was an old man. My disappearance will have hit him hard.'

'Then you should be king!' cried Snowbone. 'You should get rid of the queen and her son.'

'One day perhaps,' said Manu. 'But not yet. I'm still young. I want to see something of the world. I don't want to sit on a throne all day, sorting out petty squabbles and marrying a princess I barely know. I want adventure! I want to go with you to Farrago.'

'But if you were king, you could raise an army,' said Snowbone. 'We could sail to the Nova Land and *really* fight slavery. We could change the world.'

'No,' said Manu. 'I will happily risk my neck, but a king is responsible for the safety of his people. I wouldn't lead them into a war that had nothing to do with them.'

'It has everything to do with them!' cried Snowbone. 'It's their world too.'

'They wouldn't see it like that,' said Manu. 'I will go with you, Snowbone, but as a friend, not a king.'

'We're here!' whispered Blackeye.

They were in a small cave, dimly lit with candles, and it was indeed crusty. All the tunnels and caves inside the volcano were rough, but here the walls seemed coated in an extra layer of dust, like powder on the face of an old, old woman. Two guards were standing by the far wall. In the wall was a niche. In the niche was a shelf. And on the shelf was the Tongue of Torbijn.

The tiddlins crept forward. They didn't know why they were creeping. There was just something about the place that made them do it: a magical, holy aura that pervaded the room, hanging in the air like breath in winter. The silence . . . the flickering candles . . . the heady scent of incense . . . the stillness of the guards . . . It was truly awesome.

The Tongue was set into a silver holder. It was dry and brown and looked just like the tongue of a small leather boot.

Snowbone reached out to touch it. Instantly the guard caught her arm.

'No,' he said, glaring at her. 'It is forbidden.'

Snowbone backed off. It seemed wrong to argue in a place like this. She would be content to look from a distance. But all the time her mind was racing, trying to think of a way to steal the Tongue. Now she'd seen it, she wanted it. She had to hold it in her hands. She didn't know why. But she did know it had nothing to do with Skua.

How could it be done? Presumably there were guards on duty day and night. They would need to be distracted. But even if she managed to take the Tongue, how could she escape with hundreds of outraged Finoans chasing her?

Snowbone glanced at Blackeye. He was obviously

thinking the same thing. His eyes were narrow with concentration.

But Manu was too distressed by the heat to care about the Tongue. He was bent double, with his hands on his knees. 'I can hardly breathe,' he gasped.

And when Snowbone looked at the guards, she saw that they too were wet with sweat, and although they appeared calm, they were taking in huge lungfuls of air.

And then there came an almighty rumble from the belly of the earth and suddenly the ground was rocking beneath her feet. The guards were staggering to stay upright. Manu fell to the floor.

'What is it?' cried Blackeye.

'The volcano!' shouted one of the guards. 'She's waking up!'

And now there came a roar, and the whole place was shaking. Screams echoed down the tunnel. Cries. Moans. Rain. Torrential rain. Only it wasn't rain. It was feet. Thousands of running feet, pattering through the tunnels.

'Run!' cried Snowbone to the guards. 'Run for your lives!'

The guards looked at each other, dropped their swords and ran. And Snowbone leapt forward, grabbed hold of the Tongue, thrust it into her pocket and ran after them, with Manu and Blackeye stumbling behind.

'Come on!' she yelled over her shoulder. 'Faster!'

She ran to the end of the tunnel and skidded to a halt. The Core was packed with people, pushing and jostling, fighting to get up the Solitary Way.

'Push!' shouted Snowbone, and threw herself bodily at the crowd.

'No!' cried a voice behind her.

Snowbone stopped fighting and spun round.

'What do you mean, no?'

'I can't,' said Manu. 'I have to go back for Filizar.'

'You can't!' said Snowbone. 'There's no time! You don't even know him.'

'He's my brother,' said Manu desperately.

'Blessed moons!' cried Snowbone. 'What is it with people and families? Oh, go on, then! But be fast. We'll wait here.'

Manu nodded and began to force his way through the crowd. And as Snowbone watched his curly black hair disappearing into the distance, she wondered whether she would ever see him again.

51

Manu had to fight for every step. A panic of people pushed against him.

'You're going the wrong way!' they shouted angrily. 'Go back! Go back!'

But still Manu fought on, taking every punch, kick and blow the terrified Finoans threw at him. On he went, searching, searching for the royal bedchamber. And when he found it – when he tore himself out from the stream of bodies and threw himself, gasping, into Filizar's cave – it was like entering another world. It was quiet. So quiet. Everyone had gone. But there was his brother, sitting on the couch, rocking backwards and forwards, staring at nothing. Abandoned.

'Filizar!'

Filizar awoke as if from a dream. He looked around and saw Manu. 'Leave me,' he said. 'Save yourself.'

'No,' said Manu. 'I won't leave you.'

'You must,' said Filizar. 'I can't run.'

'I'll carry you,' said Manu.

'No,' said Filizar. 'No.'

'*Yes,*' said Manu. 'You're my brother.' He squatted in front of the couch. 'Put your arms round my neck. Hold on tight.'

Filizar clambered on to Manu's back. Manu took his brother's flat legs into his hands and, with a deep breath, launched himself back into the river of Finoans.

❧

'Where is he?' said Snowbone for the fifteenth time. 'Where is he?'

Blackeye didn't reply. He just kept looking. 'There!' he cried at last. 'He's got him!'

The tiddlins kicked their way through the crowd. When they reached Manu and Filizar, they started up the Solitary Way together. But they were no more than halfway up when the unceasing screams from below became one unbearable, deafening howl of anguish. The whole volcano shook like a baby's rattle and a hot sea of molten rock rose into the Core.

Terror gripped the Finoans. They cried, screamed, stampeded, but that made things infinitely worse. People were falling over the edge of the Way. Tumbling like pebbles into the deadly magma sea below.

'We've got to get out!' shouted Snowbone. 'We'll burn!'

Blackeye nodded furiously and pushed ahead.

'Filizar!' cried Manu suddenly. 'Hold on!'

'What's the matter?' said Snowbone, somehow managing to turn round.

'He nearly let go,' said Manu, clearly shaken. 'He was holding on with only one hand.'

'We're nearly there,' said Snowbone. 'Just keep going.'

Finally, miraculously, they reached the tunnel that led to freedom, and when they emerged, breathless, into the starlight, Manu and Blackeye hugged each other wildly. Even Snowbone let a tear fall. She was just so glad to be alive.

But the danger wasn't over yet.

'The volcano's going to blow,' said Manu. 'We've got to get down before the lava starts flowing.'

The Finoans were streaming down the flanks of the volcano. Manu and Snowbone joined them.

'No!' cried Blackeye. 'Wait!' He was staring at the horizon. His eyes were screwed up, piercing the night. 'We need to go up,' he said. 'To the summit.'

'*Are you mad?*' cried Snowbone. 'When it blows, we'll be blasted to bits!'

'Trust me,' said Blackeye.

And Snowbone looked into his face and knew that she did trust him. With a sigh, she began to follow, with Manu bringing up the rear.

For a moment, the Finoans around them wavered. They saw their king going in the opposite direction . . . but there was no time to wonder. Shaking their heads, the Finoans turned away and began the long climb down.

Blackeye hurried onwards and upwards, clambering over the rocks like a mountain goat. Snowbone kept pace behind him. Manu struggled on, with Filizar feeling heavier by the minute. The volcano was still rumbling and roaring beneath them, as if a dragon had awakened to find his gold missing. Loose boulders were somersaulting down the mountainside in a cannonade of stones and pebbles. But then there came another noise. An insistent drone, like a swarm of angry bees. Their clothes started flapping in a wind that came from nowhere. And as the tiddlins looked up, the *Stormrunner* swept in from the sea and stayed there, hovering above them.

A ladder came down from the sky. It danced in the sunlight. Wiggled enticingly like a worm on a hook. And still it came down, closer, closer.

'Come on,' said Manu urgently. 'Come on. It's going to blow.'

The ladder was within reach. Blackeye caught hold and beckoned to Snowbone. He held it steady while she clambered on and started climbing. Manu followed, with Filizar still clinging to his back. As Blackeye brought up the rear, there was a shout from above – 'GO!' – and the *Stormrunner* accelerated away, with the ladder swaying beneath and everyone desperately holding on.

And Snowbone was just about to curse Skua for

flying recklessly when the sky exploded so violently, she thought the end of the world had come. The *Stormrunner* rocked uncontrollably. The air spun in a cauldron of smoke and ash and cinders. And down below, red rivers of death began their spidery descent.

But in the distance lay the ocean, winter-wild beneath the midnight sky. And that was where the *Stormrunner* was heading, with everyone safe on board.

PART FIVE

'Right, then,' said Skua. 'Which one of you has the Tongue?'

Snowbone glared at him. 'We didn't get it. What was it you said? Oh, yes – I remember. *The island is uninhabited.* Well, it wasn't, and guess what? The natives didn't want to give their sacred relic to a bunch of thieves.'

Skua smiled dangerously. 'Is that so?' he said. 'Then you've got a long swim home, ain't ya?' And, without warning, he grabbed hold of Filizar, lifted him high in the air and dangled him over the side of the flying machine.

'No!' cried Manu. 'Snowbone!'

'That's more like it,' said Skua, returning a furious Filizar to the deck. 'Right, little lady. Hand it over.'

'You don't deserve it,' spat Snowbone.

'Don't I?' said Skua. 'If it weren't for me, you'd still be on the volcano, burned to a crisp.'

'If it weren't for you, we wouldn't have been anywhere *near* that volcano.'

'You're right. You'd still be in Spittel Point lookin' for some mug who'd fly you halfway across the world for free.'

'Enough!' said Figgis. 'Snowbone, give him the Tongue and let's be done with it.'

With one last scowl, Snowbone reached in her pocket, brought out the Tongue and handed it over.

Skua cradled it in the palm of his hand and stared at it greedily. 'You missed your chance then, Snowbone,' he said. 'You could've wished me dead.'

'Don't tempt me,' said Snowbone.

Skua slid the Tongue into his pocket.

'Oi!' said Figgis. 'Aren't you going to make your wish?'

'No,' said Skua mysteriously. 'Not now. Not here.'

And though the tiddlins badgered him for a full hour, he said no more.

53

For six uneventful days and nights, the *Stormrunner* flew over the ocean. Everyone settled into a daily routine. Figgis couldn't sit idle, so he tinkered around, repairing bits of the machine. Blackeye climbed to the top of the rigging and pretended to be a pirate. Tigermane found a broken feather blade down in the hold and spent many happy hours repairing it. She loved the feel of the feathers between her fingers and liked to imagine the exotic places the *Stormrunner* had visited over the years. Manu and Filizar just talked. They had so much to say and so many memories to share, the days flew by without them even noticing.

Snowbone simply watched the sea. She liked the emptiness: it was full of possibilities. She breathed in the briny air and savoured the salt on her tongue. Sometimes her head felt tight and the sea soothed her. The endless blue bathed her eyes and eased her soul.

No one realized how troubled Snowbone was. She kept her worries well hidden. But late at night, sitting under the stars, she would think about things. It was something Manu had said: *A king is responsible for the safety of his people.* She wasn't a king, but she was a leader. People were following her orders, accepting her decisions, trusting her judgement. With trust came responsibility. Why hadn't she realized that before? Thinking back to the raid . . . had she been reckless? Should she have planned it better? Cared more? She could have lost them all.

But at the time she had thought she was doing the right thing. She had believed her army was invincible. Wood was stronger than flesh, right? But it hadn't been about strength in the end. It had been about experience. The slavers had bucketloads of that. She had none. She was young. So young.

Now she was leading her friends into danger again. They trusted her to keep them safe. How could she promise to do that?

And why had she ever doubted Manu? He was so brave and noble and wise. Everything a prince should be. She knew that when he became king, his people would adore him. Follow him anywhere. She used to think she deserved that, but now . . . no.

It was hard being a leader. Being tough all the time, making decisions, ordering people around . . . She didn't mean to be bossy, but she had to push sometimes or things would never get done. Did the others realize that?

So many questions! No wonder Snowbone had headaches.

54

'There it is!' cried Blackeye. 'There's the Nova Land!'

The tiddlins peered into the distance and were disappointed. There was nothing but a muddy mark on the horizon. But in time it grew sharper and soon they could see the new land: flat, wide, grey. And then, out of the bleak landscape, rose a town. *Farrago!* Ten years ago, it had been nothing but half a dozen huts and one dirt track. Now the skyline was a jumble of towers, spires, buttresses and gables. Farrago was growing so fast, the official town boundary lay somewhere in the middle of the ever-expanding sprawl. It was more than a boomtown. It was a phenomenon. A wonder. A hot, seething metropolis with the worst reputation in the civilized world.

Hanging over the rails of the flying machine, the tiddlins could see it all, spread out before them like a picnic feast. They could see the harbour, curved like the jawbone of a whale, and packed so tightly with ships that a sailor could walk from one side to the other without getting his feet wet. And behind the harbour, the old town: a riot of rooftops, scored with alleyways.

But the *Stormrunner* was veering left, away from the sea, heading for the airfield. Soon Stellan had landed her in one of the bays.

'Well!' said Snowbone. 'Here we are!' She rubbed her hands together, eager for action. 'Now, first things first – we need to find That Woman. So what I would suggest is this: Manu, you take the right side of the airfield. Blackeye take the left. Figgis take the middle. Ask anyone and everyone whether they've seen the *Esmerelda*. We'll wait for you here.'

Manu asked everyone, but the reply was always the same: *no*. Just when he was losing hope, he found a gnarly old man sitting on a barrel, smoking a long clay pipe. And when Manu asked him, 'Have you any news of a machine called the *Esmerelda*?' the old man said, 'Aye, I do.'

'Really?' said Manu.

'Aye,' said the old man again. He spat out a long grey gob of spittle. 'Comes in from Ashenpeake yesterday. I knows the captain – Scuttle, he's called – and we're standing at this very spot when a merchant comes over and asks him if he'd care to pick up a load of timber. So Scuttle says aye, he would, and he's gone within two shakes of a dog's tail.'

'He had a passenger on board,' said Manu.

'Aye, that's right,' said the old man. 'Good-looking creature. I have her name.' He thought hard. '*Tarn.* Aye, that's it. *Tarn.*'

'Did she go with him?'

'Nay, lad! Why would she want to go to the Northern Wilderness?'

Manu shrugged. He had no idea what the Northern Wilderness was like. He thanked the old man and sprinted back to tell the others. But when he reached the *Stormrunner*, he found his way blocked. A gang of star sailors were crowding round the boarding ramp, noisy as a flock of gulls.

'You're too late for the reward,' said one. 'They've taken 'em.'

'What?' said Manu.

'Those runaway slaves that were hiding on board. They've taken them.'

Manu raced up the ramp. Scanned the deck. Found Filizar, crouching in a corner, curled up, shaking.

'I tried to stop them,' said Filizar. 'I tried but –'

'*Ssh!* You're all right now,' said Manu. His brother's forehead was cut and bleeding. He wiped it gently. 'Who were they?'

'I don't know,' said Filizar.

'Slave catchers,' said Skua, coming up behind. 'They pick up runaways and sell 'em on.'

Down below, the clamour suddenly grew louder. There were shouts now and footsteps on the ramp.

'Didn't you try to stop them?' said Manu.

Skua said nothing, just smirked.

'*You told them*,' gasped Manu.

'What's happening?' said Figgis, with Blackeye beside him. 'Where are the others?'

'Gone,' said Skua. He pulled a moneybag out of his pocket, tossed it in the air and caught it again. 'And they ain't coming back.'

'You treacherous, loathsome rat of a man,' snarled Manu. 'I hope you rot in chains for this.'

Skua laughed and sauntered off down the ramp.

'Come on,' said Manu, taking Filizar on to his back. 'We're going.'

'Where?' said Blackeye.

'Anywhere,' said Manu. 'Somewhere you can't be found. Oh, why didn't we realize?'

'What?'

'Most Ashenpeakers here are *slaves*,' said Manu. 'Did no one look at you strangely when you were asking questions?'

'They did, now you mention it,' said Figgis.

'We've got to go,' said Manu, and, with him leading the way, they disappeared into the dirty back streets of Farrago.

55

The slave wagon bumped along the rough road, with Snowbone and Tigermane rolling around in the back of it. They couldn't jump out – they had iron shackles on their ankles and a chain securing them to the wagon floor.

'That Skua!' said Snowbone. 'I'd like to skewer *him*, on a sharp pole over a hot fire, double-dealing scumbag that he is.' For the umpteenth time, she bent down and examined the shackles. 'But there's one thing I don't understand. If he was being paid, why didn't he wait till Blackeye and Figgis were back?'

'Too risky,' said Tigermane. 'Can you imagine the fight with all of us there? No, better to be paid for two than lose four.'

'I can't believe I let them get us,' said Snowbone angrily.

'Don't be so hard on yourself,' said Tigermane. 'You didn't see it coming. None of us did. And once a net is over you, there's nothing you can do.'

'I should have fought harder.'

'If you'd done that, they would have hurt Filizar. Forget it. It's over.'

Snowbone fell silent. They listened to the wheels rumbling along the road and the wind whipping the canvas cover.

'Where do you think they're taking us?' she said at last.

'I have no idea,' said Tigermane. 'But I think we're about to find out.'

The wagon was slowing. Then it stopped and lurched as the slave catchers jumped down. Next came voices – easily heard through the canvas – as a price was agreed. Then a flap was opened and the girls saw the ruddy faces of their captors peering in.

'Time to go,' said one. He took a key from his belt and unlocked a padlock, freeing the chain that passed through the shackles. 'Out,' he growled.

The girls emerged, blinking, into bright sunshine – and found themselves in the middle of nowhere. There was nothing to be seen in any direction. No trees, no bushes, no houses, nothing. Just the road they'd come in on. Snowbone felt her heart sinking. They couldn't escape from here. There was nowhere to escape to.

With a grunt, one of the slave catchers dropped to his knees and removed the shackles. Then he joined his mate on the wagon, turned the mule in the dust and they started back for Farrago. The girls were left with a great barn of a man, as wide as he was tall, with a thick thatch of black hair.

'My name is Dunamis,' he said. '*Mister* Dunamis to you. I am the master here. Come.'

He started walking and the girls followed. Snowbone couldn't help staring at the master's monstrous body. He was wearing nothing but boots, a vest and a huge pair of baggy shorts – definitely not enough to contain the mounds of lumpy, bumpy flesh that covered his bones. At first, Snowbone was hypnotized by his backside. The canvas shorts were straining and bulging as the blubber rearranged itself inside them. Then her eyes descended to his legs. The white flesh was rippling with each heavy step, like two pillars of porridge. Snowbone felt her stomach churn. She wondered whether she could ever face breakfast again.

Suddenly Dunamis veered left, and the girls saw why: the ground ahead fell away into a vast quarry. The air was thick with dust and clamour: the tinking of pickaxes, the *poom* of explosives, the rattle of dislodged stones. The quarrysides were crawling with workers. They clambered over the stones like spiders, breaking off pieces here; hurling them down there; carrying loads on their backs in wicker baskets. Way down below, Snowbone could see several rows of wooden barracks. She assumed that was where the workers lived.

Dunamis was still lumbering on, leading them down into the bowels of that terrible place. Snowbone looked at the workers as she passed. They were covered in

dust, but she could tell they were Ashenpeake slaves –
adults mostly, but plenty of youngsters too, struggling
under enormous loads. Snowbone was quivering with
anger at the injustice of it all.

'This will be stopped,' she muttered. 'I will make
sure of that.'

Dunamis took the girls to a shed, where he gave
them a pickaxe and a basket each. Then he pointed
a fat finger at the quarryside and said, 'There's a
space there, see? You chip off the stone, fill your
basket and bring it down here to the wagons. Empty
it, go back up and start again. You understand?'

The girls nodded.

'I didn't hear you,' said Dunamis.

He leaned in so close, the girls could smell what
he'd had for dinner. Broccoli and beans.

'Yes, Mister Dunamis,' they chorused.

Dunamis grunted in satisfaction, and the girls
turned and began the steep climb into slavery.

❧

The day seemed to go on forever. The girls were
strong, with great reserves of stamina, but as the sun
snailed across the sky, they felt a creeping tiredness
in their limbs. They were panting, grunting, moving
slowly, but still they toiled on. They had to. Dunamis
and his overseers were watching.

Snowbone realized they were in no great danger
as long as they stayed where they were. Far away to

their left, things were much scarier. Men were dislodging enormous boulders, which hurtled down the quarryside with terrifying force. Anything in their path was squished like a fly. Snowbone hoped the men didn't come any closer.

But although the girls weren't in any danger, they were suffering. Snowbone studied her arms. They were pitted and chipped. Her fingertips were rough and splintery. Her joints were stiffening. She reckoned the heat and dust were drying her out.

There was a young girl working to her right. She had a friendly face, so Snowbone decided to ask how long she had been at the quarry.

'Five years?' said the girl, struggling to stand upright. 'I don't really know. Time has no meaning here.'

'What's your name?'

The girl looked around to see where the overseer was. 'We're not allowed to have names here,' she whispered. 'But if I had one, I'd like it to be Daisy.'

'So tell me, *Daisy*,' said Snowbone, relishing the naughtiness of the name on her tongue, 'do you have family?'

'No!' said the girl, smiling. 'I'm a slave! I don't have family. That's for humans.'

Snowbone couldn't believe what she was hearing. 'How can you put up with this?' she said. 'Don't you get angry?'

'Sometimes,' said Daisy, 'but what can we do? We just hang on and try to help each other.'

Snowbone returned to her work with a passion, smashing her pick into the hard rock. Every stroke was a blow against slavery. Every cascade of stones was the crumbling of the system. Every new ache in her body was a sign to remind her that she was still alive. Still fighting.

And one day she would win.

56

Manu slipped into the back alley, clutching his bags. He slid into a doorway. Waited. Listened to hear if anyone was following. Satisfied it was safe, he walked on. Paused briefly by a shabby black door. Turned the handle and stepped inside.

'Food!' He grinned, holding the bags high. 'All thanks to Filizar.'

'What's one ring when I have so many?' said Filizar, wiggling his jewelled fingers in the air. 'I'll probably lose them all by the time we're through, but I don't care.'

'I'm just glad you've got something worth selling,' said Figgis. 'We can't eat fresh air.'

'You'd have a hard job finding any of that in this town,' said Manu. 'It stinks out there! It's hot and muggy – and I've never seen so many people in my life. Every street, every building is packed.'

'Except this one,' said Blackeye, glumly indicating the workshop they were in: the oil-stained walls, the cobwebs, the rusting machines,

235

the empty sacks they were intending to sleep on.

'We were lucky to find it,' said Figgis. 'It'll do.'

They began to eat. The food cheered them a little, but the general mood was still miserable. Damp and clinging, like a rain-soaked coat they couldn't throw off.

'What are we going to do?' said Manu. 'Farrago is like another world. When you're out there, in the thick of it, it's completely overpowering. I felt dizzy just looking up at the buildings. Where do we begin?'

'I don't know,' said Figgis with a sigh. 'I can't remember ever feeling so helpless. Back home in the forest, I felt like this when the slavers came. But then Snowbone arrived.' He smiled at the memory. 'She was only small, but she was so fierce! So confident. She gave me hope. That's what it was: hope. And it shames me to admit it, being a grown man an' all, but I felt safe when she was around. Now . . .' He paused, wanting to choose the right words. 'With Snowbone by my side, I felt anything was possible. Now I'm not so sure. I don't know where we go from here, and that scares me.'

No one spoke. Figgis had spoken for all. The sounds of the metropolis filtered in through the cracked windows. The rattle and hum of the traffic. The banging and hammering of construction gangs. The hustle and bustle of the people.

Suddenly Blackeye sat up straight. *Why hadn't he thought of it before?* He turned to his friends, and his gaze was so bright, it was frightening. 'I think I can find her,' he said. 'Right now, without leaving this room.'

He went over to the empty sacks and started to gather them. 'It's something Butterbur taught me,' he said. 'Late at night, when you were all in bed.' He piled the sacks into a reasonably comfortable heap and sat on top. 'I'm going to go on a journey,' he explained. 'My real body will stay here with you, but my shadow-body will fly away and, hopefully, find the girls. When I'm gone, you won't be able to talk to me. Don't touch me; I need to concentrate. Just watch over me, eh?'

And with that, Blackeye lay down on the sacks, closed his eyes and said no more.

57

Blackeye breathed deeply, concentrating on each breath, feeling the air moving up his nose and out of his mouth. In, out. In, out. Soon he felt the familiar heaviness creeping into his limbs. In, out. In, out. He started to think about where he wanted to go. He pictured Snowbone: her grey eyes; her mischievous smile; her white hair, curling like wood shavings. And soon the heaviness was slipping away and he was floating towards the workshop ceiling. Looking down, he could see his friends. They were crouching by the empty shell of his body, looking at each other in amazement. And Blackeye floated higher, out through the roof and up into the sky above Farrago.

It was twilight: that magical, middle moment when the sun has gone home to supper but the moon is running late and simply *won't* come out till she's washed her face. And the sky, glad to be free of the pair of them, clothes himself in purple with a smattering of stars at his hem. And the people, wandering through a world that is neither grey nor black but somewhere in between, look twice at everything, because nothing is quite as it seems any more, and they might, just might, be looking at a fairy or a unicorn.

And Blackeye, flying low and invisible over the rooftops, thought he had never seen anything so beautiful as the night and this town, embracing like lovers. The lights on the ground outnumbered the stars in the sky. Gas lamps puttering on street corners. Oil lamps smoking in saloons. Lanterns swaying in the hands of night watchmen as they came on duty. Candles, comfort lighting children to bed, to stories, to dreams.

But Snowbone wasn't in the city. Blackeye knew it instinctively. He wheeled in the air and headed back to the harbour. Flew down over the great magpie's nest of rigging and ropes. Soared out into the bay. Swept along the beach. But she wasn't there either.

Blackeye stopped flying and allowed himself to drift. *Remember what Butterbur said. Listen to your heart. Feel your way.*

Then he heard it. A whisper on the wind. A call. A sigh. A sleepless prayer.

Find us.

Blackeye grinned and started flying. Back over the town and beyond, into the wilderness. Here there were no lights to cheer him. No landmarks to guide him. But still he flew on, following the call, feeling it strengthen by the minute. He was hurtling through the night now, like a stone from a sling. Faster, faster, faster. Then he noticed a yellowy glow up ahead and, when he got close, he found it was a quarry, lit with work lights.

There was no one around. Just a dog, sniffing for scraps by a bin. But Blackeye felt drawn towards one of the barracks. He dropped down, through the roof, though the ceiling, into darkness.

He was in a room. A tiny, box-like room with three beds, one of them empty. But in the other two: Snowbone and Tigermane.

Blackeye floated over to Snowbone's bed and whispered her name. She didn't waken. 'Snowbone,' he whispered again. '*Snowbone.*'

She began to stir. Was there a draught? Had the skylight window fallen open? She turned in her bed and opened her eyes.

'*Blackeye?*' She thought she was seeing a ghost. It looked like Blackeye, but he was transparent. She could see a nail on the wall behind him. 'Have you come to rescue us?'

'I can't,' said Blackeye. His voice was strangely distorted, as if he were talking through water. 'I have no body.' He reached out towards Snowbone, patted her arm and his hand passed right through her. 'I can't open locks or bolts.' He looked around the room. 'I assume you're locked in?'

Snowbone nodded. 'This door's locked and the one at the end of the corridor. The window is barred. The walls are wood, but very thick.'

'I'll come back with Manu,' said Blackeye. 'Tomorrow night. Hang on till then.'

He smiled and closed his eyes and was gone. Out of the barracks, out into the night, flying, flying back to Farrago. In time, the moon appeared from behind a cloud and he saw the road they would need. Then he saw the town again, a bright bead of light on the horizon. And Blackeye flew down over the jagged rooftops, down into the workshop, back into his body and opened his eyes.

His friends were still there, exactly as he'd left them. Three big, scary faces staring down at him like moon daisies.

'Well?' said Figgis.

'No problem,' said Blackeye, with a wink. 'We rescue them tomorrow.'

58

Snowbone told Tigermane the good news as soon as she awoke.

'I can cope with anything today,' said Tigermane as they trekked up the quarryside that morning. 'Do you know what I mean?'

'I do,' said Snowbone. 'But keep it quiet, eh?'

As they reached their workplace, Snowbone noticed the men with explosives had moved closer. Not dangerously close, but the noise would add to their discomfort. She shook her head despairingly and began.

BOOM! The first explosion reverberated around them. A choking cloud of dust rose majestically into the air and an avalanche of stones rattled down the quarryside. The men waited for the dust to settle, then started work.

First they searched for cracks in the stone face. Then they took long iron bars and prised them in. Finally, after some strenuous pushing and pulling, they dislodged the mighty boulders, which rolled down unstoppably to the wagons below.

The men worked all morning, loosening stone after stone. Snowbone kept her eye on Tigermane. She didn't want her getting too close. This was dangerous. Out of control. The men were reckless. They never looked down. Someone was bound to get hurt. It was just a matter of time.

It was late in the afternoon. Snowbone had been thinking. Now she stopped working and turned to Daisy, who was working alongside her again.

'Do you know where slaves come from?' she said. 'I don't mean originally – I mean here, in the Nova Land?'

'No,' said Daisy. 'I've never been away from the quarry. I have no idea.'

'I know,' said a man behind her. 'There's a slave market at Barrenta Bay. It's on the coast, north of Farrago. All the slave ships unload there.'

Snowbone nodded her thanks. *Barrenta Bay*. She would remember that.

She took a deep breath, stretched and looked around. To her left, a man was trying to free an enormous piece of stone. He was pulling the bar savagely, angrily, shouting encouragement to himself. Eventually, with a great cry, he set the mighty stone loose.

The boulder bounced down the quarryside like an

enormous football. As it descended, it seemed to take on a life of its own. Every new bump sent it spinning: joyous, wild, free. And then, halfway down, it hit a sharp outcrop of rock. It spiralled crazily through the air and Snowbone, watching from above, saw instantly that it was going to crush one of the slaves below.

Oh! It hit him before she could call out. A cloud of dust rose, obscuring her view. She began to run, bounding over the rocks like a rabbit, down to the fallen man. When she reached him, she found he hadn't been crushed. The boulder had caught him sideways and thrown him into the air. But he was in a shocking state. Snowbone was glad he was unconscious.

But as Snowbone stood there, feeling sick to her stomach, an incredible thing happened. Two slaves picked up the broken body of the man and, as they carried him down the quarryside, the other slaves started cheering. *Cheering!* They were clapping, whistling, stamping their feet, laughing out loud, hugging each other, dancing in dust circles.

Snowbone couldn't believe it. She grabbed the arm of a woman beside her. 'What's going on?'

'We're celebrating!' cried the woman. 'He's escaped!'

'What?'

'He's free!' said the woman. 'He isn't a slave any more.'

Suddenly Snowbone understood. 'Where are they taking him?'

'To The Forest,' said the woman. 'The master's men will take him there on a wagon. He'll Move On in peace and live there for evermore. They say it's a beautiful place – a green valley covered with ashen trees. We all hope to go there some day.'

Snowbone looked at the woman's face. It was so radiant with hope, Snowbone couldn't bear it. If there was such a place – and she strongly doubted there was – it wouldn't be there for long. Not now, when slavers had learned the value of ashen sap. That slave they were carrying had no real future. A couple of years, perhaps, before they cut him down.

Snowbone stumbled back up the quarry, blinded by angry tears. 'Tonight,' she said to herself. 'Tonight we go. And we keep on going until Barrenta Bay is burned. Every timber of every wall – burned!'

59

It was the darkest of nights. No moon. No stars. Manu smiled. Just what he wanted.

With Blackeye keeping lookout below, he shinned up the drainpipe and swung on to the barrack-house roof. Then he padded across the timbers, counting the skylight windows as he went. He stopped at the fourth, knelt and peered through. There were the girls, waiting for him! He grinned and tapped lightly on the glass. They looked up and waved.

Manu studied the skylight window. Perfect! It opened outwards. He undid the catch and eased it open. Then he took a rope from round his waist – and there was no chimney pot to tie it to.

'*Oh, bugs and bones!*' He had to think fast. He ran back across the roof and whispered down to Blackeye, 'Come round to the window.'

Once Blackeye was there, Manu threw him one end of the rope. Blackeye tied it to the window bars and Manu lowered the other end down into the girls' room.

Tigermane climbed it first, with Snowbone behind

her. They followed Manu across the roof, down the drainpipe and into the darkness behind the barracks.

'We have to be fast,' said Manu. 'The work lights don't cover all the quarry, but where they do, they're dazzling. Follow me. Keep to the shadows.'

He set off. Snowbone followed, her mind a whirl of emotion. She was overjoyed to be free. Dizzy with excitement. But she couldn't forget the slaves she was leaving behind. It pained her to think that they would waken to a day exactly the same as the one before. Bleak and brutal, with only the hope of a serious accident to brighten it.

'Where are we going?' whispered Tigermane.

'We have a wagon,' said Manu. 'It's not far.'

They ran on. It was so dark, the girls didn't see the wagon until they were upon it. Figgis jumped down and opened the canvas.

'I am mighty glad to see you,' he said, beaming. 'Climb aboard!'

'Where are you planning to go?' said Snowbone. 'I want to go to Barrenta Bay.'

'We can talk later,' said Figgis. 'Right now, we just need to go.'

Snowbone heard the wisdom of his words. She clambered into the wagon and settled herself between Filizar and Blackeye. Figgis clicked the reins and the wagon began to move. The gentle, rhythmic rocking calmed her . . . the drama of the day faded away . . . and she slept.

60

At dawn, Figgis sighted a copse and turned the wagon towards it. They could rest there for the day, concealed by the trees.

Over lunch, Snowbone told them about Barrenta Bay.

'Do you think That Woman will be there?' said Blackeye.

'I don't know,' said Snowbone. 'She could be anywhere. I hate to say this, but I think it's time to forget her. The slave trade isn't one woman – it's a massive operation, and we need to tackle it. Barrenta Bay is the heart of the system. If we hit it – hard – we can really do some damage.'

'If I'm driving, we can travel during the day,' said Manu. 'I won't get stopped: I'm black. I'm respectable. And if anyone does question me, I'll say you're my slaves.' He prodded Blackeye playfully. 'You, boy – polish my shoes!'

Blackeye fell to his knees and began to scrub

Manu's scuffed boots. 'Please, sir!' he said. 'Don't beat me, sir!'

The friends laughed.

'Don't!' said Snowbone. 'It's not funny!' But even she couldn't help smiling. Blackeye looked so ridiculous, grovelling on the ground.

'Better get packed up, then,' said Figgis. 'Let's find these no-good Barrenta slave dogs and give them what for!'

In a flurry of activity, the pots and plates were washed and stacked. The fire was dampened. The mule was retrieved from the watering hole. The Ashenpeakers clambered into the back of the wagon. The Balaans took the privileged place up front and they were off again, bumping down the road to Barrenta Bay.

Manu followed the coastal road for one, two, three days, with the traffic growing steadily heavier. Eventually the road reached Barrenta Bay: a great fat belly of water, with a yellow belt of sand and a fine, bright buckle of a town.

Snowbone heard Manu's whistle of surprise and poked her head through the canvas flap behind him. 'What is it?'

Manu pointed ahead. 'Barrenta Bay. I wasn't expecting anything as grand as that,' he said. 'I thought there'd be a bit of harbour and the market. That's all.'

'There's money in misery,' said Snowbone.

'Can you pull over?' said Filizar. 'I want to get in the back.'

'Why?' said Manu.

'I don't want people looking at me,' said Filizar.

'They shouldn't be looking!' said Manu angrily. 'You have a perfect right to be there. If anyone says anything, they'll have me to deal with.'

'You see?' said Filizar. 'This is why I want to go in the back. I don't want trouble. We need to slip into town unnoticed. People will look; they can't help it. I can deal with that, but now is not the time.'

Manu grunted, but he did what his brother asked and they entered the town.

What a fabulous place! Manu drove down the main street, staring at the buildings. To him, slavery was a sordid business, and he'd assumed most people felt the same. That was why the dealing was done in Barrenta Bay, away from Farrago and anyone who might object. How naive he'd been.

Snowbone was right. There was money here. Every day someone made a fortune, and the town made sure it was spent. Every whim, every desire could be satisfied. There were saloon bars, ripe with smoke and clattering with dice. Gun shops with racks of rifles and bright bags of bullets. Dress shops, frilly with lace and feathers and finery. General stores, barbershops, bathhouses. Liveries to care for your horses; undertakers to care for your dead. It was charming and civilized – but it was a facade. Behind the elegant town lay its real, dirty business.

Manu turned left at the end of the street, followed the signs and there it was – the slave market. It lay at the end of a wide, dusty track, squatting on the landscape like a great brown toad: a mass of storehouses, sheds and pens. In an adjoining field, a dozen or more wagons had pitched camp. Manu joined them, unhitched the mule, fed and watered her – all the while nodding greetings to the traders around him – then climbed into the back of the wagon.

'Right,' he said. 'What do we do now?' He slumped back against the canvas and wiped his brow with his sleeve. He felt drained by it all.

'Make plans,' said Snowbone. 'When you're ready, I need you to scout around. See the lie of the land. I need to know everything.'

Manu understood. She was really saying, *I don't want this attack to be like the last one.* He nodded. He couldn't bear to lose anyone either. They all meant too much to him now.

'There's a watchtower, right in the middle of the compound,' he said. 'I saw it on the way in. If I can get up there, I'll have a perfect view.'

Manu was right. When he climbed it, half an hour later, he could see everything. To the west of the tower stood a huge warehouse, much bigger than all the other buildings on the site. It was full of eggs: he could see the crates being loaded on to wagons. To the east was the marketplace, with a semicircular bidding arena, dozens of outdoor pens and a solid brick building – presumably for holding slaves on market days. To the north was some sort of factory building, with chimneys that poured a steady stream of smoke into the afternoon sky. To the south were log cabins, where the workers lived. Nothing exciting. Manu was just about to turn his attention back to the marketplace when one of the cabin doors opened and someone came out.

Manu gasped. Even at this distance, he could see who it was.

It was a woman. That Woman. Tarn.

61

Manu sprinted back to the wagon. 'I've found her!' he gasped. 'That Woman! She's here!'

Snowbone grabbed his arm. 'Are you sure?'

'Absolutely. There are cabins round the back of the marketplace. I saw her come out of one.'

'Can you remember which?'

He nodded.

'Oh, Manu,' said Snowbone. 'This is more than I'd hoped for!' She considered the options. 'We'll get her tonight. *Oooh!*' She shook her frustrated fists in the air. 'I want to get her now! But it's too risky. We'll have to wait until dark.'

'In the meantime,' said Figgis, 'let's get the kettle on. A nice cup of tea will go down a treat right now. And after that, Manu, perhaps you could do a bit more snooping?'

'Gladly,' said Manu. 'There's something I want to investigate further.'

Manu headed straight for the factory building. The smoke was still pouring out, thicker than ever. And there was a strange sound . . . like a sick sheep, wheezing and coughing, but much, much louder. The building was an immense wooden shed, with sliding doors at the gable end. One was partly open; Manu looked inside.

Oh! He stepped back in surprise. Here, in this hateful place, he hadn't expected to find anything as delightful as this. The shed was packed with machinery, but it wasn't cold and grey and mechanical. It was enchanting. Gleaming copper pipes ran from floor to ceiling, full of knobbly joints that hissed with escaping steam. Connected to the pipes were bulbous brass tanks that jiggled like boiling kettles, and they were so highly polished that the sunlight, peeping in through windows in the roof, was bounced around the room, shimmering and dancing like a host of bright butterflies.

Manu stepped inside. The shed was hot and very noisy. Towards the far end he could see another set of open doors. There were men there, unloading a coal wagon. They must be feeding a furnace. Yes! There it was! An enormous oven, long and rectangular, with a heavy door. But what could be inside? Bread? Fish? There was no tell-tale smell. Could it be bricks? Manu couldn't see any lying around. He started to search, and he was so busy looking, he didn't see the grimy hand that reached out to touch his shoulder.

254

'*Argh!*' cried Manu, spinning round.

A short, square mechanic was beaming up at him, his overalls damp with sweat. 'I'n't it grand?' he said proudly, pointing at the machinery. He pulled a spotted handkerchief out of a pocket and wiped his wet brow. 'First time here?'

'Er, yes,' stammered Manu. 'It is.'

'Come to buy?'

Manu wondered what on earth the man meant. Suddenly he realized. 'Yes,' he said. 'My family has a farm. Up north. We need some help on the land.'

'Course you do!' said the damp mechanic. 'It's hard work is farming! Will you excuse me just a minute?'

He waddled over to the oven and peered at a temperature gauge on the door. Then he took a few steps back and looked up into the rafters, where a small platform was suspended from the ceiling. He held up his thumb.

'OK, Miggsy!' he shouted. 'Let's get her cooled!'

A young lad on the platform waved and pulled a lever, and suddenly Manu was soaked with rain. Water was pouring down from a web of sprinkler pipes set high in the ceiling and, as it hit the hot machinery: *sssssss!* The steam rose like an angry rattlesnake.

Then the rain stopped, as swiftly as it had come. Manu could hear nothing but dripping and splashing and a soft wet sighing.

And cries. Wild, animal cries coming from inside the oven. And thumps. Terrible thumps, as if something were trying to get out.

'Watch yourself!' cried the damp mechanic, dripping like a nose.

Manu heard the rumble behind him and turned. Two men were coming in with a mule wagon. They positioned it in front of the oven and the damp mechanic opened the door.

The heat hit Manu like a fist. He staggered back, blinking. And then, through his watery eyes, he saw what was making all the noise. *Babies*. Dozens and dozens of newborn wooden babies, right there in the oven. They gurgled and grinned and screamed for food, and looked around and piddled and pooed. And the men loaded them into the wagon and they were driven away, bound for who knows where.

'We offer a full service here,' said the damp mechanic. 'You can take them as eggs. Store them at home. Bring them to life when you need them. But if you don't want the hassle of hatching them yourself, we can do that for you.'

'In there,' said Manu, still shaken by what he'd seen.

'Aye, in here!' The damp mechanic stroked the oven lovingly, as if it were a prize-winning cow. 'This is a Prestige Patented Birthing Machine. The only one in the country! The eggs are put in here and heated to the optimum temperature for birthing. It's scientific is this!'

'Wow,' said Manu.

'Eh, lad,' said the damp mechanic, positively glowing. 'You've got summat special to tell the folks back home, haven't you?'

Manu nodded. He couldn't speak; his voice had deserted him. But it didn't matter. No words could ever describe what he was feeling right now.

62

The marketplace, late. No sound except the dripping of a tap. The coughing of a distant mule. The velvet flurry of a bat.

A dry, dusty darkness. Pools of amber beneath random work lights. Black-line buildings. Shadow sheds. And Snowbone, flitting like a moth between them. Eyes straining in the dark. Ears attuned to the sound of silence. Feet carefully placed.

Behind her somewhere: Blackeye, Tigermane, Figgis, Manu. Like cats, slinking into the night on pouncing paws.

Filizar remains in the wagon, despite his protests.

Five minutes later. The log cabin. A single lamp. Muslin curtains. A shadow play: Tarn pacing up and down, brushing her long, long hair.

The friends watch. Fascinated. Greedy. Tense.

Snowbone prepares to give the signal.

What will they do with Tarn once they have her? The friends haven't been able to agree. Tigermane wants to hold her captive. *Tarn has inside information,* she reasons. *We could use it in the battle against slavery.* Filizar and Manu want Tarn imprisoned, with the key thrown away. Blackeye listens but makes no comment. He will accept any decision. Snowbone and Figgis hold their tongues, but their flashing eyes speak for them. Tarn will die for what she's done. Maybe tonight, maybe later, but she will die.

Snowbone looked behind her, into the shadows. She couldn't see the others, but she knew they were there. She raised her hand –

Wait! The door was opening. Tarn was coming out.

Snowbone cursed and lowered her arm. She stood up, hoping her friends would read it as a different signal. She began to follow.

Tarn headed for the marketplace. She skirted the bidding arena and passed between the pens, walking confidently through the shadows. But as she neared the main road out of the market she slowed down, as if she were listening. Then, unexpectedly, she turned right.

Snowbone and the others followed, circling her like a pack of shadow lions.

Tarn stopped at the slave holding house, opened a door and went in.

The friends gathered uneasily outside.

'We can't all go in the same door,' mouthed

Snowbone. 'Too risky.' She indicated her friends in turn and pointed where they should go. 'Round the back . . . this side . . . far side. *Listen*. I will hoot like an owl – then we all go in.'

The others nodded and crept away. Snowbone peered through a crack in the door. It was black inside. She waited a minute more. Then she took hold of the door handle, hooted like an owl and stormed in.

She couldn't see a thing. Even with the door left open behind her, her eyes were struggling to make sense of the dark. She could hear the others. She could see their outlines moving in the light spill elsewhere. But no one seemed to have found Tarn.

Snowbone crept forward, aware that the others were doing the same. The warehouse seemed empty. Where had Tarn gone?

And then she heard a rumble and a rattle and a roar and – *DOOOM!* – something immensely heavy guillotined down behind her. She reached out – and felt bars. Thick iron bars. Then someone bumped into her. Tigermane. They grabbed each other and stared wild-eyed into the darkness. Then they saw a light, way up in the rafters. A lantern, hand-held. It began to sway, and they heard the footsteps of the carrier as she descended a flight of stairs. And now Tarn was lighting lanterns all around the room, and each new lantern revealed more of the terrible truth. They were caught in a colossal cage. *All of them.*

'Well, well, well! What have we got here?' said

Tarn, sidling up to the bars and lifting her lantern high. 'Five little fishes in a net! Quite a haul.'

She looked hard at Manu. 'I know you.' The cold malice in her words chilled the air between them. 'I was aware you'd followed me out of Ashenpeake, but I didn't think you'd find me here.'

'We would find you anywhere,' said Snowbone.

'Is that so?' said Tarn. 'Then I'll have to put you where you can't follow.' She reached into a pocket and pulled out a box of matches. 'Remember your friends?' She rattled the box.

Snowbone hurled herself at the bars, sucked in her cheeks and spat hard; *thoo!* A thick gob of spittle flew through the air and landed – *splat!* – on Tarn's face.

'You evil, ignorant woman,' said Snowbone. 'Do you think by killing us you've won the war? This is just the beginning. More will follow.'

Tarn wiped the mess away. 'Let them come,' she said. 'I have plenty of matches.' Suddenly the sneer fell from her face. She drew back. Tilted her head. Listened. Ran swiftly to one of the side doors – and dragged Filizar in. 'Well, look at this!' she said. 'A little crab, come to find the fishies!'

The friends gasped as one. Filizar, their only hope – gone!

Tarn threw Filizar down in the middle of the room. Then she moved from door to door, closing and bolting them fast. Filizar looked despairingly at the others and mouthed a single word: *sorry*.

Tarn returned and stood with her hands on her hips, studying Filizar.

'Nice coat,' she said at last. 'Give it to me.'

'What?' said Filizar.

'Your coat,' said Tarn. 'Give it to me.'

Filizar unbuttoned his coat, shrugged it off and handed it over.

'You are a low-down, bottom-of-the-barrel, snake-belly thief,' snarled Snowbone. 'You'd steal teeth from your grandmother's mouth.'

Tarn wasn't listening. She was feeling the quality of the cloth. It was exquisite. The softest silk. It was like stroking a breeze. She put the coat on. It fitted, though on her it was more like a jacket. She looked at herself admiringly and slid her hand into one of the pockets. She found something and pulled it out: a handful of nuts in a twist of cloth. She smiled and ate them, then fished in the pocket again.

The friends watched her in silence. There was something strangely compelling about her actions. It was like watching a magician pulling tricks from his cloak.

Tarn pulled out a small golden penknife. She nodded appreciatively and put it back. Next, a sweet wrapped in a leaf. She slipped it into her mouth.

'I wish you'd give me my coat back,' said Filizar suddenly. 'I'm cold.'

'Tough,' said Tarn. 'I'm keeping it. Besides, you won't have any need of it where you're going.'

'I wish you'd let us go,' Filizar went on. 'I wish you'd open the cage and set my friends free. I wish you'd unbolt the doors. Let us disappear back into the night.'

Tarn swallowed the last of the sweet and laughed. 'Some chance!' She started to root in the other pocket.

'I wish I'd never come here!' said Filizar hurriedly. 'I wish I was still at home. I wish I'd never listened to this lot.'

Tarn frowned. She pulled out an old, tatty bit of leather and looked at it, puzzled.

'I wish I could fly away!' cried Filizar wildly. 'I wish I could grow wings! I wish the roof would fall in!'

'I wish you'd shut up,' said Tarn.

Filizar stumbled forward, as if an invisible fist had thumped him in the back. Frantically, he turned to his brother. Manu saw a desperate face, wide-eyed, pleading – and silent. Instantly, he understood.

'*What did you just say?*' said Manu.

Tarn glared at him. 'I said, "I wish you'd *SHUT UP!*"'

And suddenly – *wooof!* – there was a cloud of blue smoke, and when it cleared, Tarn had vanished.

63

'*Whoa!*' cried Snowbone. 'What happened there?'

'She got away!' cried Figgis in despair. 'That's what happened! We had her this close – and she got away!'

'No, she didn't,' said Filizar. 'That bit of leather she had in her hand? It was the Tongue of Torbijn. We made her wish twice.'

Snowbone stared at him wonderingly. 'You are brilliant!' she said. 'But I thought I gave the Tongue to Skua?'

'No. You didn't. But never mind that now,' said Filizar. 'I need to get you out of there.'

He looked closely at the cage. It had no door.

'I think there's a lever up there,' said Blackeye, pointing to the far end of the building. 'I can just about see it.'

'I can't manage those stairs,' said Filizar.

'You can fetch help,' said Tigermane.

'I can't reach the bolts on the doors,' said Filizar. 'And besides, they'll see you as slaves.'

'Wait!' said Manu suddenly. He had just realized

the cage had no roof. 'I have an idea. Have you ever done that thing where you hold hands and give someone bumps for their birthday? Throw them into the air and catch them?'

The tiddlins shook their heads. They had never had birthdays. But Figgis knew what Manu meant. He looked up and saw a row of parallel metal bars high in the rafters, running from one end of the room to the other. 'You want to get up there?'

Manu nodded. Figgis swiftly took hold of Blackeye's hands and stood facing him. He told the girls to do the same, then the pairs stood side by side. Manu lay on top of their arms and the tiddlins began to bounce him.

'1 – 2 – 3 – YUP!'

Manu was hurled into the air. He scrabbled with his arms, but he wasn't high enough. He fell back down and the friends caught him.

'Again,' said Snowbone.

'1 – 2 – 3 – YUP!'

Manu flew higher. The first bar was tantalizingly close. He had almost reached it . . . when he fell back down again.

'This time,' said Snowbone. 'Come on! We can do this!'

The friends gathered their energy. Tightened their grips.

'1 – 2 – 3 – YAAAAA!'

Manu was tossed like a pancake. He went up so

fast, he thought he'd splat against the ceiling. But there was the bar, blocking his way. He reached out his hands . . . and as his fingers found metal, he felt such a rush of excitement, he thought his head would blow off. But he held on, measuring his weight, adjusting his grip, and then he began to swing. Backwards and forwards, gathering momentum, till his body went full circle round the bar once, twice, three times – and he let go.

He soared through the air like a swallow, turned a somersault as he cleared the bars of the cage, caught the next bar along and did it all over again. Down the entire length of the room he went, from bar to bar, looping the loop, his feet never touching the ground. And then, when he reached the final bar, he somersaulted on to the platform at the top of the stairs, pushed up the lever, slid down the stair rail, back-flipped over to his friends and finished with a flourish.

'When this is all over,' said Figgis admiringly, 'you should join a circus.'

'I'd like that!' Manu said.

The cage creaked and groaned as the machinery lifted it skywards.

'Let's get out of here,' said Snowbone. 'We've got more work to do.'

And with a slide of a door bolt, they returned to the night and the stars.

Snowbone lit her torch and passed it to Blackeye so he could light his. Their eyes met. Just a glance, but it was enough. Now they knew: they were both thinking the same thing, *Last time we did this . . .*

But this time would be different. This time they weren't attacking people – they were attacking property. The buildings were empty. It was still dark. No one had arrived for work yet. This was a symbolic act. They were crippling the machinery of slavery.

Torches lit, the friends dispersed. To the storehouses, to the sheds, to the marketplace. Only the log cabins would be spared. In theory. In practice, they might burn too. One stray spark carried on the wind would be enough. But Snowbone was prepared to take the risk. The workers would be roused long before that happened.

The torches touched timber. A roof here, a door there. The cheap wood was dry and thin and burned easily. Soon flickers of flame were appearing everywhere, like fireflies dancing on a lake.

Snowbone caught the first taint of smoke in the air. She smiled and breathed deeper.

BOOM! The tiny crackling fire she had started exploded into life. It had found oil: a whole tank of it. Snowbone backed off as a shower of sparks illuminated the night sky.

'Yes!' she cried, punching the air. 'Give me more!' She had unleashed a monster. A writhing red demon that would suck the flesh from this hideous place and spit out the bones.

BOOM! A second explosion, over by the birthing factory. She had to go. The workers would come running. They mustn't find her.

But she wanted to watch! She wanted to soak up every smell, every sound, every taste – because it *was* a taste now. A rich, smoky, tongue-tingler of a taste. *Oh!* She licked her lips and longed for more.

Then she heard something. Running feet, coming closer. She turned. Squinted. Couldn't see.

A bell. A man. A shadow, shifting. Flames. Smoke, wind-drifting.

She had to hide, but where? *The watchtower!*

It was untouched by fire. Snowbone ran over, threw open the door and began to climb. Her feet pounded the wooden steps as she took them two at a time, spiralling round and round, higher and higher. When she reached the top, she ran over to the balustrade and looked down.

It was like being in the volcano again. There was

a sea of fire all around, with people running, shouting, panicking. But everything was so smoky, she couldn't be sure what she was seeing. She screwed up her eyes and tried to focus.

Oh! Suddenly she felt so woozy, she thought she was going to fall. She stepped back, swaying on her feet. What was going on? She'd never felt like this before. So hot. So dizzy. Waves of nausea were washing over her. She was going to faint. She was going to be sick.

She staggered back to the balustrade and clung to it. Closed her eyes. Hoped this thing would go away.

But it didn't. It got worse. There was a snowstorm in her head. A fury of flakes, swirling, whirling around. She was in a bubble, a glass bubble, and someone was shaking it. Shaking her. *Stop. Stop. Stop. Stop. Stop. Stop. Stop.*

And then it happened.

A single bolt of bright, white pain hit her between the eyes. Hit her so hard, her legs crumbled beneath her. With a wail of pure anguish, she fell to the floor in a tight curl of agony. She began to whimper, 'Go away. Go away. Please.'

And it did. Not immediately, but gradually she became aware that the pain was subsiding.

Cautiously, Snowbone opened her eyes.

Black. Nothing but black.

She was blind.

65

Figgis ran through the market with his torch, touching walls, doors, fences. Wherever he went, destruction would follow. But he had something more on his mind. Something that everyone else seemed to have forgotten. *Eggs!* There was a warehouse full of them, Manu had said so. If the warehouse was set alight with the doors locked, the eggs would hatch but the babies would burn. Thousands of them. He had to set them free.

He stopped and looked around, getting his bearings, trying to remember what Manu had said. *A warehouse, west of the tower.* He ran on and there it was: tall, wooden, with sliding metal doors.

BOOM! The first explosion, somewhere on site. Figgis grinned. *It's beginning!* He ran to the warehouse, took hold of the handle, lifted and pushed. *Rrrrrrr.* The door was well oiled. Blissfully quiet. He opened it fully, then entered the building. Perhaps there was a door at the far end? Side doors? He'd need to open them all.

Figgis walked between the aisles of crates. So many eggs! Had they all come from Ashenpeake? Apparently so. When he held his torch high, he saw ASHENPEAKE stamped on them in red paint. *They can't all be new*, he thought. *Some of these must have been here for years.*

BOOM! Figgis jumped. 'Blessed be!' he said. 'That was close. A little *too* close for my jingle-jangle nerves. Ah, now, what's that? It wouldn't be a door, would it?'

He hurried down to the far end of the warehouse and – *rrrrrrrr* – the door slid back without him even touching it. And there, silhouetted in the doorway, was a man holding a long iron bar, his face nothing but shadow.

'What's going on here?' growled the man.

He came forward menacingly, until the torchlight flickered on his face. And Figgis stared in horror at the black hair and the dark, dead eyes.

'*Aieee!*' he wailed. 'You're a ghost!'

The man said nothing, just kept coming forward. Figgis could hear a bell ringing somewhere outside. There were shouts, cries, screams. But here, in the warehouse, there was nothing. Nothing. Just the beating of his own terrified heart.

'Bless us and save us!' he moaned, desperately wanting to run but unable to. 'You're dead. *Dead!* We left you back at the camp, with a bullet in your body. I saw you fall. You're dead.'

The black-haired man paused. 'You were there?' Calm, steady, deadly now. 'Left me for dead, did you? Well, the dead can rise.' And with that, he swung the iron bar and smashed it into Figgis's body.

Dooof. The force of the blow lifted Figgis clean off his feet and threw him sideways into the crates. The torch fell from his hand, but he was too winded to care.

Dooof. The black-haired man thumped Figgis again. 'That one's for me!' he shouted. 'And this one's for Blue Boy.'

Oh! Figgis pulled himself into a ball and weathered the blows. There was no pain outside, on his body. But inside . . . *Ah!* His breath was coming in short, savage gasps that hurt like crazy. *I can't keep taking this,* he told himself. *The damage it's doing. The shock of it.*

And with that thought: *whoosh.* He was back on Ashenpeake Island. Back at the barn after that disastrous raid. Looking at ten tiddlins who didn't speak, didn't move, didn't care as their battered bodies began to Move On. And then he saw Mouse. Sweet, darling Mouse, who wanted to live a full and happy life, and Move On gently and grow in peace, undisturbed for evermore. And then he was back in the forest. In the sacred grove. Looking at his murdered family. And he felt his anger growing inside him, straining like a dog on a leash.

Figgis's eyes were closed but his other senses were working perfectly. He could smell smoke and hear the crackle of flames close by. The fallen torch was burning the crates; soon the eggs would be out and hatching. He could hear laboured breathing. The black-haired man had tired himself. Then came a grunt and footsteps. Weary footsteps, walking away.

And slowly, very slowly, Figgis uncurled . . . and then he was on his feet and running, seeing nothing but the loathsome back of the black-haired man. *EEE-YA!* Figgis flew through the air and landed square on the slaver, forcing him to the ground, laughing crazily as he felt the solid mass of flesh and blood beneath him. This was no ghost!

Figgis clambered off, grabbed the man by his jacket and spun him over in the dust. The man was dazed. His eyes were blinking, trying to focus.

Figgis took a deep breath. 'Forgive me, Mouse,' he said, 'but I have to do this.' And he curled his fingers into a fist and set his anger free.

66

Blackeye sprinted back to the agreed meeting point, wild with excitement. He turned the corner and there they all were: grinning at him, hugging him, slapping him on the back. Except –

'Where's Snowbone?'

'Is she not with you?' said Figgis.

'No,' said Blackeye. 'I thought she'd be here.'

Figgis went to the corner and peered into the night. 'She's not coming.'

The friends looked at each other in alarm.

'I'll have to go back,' said Blackeye. 'Manu – run to the wagon. Get the mule hitched. Rest of you, follow him. Figgis, take Filizar.'

'You can't go back!' said Tigermane. 'You're wooden! Manu can go.'

'No,' said Blackeye. 'Manu has to drive. And it's so bad in there, I'm the only one who stands a chance of seeing her.' He started back.

'Blackeye!' called Tigermane after him. 'Be careful.'

But Blackeye had already disappeared into the inferno.

The market was unrecognizable: a heaving, seething skeleton of fallen timbers and twisted metal. Workers with blackened faces made human chains, swinging endless buckets of water from pump to pyre, but it was too little, too late. The fire would not be quenched. It had devoured the warehouses and the factory sheds. Now it was starting on the log cabins.

Blackeye scanned the crowd for Snowbone. It wasn't easy. The workers were grown men; she was half their height.

He moved forward and fell over something. It was a baby, crawling on all fours. *Where had that come from?* Suddenly he remembered the warehouse. The baby smiled at him, and a long stringy bit of drool bubbled out and dangled down. Blackeye bit his lip and tried not to smile. He was searching for Snowbone. Things were getting serious. But the baby looked so funny.

'Get away from here,' he whispered. He patted the baby on her head and pushed his way into the crowd. The men ignored him, cursed at him, shoved him out of the way. No one seemed to care he was an Ashenpeaker. They were far more interested in the fire and how it was being handled. Every man believed he could do better and was loudly saying so, over and over again, though no one was listening. The clamour was deafening. Blackeye could hardly hear himself think.

Eventually, he fought his way free of the crowd. Took a deep breath. Calmed down. Wondered where Snowbone could be.

Then he felt it.

A strange, quickening sensation in his heart . . . a frown and a blink . . . and his shadow-sight told him what he wanted to know.

The tower.

Blackeye turned round. The feeling had gone, as swiftly as it had come. But there in front of him stood the tower. It was starting to burn. Grey tendrils of smoke were creeping up the walls.

Could she really be up there? Blackeye scanned the top, but there was no sign of Snowbone.

He moved round to the other side. No, she wasn't there. But there was *something* there. A bump on the balustrade. A bump that suddenly unfurled, thrust out an arm and hauled itself upright.

'Snowbone!' he shouted. 'Snowbone!'

Snowbone heard him. Blackeye saw her turning her head from side to side, trying to find him.

'I'm down here!' he cried. He waved at her, but she didn't wave back.

'Is the tower on fire?' she shouted.

'Yes. You must come down now.'

Snowbone shook her head. 'Go without me,' she cried.

Blackeye looked up at her, totally bewildered. 'Come down!' he yelled. 'You can still get through!'

But no sooner had he said that than the door at the bottom of the tower collapsed, and the inrush of wind sucked the flames up the stairs.

'I can't!' cried Snowbone. 'Go! Save yourself!'

'What is wrong with you?' cried Blackeye desperately. 'Come down! Now!'

'I can't! Blackeye, you must leave me. *I'm blind!*'

Blackeye stared at her. That was why she'd turned her head trying to find him. That was why she hadn't waved.

'I'm coming to get you!' he yelled.

'*NO!*' she cried, but it was too late. Blackeye was already at the bottom of the stairs, facing a chimney of flame.

He took a deep breath, put his foot on the bottom step – and froze. For the second time in his life, Blackeye felt fear. Mouth-drying, leg-numbing, giddy-sick fear. 'I can't do it,' he stammered. '*I can't do it!*' His heart was hammering in his chest. His lungs were fighting for air. He couldn't move.

The wooden walls of the tower were ablaze now. He could hear the planks buckling around him. He closed his eyes and tried to picture Snowbone. She was alone on the tower. She was blind. She would burn to death.

His leg lifted. His foot found the next step. He gasped and opened his eyes. *I can do this. I can do this.* He began to climb: eyes open, eyes closed, stumbling, fumbling, fighting on. And when he reached the top, he leapt for Snowbone with a sob of relief, hugged her close and took her hand.

'Come on,' he said, leading her to the stairs. 'We'll have to be quick.'

BOOM!

The tower spat a monstrous fireball into the sky. It exploded over the tiddlins' heads like a rocket, showering them with sparks and debris. And when Blackeye reached the stairwell, he found the stairs had been blown out. There was nothing but a dragon's throat of flame.

'Too late!' he said, spinning Snowbone round. 'We'll have to jump.'

'*Jump?*' wailed Snowbone. 'Are you crazy?'

'We've no choice. The stairs are gone.' He dragged her over to the balustrade and looked down. 'It's no higher than the masts on the *Mermaid*. We'll be fine. I'll help you up, and we can jump together.'

'No!' said Snowbone, pulling free. 'I can't do it. Forget me – save yourself.'

'No way,' said Blackeye. He seized her hand.

'*Leave me!*' cried Snowbone, blindly lashing out at him. 'Go back to the others. Be the new leader.'

'*No!*' said Blackeye, grabbing her wrists. 'If I leave you now, I'm not *fit* to be a leader. Now come on.'

He pushed her on to the balustrade and climbed up behind.

'Dear gods,' said Snowbone. 'I'm going to die.'

'No, you're not,' said Blackeye. 'I'll cushion the fall.' He wrapped his arms round her. 'Remember,' he whispered in her ear, 'you've got the best dive-bomber in the world here, missy.' And he jumped.

Whooooo! They fell so fast, they didn't have time to breathe. Yet somehow Blackeye turned in the air so he was beneath Snowbone as they landed: *doom!*

'Are you all right?' he said.

'Yes,' said Snowbone, wriggling free. 'You?'

'Not a mark!'

BOOOM!

The watchtower exploded behind them, spewing ash and flames into the smoky sky. Blackeye seized hold of Snowbone's hand and started to run, dragging her along behind him. She didn't protest. She simply tried to run faster. She wasn't scared to be running blind. She was holding Blackeye's hand. The world was spinning around her, but that point was fixed. Firm. He wouldn't let go, she knew it.

Blackeye sped on. A band of gold had appeared in the east. There was no time to lose.

Manu was waiting with the wagon. He opened the canvas flap and Blackeye helped Snowbone in. Then Manu climbed up front, clicked the reins and they were off, down the road, into the dawn. A little black keyhole against the shimmering sky.

PART SIX

67

Manu drove the wagon north, with no destination in mind. His only concern was their safety. Were they being pursued? Probably not. The slave market had been so smoky and chaotic, no one would have noticed them leave. But still he would feel happier once Barrenta Bay was far, far behind.

He drove till nightfall, when Figgis took the reins. In the morning they swapped places again and Manu pushed on until midday, when he unexpectedly found a perfect place to pitch camp. It was a lee on the side of a valley – a sheltered spot, out of the wind. The view was breathtaking: soft, slumbering hills, with a river meandering through and a balmy blue sky above. It was blissfully quiet. Just the drone of an early bee and the bleat of a passing goat . . . and the crash-bang clatter of pans as Figgis unpacked his kitchen. The friends couldn't believe one man could make such a row! But they didn't complain. Here in the wilderness, Figgis was making it feel like home.

Snowbone sat on a hummock of grass, enjoying the scent of the spring flowers and the feel of the sun on her face.

'From up here, the trees look like broccoli,' said Blackeye, sitting beside her. 'Had you noticed? Oh! I'm sorry, Snowbone.'

Snowbone smiled. 'It's OK. You can't remember all the time.'

Blackeye looked into Snowbone's milky eyes and wondered how she could stay so calm. She hadn't cried. She hadn't raged. She had simply accepted her loss. But it wasn't like Snowbone to give in without a fight. He was worried about her.

'Dinner's ready!' called Figgis. 'And if I say so myself, it's well worth having.'

Snowbone stood up, reached for Blackeye's arm and together they joined the others. Tigermane placed a steaming bowl of rabbit stew in Snowbone's hands.

'Careful,' she said matter-of-factly. 'It's full and very hot.'

Snowbone nodded her thanks. Tigermane was great; she didn't fuss. Not like Figgis, who clucked around her like a mother hen. Still, he meant well.

Snowbone placed the bowl on her lap to cool. 'Filizar?' she said. 'Now we've got the time, will you tell me exactly what happened to Tarn? When she disappeared, you said it was the Tongue of Torbijn, but I gave that to Skua.'

Filizar grinned. 'You didn't! The Tongue you stole was a replica. I had the real one in my pocket.'

'You're kidding!' said Blackeye.

'I'm not!' said Filizar. 'One of my counsellors gave it to me, as soon as I was old enough. It was such a precious thing, he didn't want it to be stolen. So he made a replica, and that was the one you took from the Crusty Cave. No one knew except him and me. Not even the guards.'

'So you sent us along to the cave, knowing you had the real one all the time?' said Snowbone.

'Yes,' said Filizar, with a giggle. 'I wanted to impress you! The real Tongue was nothing special, but the cave was great.'

'It was fantastic!' agreed Blackeye. 'With the guards and the candles and everything, the atmosphere was just incredible. So holy. So magical. I really believed it.'

'So did I,' said Snowbone. 'Oh, I wanted that Tongue. I *had* to have it. There seemed to be some kind of aura – some enchantment – that made me long to touch it.'

'I felt that too!' said Blackeye.

'But now you say it was a fake,' Snowbone went on. 'It had no power at all. So why did we feel like that?'

'Because you wanted to!' laughed Filizar. 'Whether

it was real or not, the Tongue promised the same thing: the power to make your wishes come true. That's a very seductive thing. You wanted the Tongue to be mysterious, powerful, desirable. When you found it, in that fabulous cave, your imaginations did the rest.'

'Would you believe it?' said Blackeye. 'Filizar, you are a cunning little fox.'

Filizar winked. 'That's me!'

'But what about the real Tongue?' said Tigermane.

'Well, like I said, I had it with me,' said Filizar, 'but I'd completely forgotten about it until Tarn took my coat. Then I remembered, and I couldn't believe my luck when she started rummaging in the pockets. I was so excited, I thought I'd pee my pants! And I thought: *if only I can get her to wish twice* – because you know you can only wish once, don't you?'

Everyone nodded.

'So that's why I started to goad her: "I wish I could do this. I wish I could do that." I wanted to put that word – that idea – into her head. And it worked!'

'Brilliantly,' said Manu.

Filizar looked at his big brother and glowed with pride.

'I wonder where Tarn went when she disappeared?' said Blackeye. 'Do you think she's dead?'

'I don't know,' said Filizar. 'I suppose so.'

'There's still something I don't understand,' said Snowbone. 'If you had the Tongue with you all the time, why didn't you use it before? You could have brought us back from the quarry. *Oh!* You could have wished for –'

'– a better body? That is what you were thinking, isn't it?'

Snowbone almost blushed.

'There were two reasons,' Filizar explained. 'Like I said, I genuinely forgot I had it. But more importantly, I couldn't make another wish. I'd already used it once.'

'When?' said Blackeye.

'In the volcano, when we were trying to escape. I wished someone would rescue us.'

'*Skua*,' said Snowbone. 'That's why he came for us.'

'That's why you let go of me!' said Manu.

Filizar nodded. 'I had to let go so I could hold the Tongue.'

'And carry death within his hand,' said Tigermane.

'What?' said Snowbone.

'*And carry death within his hand*,' said Tigermane again. 'The prophecy, remember?'

'No,' said Snowbone.

Filizar reminded her:

'When winter waves throw the king from the sea
   The queen still dreams of ascendancy
   And the king upon the gilded throne
   Laments what never shall be known

When the sea turns red and the rivers rise
And the storm bird o'er the summit flies
The King of the Sea shall leave this land
And carry death within his hand.'

'You see?' cried Tigermane. 'It all makes sense now! *When the sea turns red and the rivers rise* – that's the volcano erupting and the lava flowing out. *And the storm bird o'er the summit flies* – that's the *Stormrunner* coming to the rescue. *The King of the Sea shall leave this land* – that's you, Filizar, leaving Finoa. *And carry death within his hand* – that's the Tongue. You'd used it once already, so you were carrying something that would kill you if you used it again.'

'What about the rest?' said Filizar eagerly. 'Does that make sense too?'

Tigermane thought for a moment. *'When winter waves throw the king from the sea* – you were washed up on a beach. *The queen still dreams of ascendancy* . . . Hmm. Your mother, the queen, had hoped that you would be king one day. That wasn't going to happen, but she was dreaming of having another child. *And the king upon the gilded throne* – that's your father – *Laments what never shall be known* . . .' She took hold of Filizar's hand. 'I think this means that you won't ever meet him,' she said gently. 'But also, it suggests that he never saw you, and that made him desperately sad.'

'So my father didn't get rid of me?'

'No,' said Tigermane. 'He didn't. I don't think he knew anything about it. It was your mother who got rid of you. She probably told him you died at birth.'

Filizar's eyes were silver with tears. 'I'm glad it wasn't him,' he said.

'Our father was a good man,' said Manu fiercely. 'One of the best. He would never do such a thing. It was always *her*.' A spasm of anger passed through him and he scowled.

'You know what else this means, don't you?' said Blackeye brightly, trying to lighten the mood. 'Filizar, you really were the king from the sea!'

'So I was,' said Filizar. 'I thought the prophecy was just a lucky coincidence!'

'There's one more thing I want to know,' said Snowbone, who had happily devoured her stew while Tigermane took over the proceedings. 'If you had the *real* Tongue, Filizar, what exactly does Skua have in his pocket?'

'The tongue of a dead goat!' said Filizar, and, to everyone's relief, he giggled again.

68

A crack of lightning splintered the evening sky, disturbing the crows in the distant trees. A rich rumble of thunder followed, snapping at its heels like an eager sheepdog. In the wagon, the friends sat and waited for the inevitable rain.

They had been camping in the lee for three days, eating, sleeping, relaxing. Trying to ignore the question that buzzed around them constantly, like a bothersome bee.

Snowbone especially was troubled by the question. She knew why no one was asking it. They didn't want to hurt her feelings. But it had to be asked. And so, as the first drops of rain pattered down on the canvas, she said, 'Where do we go from here?'

Everyone breathed in at once. It wasn't dramatic, but Snowbone could feel it. She was sensitive to such things now.

'We have to talk about it,' she said. 'We can't sit here forever. There's a war to be won.'

Still no one spoke. Snowbone could hear them shifting in their seats.

'Barrenta Bay was a great success,' said Filizar at last, starting them off. 'The whole place was completely destroyed and, as far as we know, no one was hurt.'

Figgis dug him in the ribs, but Snowbone hadn't flinched. Her blindness wasn't a wound. It had been creeping up on her for weeks.

'It was a great symbolic victory,' Snowbone agreed. 'But we haven't beaten the slavers. They will rebuild the market, bigger than ever.'

'Mouse was right,' said Blackeye. 'We can't stop slavery. It's all over the country. All over the world! There are too many people involved.'

'No,' said Snowbone, shaking her head angrily. 'I don't accept that. We must be able to do something. We're just not thinking right.'

She fell silent. The rain was heavier now, drumming on the canvas. The friends listened to it fall and tried to think of a way forward.

'Perhaps we should look at it differently,' said Tigermane. 'Instead of trying to stop slavery, we could think about setting the slaves free.'

'Isn't that the same thing?' said Blackeye.

'Not quite,' said Tigermane. 'We've been attacking the system – property and machines. That's a battle we can't win. The slavers will just rebuild. But if we could find a way of releasing the slaves . . . I don't know. It's just a thought.'

'It's a fantastic thought!' said Snowbone. 'Do you remember that man, back at the quarry? When the boulder hit him, the slaves were overjoyed because he wasn't a slave any more. He was free. He was Moving On.'

'So if we could get the slaves to Move On – all of them, all at once – they'd be free!' said Tigermane.

'No more slavery!' cried Filizar.

The friends went wild with excitement. They bounced up and down so hard, the wagon was shaking like a wet dog.

'Ah now, hold on here,' said Figgis above the racket. 'This is easier said than done! For one thing, Ashenpeakers can't Move On at will. Something has to trigger the process. And another thing, the slaves won't be allowed to live happily ever after. If they Move On, the slavers will kill them for their sap and ship in more eggs.'

Everyone stared at him, utterly deflated.

'I'm sorry,' he said. 'But it's true.'

Lightning illuminated the wagon and Figgis saw just how devastated his friends were. A deafening roll of thunder filled the sudden silence. 'I think we should go home,' he said. 'Snowbone, I want to take you to Butterbur. She's the only one who can possibly help.'

'I don't want to go,' growled Snowbone. 'I want to finish what I came here to do.'

'You can't,' said Figgis. 'You have to accept that.'

'No,' said Snowbone sulkily. 'I won't.'

But in her heart she knew Figgis was right. Perhaps one day the war against slavery would be won, and someone would be a hero. But it wouldn't be her. She had to accept the truth. It was over.

69

Blackeye lay in the back of the wagon, sandwiched between Figgis and Manu. He couldn't sleep. For hours he had been listening to the rain, thinking over what had been said. They had come so far, overcome so many obstacles . . . To give up the fight now seemed stupid. But Figgis was right. The slaves couldn't Move On, even if they wanted to. Until they could, nothing would change.

What an unfair world it was! Ashenpeakers were the oldest race on earth. They were incredible people: strong, noble, brave. But they were vulnerable. As eggs, as children . . . even as ashen trees. *What must the Ancients be feeling,* he thought, *when they look into this world and see what's happening? Do they wail and moan and throw themselves around in the Otherworld? Or do they just sit there and do nothing?*

Blackeye sat up. An unbelievable thought had just come into his head. *Do they know?*

He stared into the darkness, holding his breath. It was suddenly starting to make sense. He had been puzzling over the Ancients for weeks. He couldn't understand why they did nothing to help when their people were clearly suffering. Now he knew why. The Ancients didn't know! They were getting on with their own lives, down in the Otherworld. They weren't even watching.

If they knew what was happening, they would do something. They would bring an end to it all. Wouldn't they?

There was only one way to find out.

Blackeye leaned back against the wagon side and made himself as comfortable as possible. He closed his eyes and concentrated on his breathing. In, out. In, out. Soon he felt the familiar heavy-to-light sensation and he was off, out of his body, out of the wagon, out into the rain. But the raindrops passed right through him in a strange, tingly kind of way. Blackeye smiled, turned in the air and headed out to sea.

Over the waves, under the moon, into the east he went. Over sailing ships that snailed across the ocean, leaving their trails behind them, silver as starlight. Over islands, secret-sleeping, scattered like cushions on the wakeful waves. Over sage whales, barnacle blue, singing sea songs older than time.

On he went, till the Indigo Ocean became the Silverana Sea, and the water lapped clear. Here he saw a great graveyard of ships: keels sticking out of the seabed; masts reaching for the light, stark and bony like dead men's fingers; and an immense wall of seaweed surrounding them all, so thick that no living man could pass.

Finally, he saw the formidable bulk of Ashenpeake Mountain, with the island slumbering beneath it. And as soon as he had cleared the coast, he flipped on to his back and started to descend.

Down into the darkness he went, savouring the moist, peaty air. Down, down, down into the belly of the earth: the Otherworld. Into the tunnels, just as he remembered them, with their strange half-light and serpentine turns. Into the caverns with their root-rafter ceilings, where the souls of the ashen trees flickered and danced like frost fairies.

But Blackeye had seen these things, and he had no time to waste. He moved on, descending to a much lower level. Here the atmosphere changed. It felt curiously charged, like the hour before a thunderstorm. The air was perfumed with the scent of sandalwood, and the light was pearly, shifting, and swirling iridescently in all the colours of the rainbow.

And here, in a vaulted chamber, he found the Ancients. All nine of them, fast asleep on magnificent wooden beds. It was the breath from their slumbering bodies that perfumed the air and set the light shimmering.

Blackeye's jaw dropped. An overwhelming sense of awe washed over him. In the presence of these beings he felt very small and unimportant.

He tiptoed between the beds. They were intricately

carved with flowers, leaves, buds and berries, and each bore the name of the Ancient sleeping upon it. Pel . . . Edda . . . Fig . . . Bekkle . . . Gil . . . Kip . . . Ama . . . Sol . . . Tunni. Blackeye couldn't help smiling. It was sweet, like a nursery.

Blackeye was growing bolder. The Ancients were deep in slumber. He dared to move closer.

What majestic beings these were! Twice the size of any Ashenpeaker. The males had long, flowing beards with elaborate curls. The women had braided hair and elegant robes, girdled at the waist. All were lying absolutely still, like statues carved from the finest ash. Perfectly at peace, undisturbed for centuries.

With a jolt, Blackeye suddenly remembered why he was there. He needed to speak to these people. Oh, but who would dare wake them? Not he. They were so mighty. So wondrous. So terrifying.

Blackeye mustered his courage and moved closer. *Doi-oi-oi-oi-oing!* A small golden bell hanging from the roof rang out. He hadn't seen it dangling and somehow he'd walked right through it, setting it ringing. It wasn't a clamour; it was a warm, smooth, melodious sound. But it was enough.

To Blackeye's horror, there came the dry groaning of timbers. Eyes opened. Fingers stretched. Limbs loosened.

And in a single movement, the nine sleepers sat up in their beds, swivelled their great heads and saw him.

70

'What . . . do . . . you . . . want . . . boy?'

The voice seemed to rumble from the guts of the earth, the words coming together like travellers at a crossroads. Unfamiliar. Weary. Cautious.

Blackeye turned to the sleeper that had spoken – Sol – and wanted to be bold. But when he looked into the Ancient's eyes, his courage trickled away.

'What . . . do . . . you . . . want?'

Blackeye gulped. His mouth felt as dry as an old man's slipper. 'I have to speak to you, sir,' he stammered.

'Then . . . speak,' said Sol.

'No . . . wait,' said one of the females, Ama. 'I am . . . not ready . . . to listen.' She clicked her long, tapering fingers and suddenly a well appeared in the middle of the chamber. A low well, with stone sides, strangely carved and brimming with black water.

Ama walked stiffly to the well, pressed her lips to the water and drank. When she had finished, she stretched, and the years fell away from her like leaves. Suddenly she was tall and slender as a willow. Lithe and lovely. Blackeye couldn't help staring. She was magnificent.

Ama smiled at him seductively. 'Now I can listen,' she purred. She dipped her hand back into the well and brought it out dripping with water. 'Drink,' she said. And to Blackeye's astonishment, she held her hand up to his lips.

Blackeye looked at her fingers. At the drops slipping between them. He looked at her face, with its unfathomable eyes and full, wet lips. And he lowered his head and drank

The water coursed through him like a moorland stream. Cold, wild, free. He smacked his lips and looked for more. But Ama had gone.

The Ancients drank from the well in turn, while Blackeye wondered how on earth he'd managed to drink when he had no body. *It must be this place*, he thought. *These people*. Suddenly anything was possible.

'Come,' said Sol, slowly beckoning.

Blackeye followed him into a second chamber. Ama was there already, sitting serenely upon one of nine beautiful wooden thrones, and soon the others joined her. Blackeye stood confidently before them. Perhaps it was something in the water, but his courage had returned, like a mouse when the cat's gone by.

'You have something to tell us,' said Sol. 'It must

be important for you to venture so deep into the Otherworld.'

'It is,' said Blackeye. 'Desperately important.' And he took a deep breath and told them everything.

71

By the time Blackeye had finished speaking, Sol was pacing up and down in a terrible temper. Fig was standing behind his throne, gripping it viciously. Ama had her eyes closed, but her face was pained, not peaceful. Tunni and Bekkle were openly weeping. The other Ancients were staring at him, horrified.

'To think this was happening while we slept,' said Gil in disgust. 'So much time wasted.'

'Why didn't our people do more to save themselves?' said Fig angrily. 'Why didn't they fight? We gave them courage and stamina and tenacity.'

'It seems we didn't give them leaders,' said Ama. 'This . . . *Snowbone* . . . is something new. Something rare.'

'What is to be done?' said Tunni. No one answered her. 'Something *must* be done!'

'If I may . . .' said Blackeye.

'Indeed you *must*,' said Gil. 'You have more than earned the right to counsel us.'

'If the slaves could Move On, they could escape into another, better way of living,' said Blackeye.

'That is easily done!' cried Tunni. 'We could make them all Move On, just like that!' She clicked her fingers.

'Wait,' said Edda. 'Some of the slaves might not want to Move On. They might have families. Their lives might be tolerable.'

'I don't think slaves are allowed families,' said Blackeye. 'The girl at the quarry said so.'

Edda smiled. 'With respect to that girl, her knowledge was limited to the quarry. I imagine that elsewhere slaves are encouraged to pair off and breed.'

'Moving On has to be a matter of personal choice,' said Ama. 'If an individual feels the time has come, he must start the process consciously – with agreed words and gestures.'

'Like casting a spell?' said Blackeye.

'Exactly,' said Ama.

'But what happens then?' said Blackeye. 'How do we stop the traders cutting down the trees for their sap?'

'We make the sap worthless,' said Kip. 'Again, that is easily done. The sap of a living ashen tree will continue to be potent – it must be, otherwise the tree will not grow and flourish – but if the central vein is cut, the sap will sour and lose its healing properties.'

'Then . . . it's done!' said Blackeye breathlessly.

'The slaves can escape and live long and peaceful lives as ashen trees! It's done!'

'It won't happen overnight,' said Edda. 'Some lives will still be lost. And there are still many eggs to be bought. But one day, when the last living slave Moves On, it will be over. Forever.'

Blackeye had a tear in his eye and a lump in his throat. He blinked and swallowed hard. This was no time to blubber. 'I have to go,' he said. 'I have to get this thing started.'

'Wait!' cried Tunni. 'Haven't you forgotten something?'

Blackeye didn't think so. He shook his head.

'Oh, you over-eager boy!' laughed Tunni. 'You don't know the Moving On spell!'

72

Blackeye floated back down the tunnel. He was so elated, he felt he'd float even when he was back inside his body. Like a feather – or a balloon! Figgis would have to tether him to the wagon, with a string round his ankle. He'd float in the air and wave at everyone: *I'm soooo happy!*

He knew he should be flying back to share the good news, but he wanted to stay in the Otherworld just a little longer. The caverns were so beautiful. So magical.

He drifted along, simply enjoying the moment. Soon the lower level was behind him and he was back in the peaty, half-lit burrows of the upper level. Then he reached a fork in the system and suddenly felt a strong desire to go left. He made the turn and followed the tunnel into a cavern. Whatever force had drawn him there seemed infinitely stronger now. It was lifting his chin. Making him look up.

The roof was a tangle of tree roots, with a host of souls darting and flashing between them. But

Blackeye was drawn to one particular soul-light. It was small: no bigger than his thumb. Blue as forget-me-nots. And it was flickering more than the others, as if it were new and unused to shining.

Blackeye gazed at it, though he didn't know why. Then he felt a strange sensation between his eyes and, for one heart-stopping moment, he thought he was going blind, like Snowbone. But he wasn't. It was his shadow-sight, moving and moulding and misting and holding an image before him: *Mouse*. She was standing in the middle of a wood, lovely as ever, watching him with her soft brown eyes. But her feet were rooted to the ground. Her fingers were twisted and twiggy. The flesh on her arms was rough, knotty. And she opened her mouth and breathed a single word: *goodbye*.

The vision disappeared. Blackeye was staring at the flickering blue light again. This wasn't any ordinary soul. This was Mouse's soul. She was Moving On.

If that is her soul, thought Blackeye, *those are her roots. She's up there. She's right overhead. I'm down in her grave!*

Suddenly, Blackeye was lost. He was spinning in a whirlwind of love and grief and panic and fear. He couldn't think of anything but Mouse. Her smile, her laughter, her chocolatey eyes.

Thuum. A footfall in the tunnel. Blackeye didn't hear it.

Thuum . . . Thuum.

How could he hear it? He could hear nothing but *goodbye.*

Thuum . . . Thuum.

It was coming closer.

Thuum . . . Thuum.

It stopped. Sniffed. Sensed. Came.

Thuum-thuum-thuum-thuum-thuum-thuum-thuum!

WHOOOF! The air buckled around Blackeye as the massive paw came down. Dagger claws sliced through his shadow; he rippled like water. But Blackeye was still standing. His real body was safe on the wagon.

A bone-rattling roar rocked the cavern and split the tunnel floor. Blackeye spun round. The roof was raining stones, but he could see what he was fighting – the Spirit of Ashenpeake Island. An immense badger, bigger than a barn, with bat-black eyes and a mouth like a storm-cellar door.

WHOOF! The paw cuffed him again, and the world seemed to bend in on itself. The badger roared and reared again, and Blackeye was amazed to find himself still there, unharmed. But could his shadow take this beating? He didn't know. He was feeling weaker by the second.

WHOOF! The badger swiped again. Blackeye didn't see it coming. All he saw was the black-and-white muzzle, with the dead red eyes and the tombstone teeth. And as he gathered his strength and tried to find his breath, those terrible teeth seized him by the scruff of his neck. The badger shook him hard, back and forth, like a dog with a rat. Then it tossed him up into the air to break his back.

And that, for Blackeye, was enough. He closed his eyes, caught his breath and kept on flying. Out of the earth, into the sky, over the ocean. He stopped for nothing, thought of nothing, felt nothing but a burning desire to return to his body and the safety of himself.

And when he saw the mountains below him . . . and the wagon safe in the lee . . . and Figgis boiling water . . . and filling a pot for tea . . . Blackeye thought he would explode with happiness.

But he didn't. He simply fell back into his body and opened his eyes. Smiled at the anxious faces surrounding him and whispered, '*I've done it.*'

73

'How do we know the spell works?' said Tigermane. 'We can't try it ourselves – we might Move On!'

The friends were breakfasting outside, under the storm-washed sky.

'I don't want to be a tree!' said Filizar, contorting himself into a hideous tangle of limbs and tongue.

Everyone laughed – except Blackeye, who hadn't told them about Mouse, and Snowbone, who was looking thoughtful.

'I'll try it,' Snowbone said suddenly. 'Right now. I have nothing to lose.'

'Snowbone!' cried Figgis. 'How can you say that?'

'It's true,' she said. 'I told you yesterday – I want to finish what I started. This seems the perfect thing to do. I wouldn't mind staying here, on the hillside. It's lovely – you've all told me so. Perhaps my sight will come back as I change. Who knows? I might be able to see it before I go.'

'No!' said Figgis again. 'You can't Move On! You

308

think you're doing a big thing, but you're not. You're being selfish.'

'Selfish?' Snowbone gasped. 'Giving up my life as an Ashenpeaker to help end slavery is being selfish?'

'Ah, don't play the martyr with us,' said Figgis. 'We know your game. You're scared. You can't see any more, it terrifies the wits out of you, and you'd rather be the hero than have anyone's pity. Well, I'm sorry if my caring offends you, but the truth of the matter is this: we're your friends. We love you and we'd miss you if you weren't here. So that's why I say you're being selfish. If you stopped to think about us, just for one minute, you wouldn't be so quick to leave.'

Snowbone was flabbergasted. Would they really miss her? They'd miss Manu or Blackeye or Figgis, but not her. *Would they?*

'I'm sorry,' she said in a small voice. 'I didn't think.'

'No, you never do,' said Figgis. He looked at her, sitting on the step of the wagon. She was pale and frail. Forlorn as a fledgling. 'Oh, come here, you daft lump!' he said, and he put his arm round her and hugged her close. And for the first time in her life, Snowbone hugged him back.

She didn't see what happened next. Figgis turned to the others, his face a wide mask of surprise. The friends grinned. They were as surprised as he was.

'If you want someone to try the spell, you could ask that girl at the quarry,' said Filizar.

'Daisy?' said Snowbone. 'I suppose so. No, you're right! She'd be perfect. She could escape and spread the word at the same time. *Oh!*'

'What now?' said Figgis.

Snowbone shrugged. 'I just realized – I can't go back and tell her.'

'No, you can't,' said Tigermane. 'But I can.'

74

It was after midnight, some days later, when Tigermane opened a skylight window and peered down into the gloom of a barrack room.

'Daisy,' she whispered. 'Daisy.'

There was a movement down below. Daisy's sleep-bleary face looked up. 'Tigermane? I thought you'd gone.'

'I had,' said Tigermane, 'but I've come back. I want to help you escape.'

'Escape?' said Daisy, still half asleep. 'Why? I mean – how?'

'Listen!' Tigermane told Daisy the plan.

Daisy shook her head. 'I don't know,' she said slowly. 'I would like to escape, that's true. But . . . well, I'm scared! Suppose it hurts. And what if the spell doesn't work properly? I could end up stuck between two worlds. Half-tree, half-girl. Never able to Move On. That would be just horrible. No. I'm sorry, Tigermane, I can't do it.'

'Please, Daisy!' said Tigermane. 'Please! We must get this thing started.'

'I understand that,' said Daisy. 'But I don't want to go first.'

'I don't mind,' said a voice. Another girl, looking up. 'I'll try,' she said. 'I'm not scared. I would do anything to get out of here.'

And Tigermane looked down at the girl's hopeful little face and thought, *If I can save just this one, it will all have been worth it.* 'OK,' she said. 'This is what you must do.'

The girl listened carefully. 'Right,' she said, with a reassuring smile for Daisy. 'Here goes!' She took a deep breath and covered her eyes with her hands. 'I wish to Move On,' she said. She covered her ears. 'I wish to Move On.' She covered her heart. 'I wish to Move On.'

Tigermane watched her, hardly daring to breathe. 'Can you feel anything?'

'No. I feel exactly the same,' said the girl, bitterly disappointed. She looked up and Tigermane saw her eyes were bright with tears. 'It's not working. *Oh!*'

'Is it starting?'

'Yes. Yes!' Suddenly the girl was smiling, and holding her belly. 'I feel . . . tingly. All over, but especially here. Oh!' She began to breathe deeply. Steady, satisfying breaths. 'Oh! Daisy! It's really nice. I feel really good!'

The hoot of an owl drifted through the night.

Manu, on guard outside, was sending a warning.

'I have to go,' said Tigermane. She had never felt less like moving in her life. 'Please, please, *please* tell the others. Daisy – promise me you will.'

And Daisy looked at her friend's radiant face and said, 'I promise. Tomorrow, I will tell everyone I meet. And tomorrow night . . . I'll be brave. I'll say the words and join my friend.' She took hold of the girl's hand and kissed it.

Manu hooted again.

'I *have* to go,' said Tigermane. 'What's your name? My friends will want to know.'

'I don't have one,' said the girl.

'Then I'll call you Snowdrop,' said Tigermane. 'Because it's the first flower. It's brave and beautiful. It blooms while it's still winter and brightens the darkest of days. Thank you. Thank you both.'

Tigermane melted into the shadows and, with Manu by her side, ran back to the wagon.

'Did she try it?' asked Manu once they were safely out of the quarry.

'No, but her friend did,' said Tigermane.

'Does it work?'

Tigermane pictured Snowdrop: her dark, excited eyes; her luminous face; her wonderful smile. 'Oh, yes,' she said. 'It works!'

75

The friends returned to Farrago cautiously. Slavery was far from over; they had to be careful. Manu drove the wagon to the airfield, then ran back into town. He had another of Filizar's rings in his pocket. With luck, it would raise more than enough money to get them all home.

The others waited in the wagon. They were supposed to be hiding, but Filizar couldn't resist peeping out between the flaps. The airfield was such an extraordinary place, with people arriving from every part of the world. Affluent traders, stylish in velvet and fur. Prospectors and trappers with weather-beaten faces and horny hands. Adventurers and dreamers with holes in their boots and hope in their hearts.

'There's Stellan!' he cried suddenly.

'Don't let him see you,' said Figgis. He dragged Filizar away from the opening.

'Why?' said Filizar. 'Stellan's OK.'

'*Said the mouse as the cat went by*,' said Snowbone, instantly angry. 'There's no way I'm flying back on the *Stormrunner*. No way! I wouldn't care if it were the last machine on this earth, there's no way I'd –'

'Shh!' said Tigermane, peering through a hole in the canvas. 'Oh! Stellan's seen us! He's coming over!'

Suddenly the flap was pulled back, and there was Stellan, looking them over. 'Hey!' he said. 'I didn't expect to find you here!'

'If we *are* here, it's no thanks to you,' said Snowbone.

'Nay, wait a minute!' protested Stellan. 'I wasn't there, remember? Skua sent me on an errand. By the time I came back, you had gone. I was mortified! Skua had done some bad things over the years, but that was outrageous. I left him, there and then, and I haven't seen him since. On my honour! You must believe me! I thought you were legal. Skua said you had papers.'

'Papers?' said Figgis.

'Ya, papers. To show you are freeborn. Nay?'

Figgis was shaking his head.

'Have you never travelled?'

'No,' said Figgis. 'I walked as far as Kessel once, but other than that . . . no. There was no need.'

'Ah!' Stellan smiled ruefully. 'I wish I had known! If you are an Ashenpeaker and you want to travel, you need papers. Legal papers that show you are freeborn, not a slave. You get them in Kessel. It's easy – there's an office by the harbour. They don't cost anything. But you can't travel to the Nova Land without them. Well, you can, but . . . You know what can happen! Anyway, what are you doing here? Do you need a flight?'

'No,' snarled Snowbone.

'Yes,' said Figgis. 'We do,'

'Well, you have one!' said Stellan. He grinned broadly. 'My friends, you will not believe what happened to me after I left Skua.'

'No, but I think you're about to tell us,' muttered Snowbone.

Stellan flashed her a smile, though it turned to a frown as he studied her eyes. He decided not to comment.

'I stormed into town,' he said. 'Found a bar. Had a few drinks. Started talking to an old guy sitting next to me. Star sailor, he was. He told me he wanted to retire but didn't know what to do with his machine. So we talked, and we drank, and we talked some more – and then he gave her to me! Well, that's not quite true. I have to pay him off, out of the profits. But she is mine. And she's a beauty! Really fast. The *Comet* she's called. And you know, I feel bad about what Skua did. I want to put things right, I really do. So I'll fly you wherever you want to go. No charge. Anywhere in the world.'

'Anywhere?' said Tigermane.

'Anywhere!'

And so the friends returned to Ashenpeake. They arrived back on the dampest of days. The *Comet* descended through a wet fleece of cloud and landed at Spittel Point airfield. The boy with the terrible teeth tied the mooring lines fast and the friends gathered their scant belongings. It felt as if they had never been away.

'Stellan,' said Figgis, 'you're a perfect gentleman.' He shook the young man's hand warmly. 'The trip couldn't have been better. The *Comet* is a grand piece of machinery!'

Stellan smiled. 'I like to think so.'

'Right, then!' said Figgis, turning to the others. 'Let's get going! It's a long way to Bogey Bridge.'

'Wait!' said Tigermane. 'There's something I have to say. I'm not coming with you.'

'What?' said everyone at once.

'I'm not coming with you.' She smiled. 'I have had the best time, with the best people. And I am *so* proud of what we've done. But now it's over . . . I want more! I want to see the world. There's so much out there, waiting to be discovered. I've spoken to Stellan and he's been very kind. He's offered me a home and a job, for as long as I want.'

'On the *Comet?*' said Blackeye.

'Yes! I'll be mending the feather blades, fixing the rigging, cooking, cleaning – whatever needs doing. We're going to fly to Kessel first, so I can get my papers, and then we'll be off.'

'That's great news,' said Manu. He kissed Tigermane on the cheek and gave her a cuddle. 'We're going to miss you, though.'

'I'll miss you,' said Tigermane. 'Oh, this is the worst bit! Saying goodbye. Give me a hug and be on your way!'

And they did hug her, even Snowbone. Then they walked away, feeling as if they had left a little bit of themselves behind, like a sock under the bed.

We'll have to get used to saying goodbye, thought Snowbone. *Tigermane was the first, but she won't be the last.*

She was right. Five of them would arrive at Bogey Bridge but only one would stay.

76

The friends barely recognized Butterbur's house. Without the snow, it looked a completely different shape. And no one could be sure, but there seemed to be fewer chimney pots and many more windows.

Blackeye rang the doorbell and they waited. Feet came running. The door was opened.

'Two Teeth!' cried Blackeye. 'You're still here!'

'I am,' beamed Two Teeth. 'Fudge is here too. We've been working for Butterbur, building a new herb garden.' He ushered them into the sitting room.

'It's great to see you, buddy,' said Blackeye. 'We've got so much to tell.'

'Then it will have to wait until supper!' said Butterbur, sweeping in.

'Aunt!' cried Figgis. He sprang across the room and kissed her on her cheek.

Butterbur smiled indulgently. 'Well,' she said, gazing at the company. 'This is a surprise! And here's a new face.'

'This is my brother, Filizar,' said Manu.

'You are very welcome, Filizar,' said Butterbur warmly. 'So! How are you all?'

She had noticed Snowbone the second she entered the room. How could she not? Snowbone was perched on the edge of the sofa, silent and lost, her milky eyes looking but not seeing. Compassion kicked Butterbur like a mule, hard, angry, right in the chest. *What have they done to you?* She wanted to gather Snowbone into her arms. Hug her. Hold her. Promise to help. But she didn't. She hid her worry well, and her welcome never faltered.

'Two Teeth, will you tell Fern we have guests? Good lad.'

Two Teeth scampered away.

'He's a joy,' said Butterbur. 'He's so happy, all day long. And Fudge – I've never known anyone work so hard. You couldn't have sent the wagon with anyone better.'

'Do you still have the sap?' said Figgis.

'I do,' said Butterbur. 'It's quite safe.'

'If everything goes to plan,' said Manu, 'there won't be any more sap. That wagonload is the last of it.'

'Is that so?' said Butterbur, raising an eyebrow. 'Then we're lucky to have it.' She glanced at Snowbone. 'Well now! You all know where the guest rooms are. Why don't you get yourselves cleaned up and we'll meet for supper in, say – an hour's time?'

The friends readily agreed and, with a scraping of

chairs and a gathering of bags, they headed upstairs.

'Not you, Snowbone,' said Butterbur lightly as Blackeye guided her by. 'It's OK, Blackeye. I'll see to her.'

Snowbone nodded and Blackeye followed the others.

'We've got some work to do,' said Butterbur, and she took Snowbone by the arm and led her away.

77

Snowbone breathed in deeply. Herbs, hay, spices . . . they could only be in Butterbur's surgery.

'Make yourself comfortable,' said Butterbur. She eased Snowbone into a soft armchair. 'I won't be a moment. I just have to fetch something.'

She moved away. Snowbone heard a rug being kicked back. Then a grunt: Butterbur was pulling something heavy. Footsteps, *tip – tip – tip* like a tap left dripping. Silence. Footsteps again.

'Can you lean back for me?' said Butterbur.

Snowbone obeyed.

'I'm going to put a few drops into your eyes,' said Butterbur. 'Try not to blink.'

'Will it hurt?'

'I don't know. I've never used this before. I hope not, but I can't promise anything.'

Snowbone sighed and opened her eyes wide.

Plip . . . Plip! Plip! Ooh! Snowbone tried really hard not to blink, but her left eye was stinging.

Plip! Plip! Plip! Ooh! The right eye now! Snowbone

opened her mouth and stretched her face, trying to keep the drops in there, working.

'Any better?' said Butterbur.

'No, not yet.'

'Let me try again.'

Plip! Plip! Plip! Plip! Plip! Oh! This was horrible! *Plip! Plip! Plip! Plip! Plip!* And still nothing. Snowbone felt her hope shrivelling inside her like a salted snail.

'Anything?'

'No.' Snowbone was glad her eyes were running. She'd be crying now.

'I'm going to try a compress,' said Butterbur.

'No . . . wait,' said Snowbone. 'I think something's happening.'

'Can you see?' said Butterbur.

'No,' said Snowbone. 'It's still black. But it feels better.'

'Relax,' said Butterbur. 'Don't fight it. Let it happen.'

Snowbone tried to relax further. She could hear Fudge outside, laughing in the garden, but she shut him out and listened to her own breathing. In, out. In, out. And suddenly the black was moving. There were shadows, shapes. Tiny bits of fuzziness. And a faint redness, as if the black were rusting away.

'Anything?' said Butterbur.

'I'm not sure,' said Snowbone.

'Take your time.'

Snowbone settled back into the armchair and kept her eyes closed. She still couldn't sec anything, just the strange ruddy glow. But suddenly it was fading . . . pulling back like a curtain . . . and she could see a forest. A lush, vibrant forest. She felt she was walking into it. The trees towered above her, their leaves fluttering silver like moths. She could feel their vigour; hear their sighs as they worshipped the sun. The grass beneath her feet was soft, springy like a mattress, astonishingly green. And she could hear it growing. Every blade of grass was whispering to its neighbour, urging it on.

There were butterflies, candy-bright. She could hear the powdery rustle of their wings as they flitted by. Hear the flowers humming as their nectar was sipped.

She walked on.

Whoo-whoo-whoo-whoo. A sound, somewhere behind her. A downbeat of wings, growing louder, louder. *Oh!* She ducked as the bird flew over her head. It sounded like an eagle, but it was only a thrush. It landed on a branch ahead of her and began to sing. And as the notes tumbled from its throat, Snowbone saw them dancing in the air like dust motes, thick and brown and warm as the speckles on the bird itself.

She wandered on through the softly rippling forest. The scent of the flowers, the sweet earth, the ripe fruit hanging from the trees . . . *Mm!* It was like drinking honeydew.

Then something caught her eye. Something small, moving beneath one of the trees. It was a stag beetle, a small but mighty warrior, rooting in the leaf litter. Snowbone studied it intently. She had never seen an insect that looked so polished. Its carapace shone like black armour. Its deadly pincers snapped the air with terrifying force. Despite its size, it was fearsome. And it was getting bigger. *Bigger*, as if Snowbone's interest were feeding it.

The beetle grew before Snowbone's eyes. As big as a boot . . . a boy . . . a boat! Now she wasn't looking *down* at it – she was looking *up* at it. The beetle towered over her: a terrible tangle of legs and feelers and bone-cracking claws.

But Snowbone wasn't scared. She could see nothing but beauty. The sun bouncing off the beetle's shell . . . the exquisite jointing of its legs . . . the precise design of its pincers.

'Oh,' she sighed. 'You are just wonderful.'

At the sound of her voice, the stag beetle began to shrink until it was no bigger than it ought to be. With a happy smile, Snowbone walked on.

The forest was thinning. The sunlight trickled through the leaf canopy like pear juice: thick, golden, luscious. And when Snowbone stepped out into the sunshine, she found a rainbow. A jubilant shout of light that tethered the earth to the sky, shimmer-shining, close enough to touch. And she stepped off the edge of the world and into the rainbow.

Kaleidoscopic colours thrummed and flashed around her. She could taste the red, sweet as strawberries. The yellow, creamy as custard. The blue, tangy as blueberries. And far, far below, she could see the rainbow's end, buried in a corduroy carpet of earth.

Snowbone slid down the rainbow to the fertile land. On her hands and knees, she started to dig, deeper and deeper, searching for the pot of gold. But the smell! The ground was rotten. Hot. Wet. Icky.

'Snowbone! Snowbone!'

Snowbone felt herself being shaken roughly by the shoulder. She scrunched up her eyes and shook her head. Everything went black. Then slowly she opened her eyes . . . and saw a pig. A pale-pink pig with a bandaged ear and a mucky mouth. And when she sat up and looked around, she found she was in Butterbur's animal hospital, on her knees, rummaging through the straw in the pigpen.

'Snowbone?' said Butterbur anxiously. 'Are you all right?'

'Yes,' said Snowbone, beginning to laugh. 'I'm fine. In fact, I'm better than fine. I can see everything. It's brilliant!'

'You gave me quite a fright,' said Butterbur. 'And poor Sausage here didn't know what to make of it.' She patted the pig affectionately. 'Why anyone would want to root in her poo is beyond her!' Butterbur helped Snowbone to her feet. 'Let's get you cleaned up.'

They returned to the surgery, and there Snowbone saw something so unexpected her heart skipped a beat. On the table stood an opened leather flagon, with a dropper beside it.

'Did you use ashen sap?'

'Yes,' said Butterbur. 'This is one of the flagons Two Teeth brought up.'

Snowbone couldn't believe it. Tarn and her gang had brought untold misery to countless people, Figgis included, but without their villainy she might still be blind. *This is crazy!* thought Snowbone. *Tarn is dead and I am the one benefiting from her crime. It's mad. Mad!*

Mad but true.

78

The meal the friends shared that night in Butterbur's house was the best ever. It wasn't just the delicious food. It was the laughter and the sense of belonging that made it perfect. And the knowledge that it would be their last together added a special flavour all of its own: a warm, subtle hint of spice that lingered on the tongue long after the meal was over.

Between them, the travellers recounted the whole adventure, while Two Teeth and Fudge punctuated it with a *no!* here, and a *wow!* there, and an *oh, you never!* thrown in for good measure.

Butterbur listened intently, saying nothing but memorizing it all. When it was over she said, 'I'm so glad you've used your shadow-sight, Blackeye. It's such a rare and precious gift. It needs to be nurtured.'

'Torbijn had shadow-sight,' said Filizar.

'Really?' said Blackeye.

'Yes. I forgot to tell you. Skua was wrong to say he was just a mapmaker. Torbijn was much more than that. He had extraordinary powers. He was a shaman, a healer. He could definitely shadow-fly. That's how he drew his maps.'

'Ah!' said Figgis. 'Now that is interesting! Stellan showed me a Torbijn map and it was incredibly precise. We couldn't work out how he was doing it long before flying machines were invented. Well, now we know!'

'I'm so jealous of you all,' said Fudge. 'I know there were times when it got hairy, but you've had such an adventure. You're heroes. Real heroes.'

'I don't think I'm a hero,' said Snowbone. 'Though when we first set out, I thought I would be. I thought it was my destiny. But it didn't work out like that. I played a very small part in the adventure. Nothing I did was particularly brave.'

'You led the attack against the slavers,' said Two Teeth. 'You led the attack at Barrenta Bay.'

'That wasn't bravery,' said Snowbone. 'That was bravado! There's a difference. Bravado is instinctive. You're so fired up, you just storm in. You don't really think about what you're doing. That's me! But bravery – real bravery – is when you understand the danger you're facing, and you feel afraid – yet you still go in. Manu ran back to save Filizar in the volcano. Tigermane risked capture to return to the quarry. Blackeye risked his life to save me from the tower. That's bravery. No, if you're looking for the real hero in all this, it has to be Blackeye. Without him, we wouldn't have won.'

Blackeye shook his head. 'Snowbone, you're not being fair to yourself. You are a hero. You're *my* hero. Without you, I wouldn't have done anything. I would still be on the beach at Black Sand Bay, building a tree house! You took charge. You spurred us on. It was your energy that kept us all going. Your energy, your belief and your commitment. Without you, we were nothing. If you could have seen us sitting in the workshop in Farrago – miserable, completely at a loss what to do – you would know that!'

Snowbone smiled. She didn't know what to say.

'If we're talking heroes,' said Figgis, 'then I didn't amount to much at all! What did I do? I made tea and washed a few pots.'

'You found the black-haired man and the blue-eyed lad,' said Manu. 'You sorted the flight to Farrago.'

'That's all!' said Figgis. 'You could have left me behind at Spittel Point and not noticed the difference.'

'No,' said Blackeye. 'That's not true. You kept us going, just as much as Snowbone. You made sure we had food and water and somewhere safe to sleep. You were like a mother to us.'

'I'm the only mother you'll ever have!' said Figgis.

'I couldn't ask for better!' said Blackeye.

'You wouldn't want mine!' said Filizar, and they all laughed.

But Manu, lying in bed later, felt his heart harden as he thought of his stepmother and her scheming.

And Figgis, lying awake in the room next door, felt every muscle tense as he thought of the fight in the warehouse. He hadn't told anyone about the black-haired man and he wasn't going to. He would lock away the memory in the darkest chamber of his heart and throw away the key. 'Some secrets aren't for sharing,' he told himself, punching his pillow to make it more comfortable. 'And dead men don't tell tales.'

79

'So what's next?' said Butterbur. 'Where do you go from here?'

It was midday. The friends had slept well into the morning. Now they were finishing a very late breakfast.

'I'd like to stay awhile, if that's all right with you,' said Figgis. 'I have nothing to go back to.'

'Of course,' said Butterbur. 'There's always plenty of work to be done.'

'Filizar and I might return to Balaa,' said Manu, 'but we need some time to think. At the moment, we're planning to go to Kessel. We could get a ship from there.'

'With his body and my brains, we'll make a great team,' said Filizar. 'That mother of mine won't know what's hit her!'

'What about you, Blackeye?' said Butterbur.

'I'm going to find Mouse,' he said simply.

No one dared press him further. His face was as bleak as a beach in winter.

'And what about you?' said Butterbur, turning to

Snowbone at last. 'I thought you might like to stay here and work with the animals.'

'I have thought about it,' said Snowbone, 'but I can't stay. Not at the moment. I'm too restless. I have to go on.'

'Do you know where you're going?' said Figgis.

'I do,' said Snowbone, and she smiled enigmatically and said no more.

Snowbone stood in the clearing and looked at what remained of Figgis's house. Nothing much. A few charred timbers, green with moss and overgrown with nettles. Half a dozen rusty pans, buckled and bent. A ceramic sink. Bed springs. A twisted fork.

She moved over to the fallen ashen trees. They lay where the tiddlins had placed them, side by side in neat rows. Snowbone sighed. 'If only the Ancients had been watching instead of sleeping, it would never have come to this,' she said. 'What a waste.'

Or was it? She couldn't escape the fact that she owed her sight to trees like these. Suddenly she felt very small and humble, and curiously cherished, as if these Ancestors were honouring her in some way. But how? They were long gone. Their souls had flown away like bumblebees, never to return. But still . . .

'Thank you,' she whispered. 'Wherever you are.'

And the leaves on the living trees suddenly rustled, as if they were talking to each other.

❧

The sun was setting by the time Snowbone reached the forest fringe. Its low rays filtered through the trees like an amber fan, drawing her to the sea. To the salt-charged air and the falling waves. To the fleecy foam and the endless sky.

Snowbone left the forest behind and stepped on to the black sand. That wasn't good enough; she kicked off her boots to feel the grains between her toes. She began to walk down the beach, but that wasn't enough either. Soon she was running, and the waves were rushing to greet her. Rolling in joyously, tossing their white-washed manes.

Snowbone stopped at the water's edge and stared out at the limitless ocean, breathing in great lungfuls of briny air: tasting it, savouring it, loving it. 'I promised I would return,' she said, 'and I have.'

She sat down on the sand and waited for the moon to rise. Slowly it came: a great silver button pinned to the cloak of the sky. Snowbone sat for hours, watching it journey across the heavens, until a band of golden light appeared at the rim of the world and the morning came.

This is such a perfect place, she thought as the sun began to ascend. *I'm not going away again for a long, long time.*

And she didn't. She stayed at Black Sand Bay for many moons, happily alone. And when she did eventually leave, it was for the most unexpected of reasons.

But that, my friends, is another story.

Afterwards

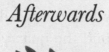

After Tigermane had gone, Daisy and Snowdrop sat in their bleak barrack room and waited for morning. When it came, the bolts were drawn back, the slaves were summoned to work, and Daisy told the quarry master that her friend was Moving On.

Dunamis stared at her like a great fat frog eying a worm. 'When was she hurt?' he asked suspiciously.

'She wasn't,' said Daisy. 'She's quite well. She's just Moving On.'

The news spread like ice cracking on a pond. *One of the girls . . . eight years old . . . fit and healthy . . . Moving On!* Then came the rumour of a spell. Magic words that anyone could say. *You cover your eyes . . . cover your ears . . . cover your heart . . . and this is what you say . . .*

By midday, the quarry was a cauldron of hot, feverish hope. Dunamis cracked his whip and spat and swore, but who was caring any more? No one. *No one!* Because seventeen slaves were Moving On. Escaping!

That night, Daisy said the spell. And elsewhere in the darkness, in a room hissing with whispers, seven boulder men realized they would have to escape. *Really* escape. They had to spread the news. If they didn't, no one beyond the quarry would ever know. Dunamis and his men would hush it up. Even if a rumour spread, the spell certainly wouldn't.

And so the next day, as the overseers struggled to cope with hundreds of slaves Moving On at once, the boulder men slipped out of the quarry unseen. They began to run. And one reached a farm and one reached a plantation. One found a factory, one found a lumber mill. One found a coal mine, one found a gold mine. And one found a ship and stowed away, and carried the news to another land.

Hundreds, thousands, hundreds of thousands! All around the world, slaves Moved On. Their owners bought more eggs, but the spell continued to spread – dedicated bands of escaped slaves made sure of that. So the owners bided their time and waited for the ashen trees to mature. They would have a bumper sap harvest, for sure! But a strange thing happened. As the first tree was felled, the sap turned foul. It was black and greasy, stinky as beer breath, and it wouldn't heal anything, not even a cut finger.

The slave market at Barrenta Bay was rebuilt, but it fell into disrepair as trade dwindled. The town declined. The shopkeepers moved away and soon it was a ghost town. Squirrels nested in the saloons. Wild dogs roamed the streets. Crows roosted in the clock tower. Time stood still.

But not the trees.

Slaves believed in The Forest: a place of peace, where Ashenpeakers could Move On and grow old together. Did it exist? Perhaps not, but the slaves *wanted* it to exist. That was why, at the quarry, they loved to see their friends carried away on the wagon. It made their dreams real.

But now, with dozens of slaves Moving On every day at the quarry, the wagon wasn't being used. The overseers were dumping people in a yard behind the master's cabin. Here there was neither soil nor water. The emerging ashen trees couldn't take root.

So they started to walk.

Slowly, slowly, by the light of the moon. Their skin turned to bark and their fingers sprouted leaves, but still they marched on: great armies of trees from east and west, north and south, converging in the darkness. And when they found water and shelter – in the lee of a hill, in the basin of a valley – they stopped. They sent their roots down into the earth, creating an Otherworld of their own, beneath this foreign land, where their souls could dance, bright as butterflies. They spread their branches into the air above, creating vast canopies of leaves, from coast to coast across the Nova Land.

And they sent their hearts across the world, singing the news:

It's over, it's over. We're free, free, free . . .

Acknowledgements

A book is like a pirate ship in full sail. It's wild. Wonderful. Gloriously exciting.

The writer is the pirate captain, standing proudly on the deck, gorgeously attired in velvet and lace, with a big fat feather in her hat.

She isn't voyaging alone. Below decks, or up in the air, clinging to the rigging, there are dozens of pirates beavering away, doing all kinds of things. Without them, the ship would never even leave the harbour, never mind sail the seven seas.

And so, me hearties, love and thanks to:

Adele Minchin and everyone at Puffin, especially Tania Vian-Smith, my tireless First Mate.

Yvonne Hooker and Shannon Park, best Ship's Doctors this side of the Indigo Ocean.

Pat White and Rebecca Price at Rogers, Coleridge & White, Pursers and Official Port in a Storm.

Bethan England, Jack Manuel and Daniel Rosser of the Merthyr Tydfil Exciting Writing Squad, fellow seafarers and pirate captains of the future.

Also to Beverley Robins, our very own Figgis.

Rob Soldat, Sea Sage. Never more than a wish away.

And finally thanks to Ray, Sea Dog, Husband and Work-shy Fop.